Praise for THE DAMSELFLY

'*The Damselfly* is accomplished in every way; deftly plotted and ingenious, it explores the devastating effects of the brutal murder of a promising teenager on her friends and the community around her. Sensitively handled, with beautifully drawn characters that you do genuinely care about, it's a compulsive read until the final breathing page.' – Elizabeth Haynes, author of *Never Alone*

'Multi-layered, fiendishly plotted and peopled by a cast of characters drawn with rare delicacy and skill, *The Damselfly* is a suitably gripping and original end to SJI Holliday's critically acclaimed Banktoun Trilogy.' - Eva Dolan, author of *Watch Her Disappear*

'An absorbing, intense and utterly riveting read, not only the very definition of a page-turner but one with an ending to die for. *The Damselfly* grips throughout then stops you dead in your tracks, beautiful writing, beautiful plotting from an entirely twisted genius of an author.' – LizLovesBooks

'I simply adore the Banktoun series and *The Damselfly* was no exception. I read it in a day – this is one you won't want to put down until its heart-breaking conclusion. SJI Holliday has an exciting career ahead of her.' – Jenny Blackhurst, author of *Before I Let You In*

'*The Damselfly* is everything we've come to expect from Holliday – unnerving, compelling, and grabs tight from the start. At the end she throws us something unexpected and I don't mind admitting I shed a quiet tear. Loved being back in Banktoun. Loved this book.' – Amanda Jennings, author of *In Her Wake*

'Think you're in for a cosy time of it if you move in to a small town? Read this book and have a re-think. SJI Holliday has masterfully drawn a close-knit community and illustrates just how claustrophobic knowing everyone can be. There's no court quite like the court of public opinion and nowhere is this more keenly felt than when death occurs - minds close and mob mentality rules. Where she excels is in her characterisation. With just a few words, in her trademark tight prose, Holliday brings the people in Banktoun to flawed life. This is a pacy read: a fascinating ride, and one that will keep you glued to the book, right to the very last word.' – Michael J Malone, author of *A Suitable Lie*

'Holliday has written another haunting, fast-paced thriller. *The Damselfly* gets under the skin of teenagers, families and the Banktoun community, showing that nothing is as it seems.' – AK Benedict, author of *The Beauty of Murder*

'*The Damselfly* is a fabulous, compelling read. Holliday writes with enviable assurance, creating characters that feel as real as anyone you know, and a blaster of a plot that grips you right from the get-go.' – Ava Marsh, author of *Untouchable*

'A heart-thumping thriller, packed with twists and turns, that left me breathless.' – Jane Isaac, author of *Beneath The Ashes*

'*The Damselfly* is a forceful, utterly gripping story that builds and builds the suspense until the stunning ending that will leave readers gasping. SJI Holliday's writing goes from strength to strength. She really is one of the best crime fiction authors around.' – Random Things Through My Letterbox

'Intense, unsettling, gripping and dark – another fantastic book by SJI Holliday.' – Off-the-Shelf Books

'A murder mystery which leaves you wondering who you should trust. SJI Holliday has made Banktoun a great place for readers to visit – but I really wouldn't like to live there! A five-star page-turner, I loved it.' – Grab This Book

THE DAMSELFLY

S.J.I. Holliday grew up in Haddington, East Lothian. She spent many years working in her family's newsagent and pub before going off to study microbiology and statistics at university. She has worked as a statistician in the pharmaceutical industry for over sixteen years, but it was on a six-month round-the-world trip that she took with her husband ten years ago that she rediscovered her passion for writing. Her first novel, *Black Wood*, was published in 2015, followed by *Willow Walk* in 2016. You can find out more at www.sjiholliday.com.

THE DAMSELFLY

S.J.I. Holliday

BLACK & WHITE PUBLISHING

First published 2017
by Black & White Publishing Ltd
29 Ocean Drive, Edinburgh EH6 6JL

3 5 7 9 10 8 6 4 2   17 18 19 20

Reprinted 2017

ISBN: 978 1 78530 087 5

A CIP catalogue record for this book is available from the British Library.

Typeset by Iolaire, Newtonmore
Printed and bound by CPI Group (UK) Ltd, Croydon, CR0 4YY

To my grandma and grandad for keeping me up to date with the gossip, and to the people of The Hidden Toun for providing it.

'In individuals, insanity is rare; but in groups, parties, nations and epochs, it is the rule.'

Friedrich Nietzsche

PROLOGUE

Friday, 13 January

Sometimes, Katie wished that she was dead.

If she was dead, she wouldn't have to put up with Brooke, that nasty piece of work that she had no choice but to call her sister. If she was dead she wouldn't have to spend her evenings cooking tea for the ungrateful cow, trying to keep some semblance of calm in the house that was anything but. She'd probably miss Brett, though. Her little brother wasn't so bad. A bit too quiet, maybe. A bit too ready to follow after Brooke like a lost sheep. But she couldn't blame him for that. Brooke was persuasive. Brooke always got exactly what she wanted. Brett would grow up soon enough. He'd work it out. Realise what Brooke was *really* like. A number-one grade-'A' cow.

Most of the time, Katie wished that *Brooke* was dead.

That'd make everything a lot simpler. No more arguments, no more having to make peace with her for her mother's sake. Her mother was crap, as mothers went, but she tried. Well, she tried *sometimes*.

Katie was sitting at the bottom of the stairs, lacing up her ten-eye oxblood Doc Martens. She left two holes undone and wrapped the black laces around the tops twice, tying them in a double bow. She'd tried lacing them up to the top once but they'd been too tight and it had felt like the skin on her ankles was in flames. She loved her DMs. Wore them with everything, wore them all the time – and still the soles were like new. Not like the cheap shite her sister wore. Hopefully Brooke would have bunions by the time she was twenty. Ugly, twisted feet to go with her ugly, twisted personality.

'Fucksake, cannae believe you're still wearing they things, you look a right state.'

Katie flipped her hair out of her eyes and looked up, glaring at her sister, wishing she could direct lasers out of her eyes to eliminate the little bitch. 'Piss off, Brooke,' she said. Brooke snorted and gave her the finger then flounced out the front door in her fake Louboutin stilettos, leaving it standing wide open. Just as she always did. Yet, funnily enough, it was always Katie who got the bollocking. As far as her mum was concerned, Brooke's cute little pointy chin reflected buttercups in the dark.

Before she could even take another breath, never mind stand up and walk the two steps she'd need to take to be able to close the door, another voice shot through from the kitchen: 'Shut that bloody door! What have I told you? You weren't born in a fucking barn.'

Katie sighed. Her mother should've taken her to a barn and left her there. She'd have got on far better in life with a bunch of farm animals than the bunch of bottom-feeders she had the misfortune to live with. She stood up and kicked the door shut. Then shouted back: 'Mum, *please* can I have that money? They need to know today for numbers ...'

There was the sound of a chair being scraped back, then her mother appeared in the kitchen doorway. She was wearing the pink fluffy slippers that Brett had bought her for Christmas, coupled with a wash-grey towelling robe that Katie *knew*

Brooke had nicked from BHS. She accessorised the look with a half-smoked Lambert & Butler, expertly balanced on her bottom lip, and a clump of murky brown hair in desperate need of a comb and at least two litres of conditioner.

Katie stared at her, awaiting her response.

She shook her head. 'Sorry, doll. I told you. I can't afford it.'

'You managed to find the money for Brooke to go to that open day in Stirling.'

'That's different. That was for her *career*.' She overemphasised the double 'e' in the last word and Katie felt like slapping her.

'Career? It was a day trip to some beauty school to hear about some stupid bloody diploma that she'd be too thick to pass anyway! And I know for a fact that she didn't even go. Her and two of her brat mates bought cans of cider and sat in the park all day. They nearly never got let back on the bus!'

'Who told you that?' Her mother's face shrivelled up, accentuating the lines that shouldn't really have been there yet. For a woman in her early thirties, she could easily pass for a rough-looking fifty-year-old in an identity parade. 'Brooke might not be as clever as you, wee smarty-pants, but at least she knows how to look after herself. Can you not wear something that's not black or purple for once in your life? Would it really bloody hurt to put on a bit of lip-gloss or something? All that black kohl ...' With that, she turned and waltzed back through to the kitchen: conversation over.

Katie stared at herself in the hall mirror. She looked fine. More than fine. She was far better looking than Brooke and she didn't need to walk about half-dressed and caked in make-up to show it. She twisted the little silver stud in the side of her nose and walked out of the house, slamming the door behind her so hard that the whole house rattled.

She stopped at Fleetham's to buy a packet of chewing gum and ten Berkeley menthol. The only thing that Mandy Taylor had managed to pass down to her daughter was a craving for cigarettes, probably because she'd smoked twenty a day since she was fourteen and never bothered stopping during any of her pregnancies. Katie told herself that menthol couldn't be as bad, seeing as they tasted of mint. This was the only thing she deluded herself about. Well, that and hoping to get a place in a uni far, far away; wasn't going to help her application much, though, if she couldn't even go on the subsidised school visit. She had a provisional place to study at King's College in London, but they were expecting to see her before the final decision – not a formal interview as such, but she knew they were checking her commitment. Christ, it was only a poxy bus to London Victoria and an overnight stay in a hostel. A travelcard and some lunch. A hundred and fifty quid wasn't that much, but giving it to her would mean that Mandy might have to rein in a few of her nights out. Was it really so much to ask? Bitch.

'Is that everything, hen?' The woman behind the counter made her jump and she dropped her purse on the floor. Coins rolled all over the shop. She scrabbled about trying to pick them up, while trying to avoid the feet of the boys from the year below her, who were laughing and trying to stand on her fingers.

'Thanks for helping!' Katie said, red-faced and batting at her hair that was hanging over her eyes as she pulled herself up from the floor.

The boys kept laughing. 'Look at the state of *that*,' one said, and his friend replied, 'I wouldnae touch her with yours!' as they sauntered out of the shop, all shiny trainers and freshly cultivated bum-fluff.

'Ignore them,' the woman behind the counter said. 'Stupid wee laddies.'

Katie bit her lip and fought back tears. *Pricks*. If only Hayley had been with her. She'd have told the little bastards where to

4

go. *Fucking Hayley*. She blinked back tears. She hated to admit it, even to herself, but she missed her friend. Her *ex*-friend. She looked down at the coins in her hand. A new pound coin shone brightly on top of the pile of coppers and fives. She held it out: 'I'll have a scratch card too, please. Might as well.'

The woman made a big show of holding her hands over the cards in the dispenser, wiggling her fingertips. She ripped a card off one of the rolls. 'This is the one, hen,' she said. 'Mind and come back for a wee treat for yourself when you collect your winnings!'

Katie smiled and took the card. Stuffed the cigarettes into the deep pocket of her army-green parka. 'Thanks, Mrs Fleetham.' A little bell tinkled over the glass door when she pulled it shut behind her.

She was almost at the school gates when she decided she wasn't going in. *Fuck it*. She had a study afternoon anyway, and this morning was only one of her elective subjects. Nothing to miss. She walked straight past the gates and into the huge leafy park that took up most of the centre of the town. Apart from the river, which was number one choice, Garlie Park was a favourite hang-out for skivers; but there was an unwritten code that meant no one would clipe on anyone else. If anyone was asked, they'd deny having seen her, and she'd do likewise. She pulled her mobile out of her pocket and texted Neil:

At swings. Bring coffee ☺xx

She sat down on one of the tyre swings and kicked her legs until she got into a nice rhythm, then pulled the scratch card out of her pocket and started to rub it gently with her thumbnail. She did it slowly, neatly revealing one little square after another. These weren't things she could afford to buy very often, so when she did, she liked to savour them. Even if the most she'd ever won was two quid. Sometimes she and Neil liked to make up grand tales about what they were going to do when they became millionaires. Get away from this place, that was for sure.

She rubbed off the three boxes in the top row: one five-thousand, followed by two tenners. She felt a little flutter in her stomach. Might she win a tenner this time? She rubbed the next three symbols off: a twenty-five, followed by a quid, and a 'special symbol' that would net her the jackpot of fifty grand if she got two more in the bottom row. Now *that* was never going to happen. Nor would she ever get the illustrious third tenner. She was starting to rub off the last row of three when she spotted a familiar floppy-haired figure running across the grass towards her, carrier bag in hand. She grinned and waved, and put the scratch card back into her jacket.

'Hey, babe.' Neil took hold of the ropes at the sides of her and leant forward to kiss her hard on the mouth. He tasted of coffee and chewing gum, smelled of lemon shower gel.

Katie wrapped her arms around him and breathed in the smell of his faded leather jacket; it carried a musty smell of cigarette smoke and incense that she loved. 'God, I've missed you ...' Her words were muffled from having her lips pressed up to his chest.

'Me too,' he said. Then, cupping her chin, he said, 'You OK? You look like you've been crying. Has Brooke been giving you a hard time? Your ma?'

Katie shook her head. 'Neither. Just some idiots in the paper shop when I went to buy fags. Little pricks from fifth year. Surprised they're still hanging about. They should've all buggered off by now, most of them are over sixteen.'

'Never mind them, doll. You'll be gone soon enough. A few more months and you'll be away to the big bad city ... I'll miss you!' He gave her a sly look and she slapped him on the arm.

'You're coming with me, you idiot.'

With that, he pulled her off the swing and onto the grass,

and they lay there, cuddled and content until she threw him off and sat bolt upright. 'Shit! Nearly forgot to finish this.' She pulled the scratch card out of her pocket and showed it to him.

'Ah – the famous scratch card ritual. What on earth are we going to do with the two quid this time, eh?' He pulled himself up to sit beside her, then leant over to the carrier bag and pulled out a flask. 'We can toast our win with a nice wee cup of steaming milky-coffee!'

'It's not even two quid this time.' She laughed and kissed him on the cheek. He leaned in against her as she carefully scraped off the third and final row. Another 'special symbol'. Another five-thousand. She swallowed, turned to face Neil. 'It's gonnae be a dud by the looks of it.' Her finger hovered over the final box and as she scraped it Neil said, 'Tenner!' But then they both fell silent when they realised it wasn't a tenner at all.

It was five-thousand.

Her hand shook as she gripped the card; he leant in closer and ran a finger over its surface, as if checking it was real. She could hear his breath, coming fast, mixed in with her own.

'You can't tell anyone about this. Not *anyone*. Promise?'

Neil squeezed her hand but didn't look her in the eye. 'I promise,' he said.

MONDAY

1

Polly

She'd forgotten about the gossip.

The way the slightest small thing was embellished and magnified until what started off as an annoying, buzzing midge turned into a multi-headed monster. Back in the town less than a week and already it feels like she's never been away. It'd seemed like a good idea, popping out to the post office during the first break, knowing that she wasn't on playground monitoring duties – not on her first day. What else was she going to do? She's no sessions lined up. They only passed her the pupil list at 9 a.m. and suggested she'd need at least a couple of days to go through it. Work out who it was she needed to see. Which kids needed her help first. The school had gone a term and a half without a guidance counsellor – a few more days wasn't going to make any difference. As far as she remembers, Banktoun High is a decent school, and the attached Primary is full of well-behaved kids. She's already wondering if she's going to have anything to do at all in this backwater town. Not compared to the Edinburgh estate she's just come from. *Challenging* is the only way she could describe *that* place.

Banktoun will be a breeze.

She shuffles forward a few steps as the queue drops by one. She can hear the woman at the front, loud booming voice asking for *First Class, please, the signed-for one*, enunciating her words as if she was talking to a child, not the elderly Asian man who Polly recognises as Mr Kahn, the man who used to own the sweet shop on the corner near the school, before the Andrews took it on and started making their infamous home-made chocolate traybakes.

Memories ping at every turn, not all of them good.

She's tried and failed to tune out the whispering women huddled at the narrow counter at the side of the shop, filling in forms before joining the queue. They're taking longer than necessary, Polly assumes, using the time to skive off from the supermarket where they're meant to be now, their crisp blue uniforms giving them away. Polly glances over at them. Various leaflets are scattered across the counter. Broken chains dangle off the edge, the pens they once held nicked long ago.

'It has to be something bad if the flashers were on, doesn't it? Those bairns are in trouble so often, they've practically got their own policeman.'

Laughter.

'I heard it was something to do with the oldest one.'

'Katie? Nah. She's the only undamaged fruit in that bowl. What'd the police be wanting with her?'

'I don't know, Sheila. But mark my words, there's something going on up at that hoose, and it dusnae sound good.'

Cashier Number Three, Please.

Polly blinks and walks forwards. She's no idea who they're talking about, but some family are clearly the focus of the town's idle chatter today. She wonders about the police car, though. Wonders if that nice policeman is still working here. She'd seen him a few months ago, at her cousin's funeral. She'd ended up having a terrible argument with Simon at the graveside, just to add to things.

12

Awful, awful day.

But that didn't mean he was still around, did it? Some people manage to escape this place. 'Remind me why it is you've come back here?' she mutters to herself.

'What can I help you with, please?'

Polly pushes a pile of papers into the tray, and Mr Kahn opens the slot at the other side and pulls them out. He grins at her through the glass.

'Haven't seen you for a long time,' he says.

Polly smiles. 'I've been away for a bit, Mr Kahn,' she says. 'But then this new job came up and I wondered if maybe it was time for me to come back. I just need to get these documents witnessed. I wasn't sure who to ask. I wondered ...'

Mr Kahn winks. 'No problem, love. I'll vouch for you.' He scans through the documents, flipping them over. 'Ah, taking over your parents' house, are you?'

Polly nods. 'It's been rented out for years, but, well – there didn't seem much point in me moving in anywhere else. It's been empty since the summer. Last tenant left it in a hurry. Needs a bit of work ...'

She lets her sentence trail off, looks away from Mr Kahn's sympathetic eyes. 'If you need any help, you know where I am,' he says. He signs the forms, then slips the pile into the envelope that Polly has already addressed. 'Special Delivery?'

Polly feels her hand go to her stomach. She presses gently into the still soft flesh. Blinks away tears.

'Yes. Thank you.' She touches her bank card against the contactless reader to pay. Mr Kahn slides the receipt through the drawer and she takes it and walks quickly from the counter before the tears can make an unwelcome appearance.

Not for the first time, she wishes she had someone waiting for her at home, someone to cook her dinner and ask her about her first day. But she burned that bridge when she told Simon she was leaving. She'd felt a bit sorry for him in the end; he clearly thought things could continue as they were forever. But Polly couldn't stay in that rut any more. Especially not now.

She stands on the steps, fumbling in her pockets for her gloves. Puffs of air hang like clouds in front of her face. Out on the street, the sounds of sirens disappear into the distance. Ambulance, maybe? Not that unusual. But something about the sound makes her feel uneasy. The gossiping old biddies mentioned police too. A lot for this small town on a quiet Monday morning. A prickle of fear runs down her back, like ice sliding down a car windscreen. Something has happened. Something has definitely happened.

Something bad.

Remnants of dirty slush are banked up against the kerb. She glances across at the Rowan Tree, but the place is in darkness. Too early. He wouldn't be in there now, would he? She keeps her head down against the biting wind. Her feet crunch on the salty pavements as she hurries back along the street to the school, hoping that her instincts are being magnified by a sudden rush of hormones. Hoping that her paranoia is unfounded. It's her first day in her new job. A fresh start. Away from Simon and his measured apathy. But the churning in her stomach refuses to go away.

She sees the police car just as she turns the corner. Parked right outside the school gates, on a double yellow line. Melting ice drips slowly from the back of the car, leaving a small puddle on the ground.

Bad. I knew it was bad.

She walks faster. Faster. Starts to run.

2

Louise

She feels sharp stones under her feet, poking up through the worn rubber soles of her trainers.

Need. New. Trainers.

She coughs, and pain burns down through her lungs. She knows she's going too fast, that she can't possibly keep up this pace, but she's enjoying the feeling of the cold sea breeze whipping across her face. She breathes in deep through her nose, inhaling the briny air.

The sun is a bright orange ball, low in the sky, illuminating the hills across the other side of the Firth of Forth.

Keep going. Keep going.

She can see the outline of her building up ahead, just past the hulking form of the Royal Yacht *Britannia*, permanently moored on the edge of the shopping centre, in the quay.

Finally, she reaches the end of the stony track, moves back onto the paved walkway that runs along the edge of the flats. The high-rise luxury apartments that had been built on the water's edge, in an area of the city that was undergoing major redevelopment. It's supposed to be on the tramline now, with a fast, neat route all the way up Leith Walk, along Princes

Street, out to the airport. But the money ran out and Leith is still served only by buses and not quite as regenerated as they'd promised.

But Louise doesn't care. She loves the old buildings around the docks, the grungy little pubs hidden away from the tourist throng that only ever make it as far as *Britannia* before disappearing back up to the city and the more picturesque sites of the castle and the gardens. Even if the main shopping street seems to sell more tourist tat than decent stuff nowadays, you still couldn't fault that view when you sat in a café at the West End and gazed out on to the castle rock, imagining everything that had gone before in thousands of years' worth of history.

Edinburgh. Her city. There's nowhere else she wants to be.

Outside her block, she stops, bends forwards and drops her hands to her knees. Her breath is coming out in jagged gasps as she checks her watch. Forty-three minutes. Brilliant. She's shaved seven minutes off her six-mile route, and she feels good. Her face glows hot in the cold morning air. Her legs feel wobbly, like she's properly used them for once. She's looking forward to her weigh-in at ten. She has a feeling this has been a good week. She'd even forgone her usual Friday night curry with the girls for an evening at the cinema with her cousin, and she'd managed to avoid having a hot dog or an ice cream, settling for just a small bag of salted popcorn, a Diet Coke and an oversized Tom Hardy on the screen to keep her satisfied. Could this be another three pounds lost? She hopes so. If so, then she's going to make her two-stone target even quicker than she'd hoped. And then, godammit … then she's going to make him notice her.

It's all very well to say it's what's inside that counts, but it's harder when you're older. You can't just walk into the pub and pick someone up; she'd look more like a desperate slapper than the 'empowered woman' she is perpetually aiming for. The only bonus is that she often gets told she looks ten years younger than she is, which might be another reason why the object of her desire hasn't noticed she exists, other than as a work colleague who is easy to get on with and doesn't smell of B.O. or fried egg sandwiches, a scent that quite a few of her colleagues seem to favour.

What was it with men and fried egg sandwiches? She couldn't understand why anyone would want that runny yolk dribbling out of the bread and down the edge of your hand. The thought makes her feel sick.

She pulls her keys out of the little pouch she has clipped through the laces on her left trainer, and as she starts to stand back up she is suddenly aware of someone standing behind her. She glances across the car park from her still bent position. She hadn't even noticed the car. Too busy thinking about 'Operation FitChick' and wondering if she had any blueberries left for her porridge. She stands up slowly. Turns. Plastering on a smile that says she is not at all inconvenienced by this development, when clearly she is.

'Morning. Good timing, eh? Just time for you to have yourself a shower and I'll make myself a wee tea while you're getting ready.'

This is so bloody typical, she thinks. Here I am working like a demon trying to get myself in the best shape of my life for a man, and here he is when I'm bright red, sweaty, make-up-less and wearing leggings that most definitely don't flatter my arse.

'Detective Sergeant Gray,' she says, 'Fresh from his training and bringing yet another scandal to darken our doors! To what do I owe this pleasure?'

He grins. 'I nearly didn't come back from that place, you know. Tulliallan is a nice wee spot. I'd forgotten how enjoyable it was being back at the Police College, getting three cooked meals, playing pool every night. Getting a decent night's sleep. It's nice to only be working on theory for a change. You forget what it's like in the real world. I was only there a week, but it feels like a lifetime. Trust me to come back and walk straight into this … Jesus, only me, eh? I'm starting to think I took the wrong job for a quiet life. Are we going in or not? It's freezing out here. Plus, these are getting cold and I like it when the butter melts …'

He holds up a brown paper bag and Louise smells the unmistakeable scent of fresh morning rolls.

As they stand waiting for the lift, she glances across at him. He's reading the fire regulations that are hanging on the wall. His fair hair is shorter than usual, neatly trimmed over his ears, his familiar side-burns now shorter, narrower and barely noticeable. The doors open and she catches her reflection in the mirror at the back of the lift and quickly walks in and faces the opposite way. He is humming quietly, and she's pleased to see that he's happy. He's had some pretty awful shit thrown at him these past few months. She senses this is the calm before the storm, though. What's he doing coming here to pick her up?

'What's happening, Davie? I was meant to be going in at twelve today.'

'Something's come up. They've sent down a couple of uniforms, and Malkie's on his way, but he wants us to go and take a look. Typical that this would happen just as I'd made my new base up here, eh? Funnily enough, I'd only just got into the station when the call came in. I nearly jumped back in the car and went all the way back, but I thought you might want to come with me. Seeing as you've been there before and enjoyed it so much.'

'Where?'

'Banktoun, of course. You might be spending a bit more time back in my neck of the woods.'

She smiles to herself. Plenty of time on the car journey to ask him how things went at Tulliallan. But more to the point, plenty of time to work her charms on him. She hopes whatever he's taking her to isn't too gruesome. But if Malkie's asked her to go with Davie, it's hardly going to be an invite for a relaxed brunch and a quick read of the papers. It was times like this she wondered why it was that she was so desperate to join the Serious Investigations Unit. But then she remembers. Life would be so boring otherwise.

3

Polly

The school is buzzing with activity, despite there being fewer pupils there than usual. The bus bringing many of them from the villages in the hills have been held up, no doubt already headed back to where they came from. Those kids might not even know that anything is wrong. Children are chattering as they file down the corridors towards the assembly room. Various calls from teachers of 'Slow down', 'No running', 'Keep quiet' are falling on deaf ears. Her heart is already hammering in her chest. The gossiping women at the post office. The police car outside. As she's unlocking the door to her office, a voice booms out from behind her.

'Ms McAllister, there you are. Emergency meeting in the assembly hall. Walk with me, I'll fill you in.'

Jon Poole, the headmaster and school rector, is wearing his black robes and carrying a pile of paperwork. His normally cheerful face is drained of colour, except for two red dots high on his cheeks. His soft grey hair flops forwards onto his face, and he pushes it away impatiently.

'The police are here. Catherine's been trying to find you for the last half-hour. Have you heard what's happened?'

His secretary, Catherine Leeming, is a striking and formidable woman, with the physique of an Olympic athlete and thick, honey-coloured hair twisted into a perfect topknot. Polly is slightly in awe of her, having spotted her rigorously ordered desk and ramrod straight filing shelves on the way into Jon's office that morning.

They march together through the side door into the assembly hall, where half of the seats are already occupied with boisterous children, the rest being slowly filled by the queues of kids making their way through the main doors. Next to the steps up to the stage, two uniformed police officers stand with their arms crossed over their chests, talking quietly to each other, glancing occasionally into the assembling audience.

Polly has to walk fast to keep up with Jon, who is striding across the polished floor as if his life depended on it. 'One of our sixth formers has been found dead. At home. The police are saying it might be suspicious. They want to talk to the children, then they want us to keep them here and give them counselling. Of all the times you could've gone walkabout, Polly ...'

'I ...' She pauses, feeling both chastised and riddled with guilt. 'I'm sorry, Mr Poole. I nipped to the post office. I was going to go through my list today. I didn't think there was anything urgent. After all, you've managed without someone for months ...'

She lets her sentence trail off, seeing Jon Poole's look of bewilderment. Why the hell did she call him Mr Poole? This is a disaster. Suddenly she feels like a pupil here again, not a staff member. She wonders if Jon thinks of her like that, too. She'd always suspected that he didn't particularly like her as a child and was surprised when he'd offered her the job. Even more surprised that he was still here after all these years. But she supposed he was only in his sixties, not a hundred and eighty like they used to think he was back when she was in her teens and he was probably only in his early forties – not much older than she is now. Get a grip, Polly! She remembers why she's here … remembers that there's a dead girl, that this is what's important right now.

'She was one of the good ones, Polly.' Jon's voice breaks, and he coughs, covering it up. He might seem like he's a perfect pillar of professionalism, but Polly knows he has a heart too. He's been at this school forever. He was deputy head when she was a pupil here, and now he's been head for so long that no one can really remember what it was like before. Even though she's been away for years, Polly can still feel the importance of this man. And she can sense his unease. His shock. It's hardly a regular occurrence, hearing news of a dead child on a Monday morning.

The two policewomen turn to greet them.

'Hello, sir. I'm Sergeant Zucarro and this is Constable Evans. We'd just like to have a quick word before you address the school, then, if you don't mind, we'd like to say a few things too. Then we'll leave you to it.'

'Will you need to talk to any of the pupils individually?' Jon asks.

'At this moment in time we're not really sure what we're dealing with,' the sergeant says. 'The SIO … sorry, the Senior Investigating Officer, said to just come and ask if we could be of any assistance at this stage. There'll be detectives taking over from us, I expect—'

'Detectives?' Polly interrupts. 'So it's a murder inquiry, then?'

The constable gives the sergeant a hard stare, and the sergeant blushes. They're both young. Can't be much older than some of the sixth years. The sergeant – was it Zucarro? – has the kind of dark, glossy hair that Polly would kill for. Constable Evans is bobbing about, taking everything in. She looks like an excited terrier, ready to pounce on someone's trainer and rip it to shreds.

'We don't know anything for sure, yet, Miss …?'

'McAllister. I'm the new guidance counsellor. It's my first day.'

The policewomen look alarmed. They smile, trying to make things a bit better than they are. 'Don't worry, Ms McAllister. You won't have to deal with anything on your own. But it will be good to have your expertise to help question the children.'

Jon pulls his robes around him and coughs loudly as he makes his way up the stairs to the stage. The room falls into silence; the waiting crowd know how to behave in his presence. Polly stands at the side of the stage and glances down at the front row as Jon begins his speech. She can't remember all of the staff's names yet. But she recognises Lucas Crisp, the biology teacher. She remembers him because of his clump of unruly brown hair and his thick, black-framed glasses, and his smile that she had found quite unnerving. She'd found him charming and endearing when he'd questioned her as part of the interview panel only a couple of months ago. She imagined he was popular with the students. She'd half-wondered, back then, if he was single. He was clearly far too young for her, but it was nice to have some eye-candy in the workplace, even if she was in no position to act on anything. She also remembers Lois Reibach, the quiet, softly spoken American teaching assistant, over for a year as part of a cultural exchange trip. Jon told her that Lois was great with the pupils, that she's eager to be involved in all aspects of their schooling. She's hoping to get her involved with some of the counselling sessions once she works out what it is she needs.

Jon coughs again, signalling the start of his speech. 'I'm sorry to have to gather you all like this today, but we wanted to make sure that you find out the information from a reliable source, rather than relying on hearsay and gossip, which, as you know, is prone to taking on a life of its own.'

There is some shuffling in seats. The air vibrates with anticipation.

'It is with much sadness that I must inform you that Katie Taylor has sadly passed away. She was found at home, in bed. At the moment, that's all we know and we don't yet know for sure if this was an accident or a result of some unknown medical condition. As we are unsure, the police are involved until the cause of death can be established as accidental, or … otherwise.'

More murmuring. Some scraping of seats. But Polly has blocked most of it out – focusing on the girl's name. Katie Taylor. Surely not … it couldn't be. Just a coincidence. There must be loads of other families with that surname in the town now. She can't be Mandy Taylor's daughter. If Mandy had a seventeen-year-old, she'd have heard about it, wouldn't she? Mandy must've been pregnant in her final year of school.

That year she spent most of her time trying to kick Polly's head in.

4

Louise

While she was showering and spending too long trying to decide what to wear, only to realise it didn't really matter, now that Davie's seen her at her worst, he has prepared them a couple of cheese rolls and made a flask of tea. She throws a pair of knickers and a new tube of toothpaste into her small overnight bag – she's always got it ready, just in case.

Despite her diet, she doesn't protest about the cheese and is impressed that he's managed to find a Tupperware box for the rolls, as well as a flask that even she'd forgotten she had. Must have been something Chris left behind. She's surprised that she's not bothered that it might be his. It's been nearly a year since they split up and at first every single reminder made her angry and tearful, but something has finally changed inside her. Now that she can see things for what they are. It's just a flask. She can't even remember the two of them using it to go anywhere together. He was hardly the picnicking type.

Davie drives, while Louise busies herself trying to pour tea into the cup and not her lap. She's vaguely aware of them driving along London Road, heading east, passing the grand Georgian crescents before hitting the new buildings that've been jammed into the gaps. Bingo halls. Chinese restaurants. A huge McDonald's where there used to be an opticians. They pass Meadowbank stadium, where she remembers once having to do a school athletics event and hating every second of it. Funny that it's taken her nearly thirty years to start running again.

'Pass us a roll, will you?'

'Is eating and driving not illegal?'

'Not yet. Anyway, what you going to do? Call the police?' He smiles, but she can see his mood is subdued. She hands him a roll and he mutters a curse under his breath as flour immediately flutters all over the front of his navy jumper, like a flurry of snow.

'Remind me again how it is you live in that big fancy apartment?'

She'd noticed him out on the balcony when she'd come out of the shower. He was gazing out towards the Forth Bridges, which were only a few miles to the west, quite the view. Not the usual place for a single, forty-something female detective constable whose family were third-generation fishmongers from the tiny village of Port Seton and who were barely keeping their heads above water, so to speak.

'I'm housesitting for my little brother. He's a broker with Standard Chartered. He's on a two-year secondment in Hong Kong and he didn't want to rent his flat out to drug dealers, who are pretty much the only people who could afford the rent on a place like this at the moment, with the way the rental market is.'

'Oh aye,' he says. 'You did tell me that. How the other half live, eh? What're you going to do when he comes back?'

She's still got eighteen months before that happens. As ruthless as it might sound, she's hoping to be in a relationship by then. Hoping the matter gets taken out of her hands. She's not expecting to ever live in a place like this again, although it's nice for a change. A three-bed semi on the outskirts of town with a man who doesn't treat her like a doormat would be a nice alternative. Maybe a wee dog, too. Or a cat even. Davie has a cat, she recalls. Cadbury. Smooth chocolatey fur. He's shown her photos. Belonged to his ex. He doesn't say much about her, but he's definitely still got the cat. He's got the scratches on his arm to prove it. She's happy with the thought of pets now. She's long given up on the hope that she might have children. Not that she's too old – not yet – but she's so used to being without them, it would be a hard lifestyle change to pull off. Especially with her job.

'Lou? What're you going to do when he comes back?'

She laughs. 'Sorry. I was miles away there. I haven't really thought about it,' she lies. She pulls a piece of roll off and pops it into her mouth, turning to gaze out of the window before he can read anything in her eyes. When she turns back, he is concentrating hard on the road. There are two lanes of traffic, and the car in front doesn't seem to be able to decide which one it prefers.

'So, fill me in,' she says.

He chews for longer than seems necessary. 'Seventeen-year-old girl. Katie Taylor. Found dead in her bed this morning. At first it looked like it might be a suicide. Pills on the bedside cabinet. No signs of a struggle. Mother came back from nightshift at a local factory, couldn't wake her up.'

They're passing the Fort now. A sprawling out-of-town shopping centre whose ineffective road layout results in a seemingly endless queue of traffic from a Friday afternoon until a Sunday night. Louise remembers going to the cinema there, years ago. One of the *Back to the Future* films. They had a DeLorean outside the entrance. No camera phones to snap photos, though; not back then.

Louise takes a mouthful of tea. It's always grim when it's a kid, even if it turns out to be an accident rather than anything

27

intentional: always grim. The parents sink in on themselves. No one can comprehend it. She remembers the first time she had to go and tell the parents that their child was never coming home. An accident on the bypass. Joyriders. All four died and the oldest one was only sixteen. That'd affected her for a long time afterwards. The expressions on those people's faces as their worlds had collapsed around their ears.

'Right. So what's making it look suspicious, then?' she says, already thinking up the possibilities. Marks on the body? A vital piece of evidence found nearby? Maybe it was just completely out of character – but then, who knows everything about their teenage kid these days? All that cyber bullying – stuff that they're so ashamed about they could never tell their parents…

'Doctor wasn't convinced by the scene. Said it looked staged.'

'Been watching *CSI*, has he?'

'He used to be a pathologist, retired and went back to being a locum GP. He was the one called out. Just coincidence. A good one. For us, I mean. Another doc might not have been so aware. Might've been nothing for us to examine.'

'What do you mean, "staged"?'

'The way the pills were spilled on the side. The way she was lying in the bed. Her arms were close to her sides, the blankets tucked in around her.'

'Blankets? I didn't think anyone had blankets these days … I always have to untuck them in hotel rooms. I hate my feet being trapped.' Not that I've been in a hotel room for a while, she thinks. She shifts in her seat, feeling the waistband of her trousers digging into her stomach. Why the hell did she choose this pair?

Davie ignores her, carries on. 'He took photographs on his phone. Made sure he took some of her undisturbed, then during his examination. He couldn't be certain, but he said it looked as if she had fresh bruising on her arms and legs. It was unusual enough for him to be concerned.'

'We caught a lucky break there, then. Another GP ... someone without his experience. We could've missed this altogether. I mean – hopefully it's nothing. The bruising could be unrelated to her death. But if it's not ...'

'Exactly,' Davie says.

Louise catches a glimpse of the town sign as Davie indicates off the roundabout and wonders what idiotic council pow-wow came up with the cheesy slogan.

Welcome to Banktoun
Twinned with Le Havre, France
Le Happiest Town in the County

5

Neil

Neil wrenches a branch from where it's been stuck to the ground with several days' worth of frost and chucks it into the river. There is a thin layer of ice on the surface and it breaks easily as the branch cuts through it, disappearing into the depths below.

Bloody Katie.

He should be on his way to school now, but he's already decided he's not going in. He unsticks a couple of smaller branches (twigs, really) and throws them in. Digby's Deathhole. One of the nicer spots along this stretch, despite the name. No one is likely to be swimming in there for a good few months yet, though. No one is quite that stupid.

Today was meant to be a special day. He'd sat with Katie in her bedroom and they'd discussed it all. Worked out what to do. They were going to get a bus to town and walk up the bridges. He liked it up there. A nice part of the old town, full of nooks and crannies, old buildings, cool cafes. Pubs, too. As long as they weren't in their school uniforms, they'd get into some of the pubs up there. It was close to the university, and most of the freshers were only a year older than him and

Katie. Katie could easily pass for eighteen, and despite his baby face he had perfected an older look with his clothes and his perpetual scowl. People often thought he was a grumpy bastard, but it couldn't be further from the truth. He just liked that moody look. He practised in the mirror, getting the scowl just right. Then he'd add a bit of eyeliner that was so subtle you'd barely know it was there – but it made his eyes stand out more. Brought out the deep green.

He'd describe himself as intense.

Nice.

But he had a temper, just like anyone else. And Katie trying to change the plans at the last minute had pissed him right off.

'I know it's not what we agreed,' she'd said. Her voice had become that high-pitched whine that really grated on him. Why did girls do this? Didn't they realise it was a signal for guys to switch off and not listen to another word until they started speaking normally again? 'But I think it's better this way. Safer. You know that everything will be fucked if anyone finds out about this money.' He'd been picking at a scab under his chin at this point. A shaving nick that he was refusing to leave alone, enjoying the sting each time he ripped off the healing piece of skin. 'Neil ...' She'd poked him in the ribs then, and he remembered her saying money, but that was really it.

'What? Sorry, I didn't hear you. Say that again.'

'I knew you weren't listening to a word I was saying.' Her tone had turned petulant now, and to emphasise this she'd angrily pulled her T-shirt back down over her bare breasts and slid up to the top of the bed, hugging her knees to her chest.

'Babe—'

'No. I've told you. I'm going to give the scratch card to someone safe. Someone *neutral.* Then when the time's right, when I'm sure Brooke's not sniffing about, then we'll go and cash it in. There's plenty of time. You've got one hundred and eighty days. I checked on the website.'

Brooke ... why did she have to mention Brooke? He'd shuffled up the bed towards her, tried to remove her hands from her knees but she'd pressed down harder, not letting him in. This was his punishment. *No shagging for you, Neily-boy. Not until you agree with everything I say ...* What was it with girls? Even the good ones, like Katie. They were all so bloody neurotic and controlling. They wanted it all their own way all the time.

'Where is it, anyway?'

'Where's what?'

'The scratch card, you arse. What else are we talking about here?'

'Fuck off, Neil.'

'Jesus! What's up with you? One minute you're all over me, talking about all our plans, ready to suck my dick ... next minute you're curled up there like a tight wee bitch. You on the blob or something? Fucksake ...'

He'd stopped when he realised she was crying.

'You're a prick, Neil. You know that? You're just like all the others. You're all the fucking same.'

'Oh, come on. I'm sorry. Honestly. You just ... it's just you got me horny, then you stopped. My dick's throbbing. Honestly. What you do to me ...'

He'd given her his best puppy dog smile, but she wasn't having it. 'Right. Fuck this, then. If you're not telling me where the scratch card is, and you're not up for a shag, then I'm not hanging about to hear you bloody complaining about what a prick I am. There's plenty of other wenches that'd be quite happy to take a piece of this.'

He blinks at the memory. He'd actually pointed to his crotch. He was like some sex-starved lunatic or something. No wonder she'd told him where the fuck to go. He didn't even know why he'd acted like that. Maybe just the disappointment – he'd been looking forward to their day in Edinburgh – getting the cash – celebrating. He was hoping he could convince her to get a cheap hotel. Really go for it. They'd still have most of the cash left, and then they could chat more about what she was going to do with it. It was her money, after all, but she'd made it clear that she wanted to share it between them. Made sure he knew that she saw a future with him.

He wanted that too.

Which was why he was so pissed off with himself for what he did afterwards – jeopardising that – a life with Katie – for a cheap thrill. He was normal, though, wasn't he? No one was actually faithful to their girlfriend at school, were they? If Katie told him she'd been with someone else, he'd put his balls through a shredder, but he'd still want to be with *her*. She was the best-looking girl in the school – and he was lucky that some guys couldn't see past her Gothy clothes and make-up to see what a proper catch he had.

She was all his.

Well, hopefully. He'd texted her a few times after their argument and she hadn't replied. Still punishing him. She'd stop when it suited her – she could never keep it up for that long. *You're such an idiot, Neil,* she'd say. Then she'd give him the eyes that said *I want you. Right. Now.*

He decides he'll go and find her after registration. Get her to come with him to his. His mum and dad had left early and they wouldn't be back till late. It was about time that Katie got to try out the bubble-jet bath in their fancy new en suite …

He picks up a final branch and flings it into the river, at peace with himself now – ready to face Katie and apologise for being a total dick. He can block out the rest. He can get over it, forget it happened. Assuming someone else doesn't blab. He flips up his hood, adjusts his rucksack onto two shoulders and climbs up the slippery bank. He cuts up through the trees and onto the edge of the playing fields. Picks up his pace a bit and he makes his way down the edge, keeping close to the fence until he's past the old pavilion and in line with the side

33

of the main school building. He takes his phone out of his coat pocket, checks the time. He's late. Well late. So what. He slows down again. Turns into the playground and hopes the side door is open so he can sneak into the common room without anyone seeing him.

Too late.

Pete Brotherstone, the janitor's dopey assistant, is hovering outside the door to the boiler room.

The words come out automatically. 'All right, Pete? Got any fags?'

Neil knows Pete doesn't smoke, but it's something that always winds the other boy up, so he likes to say it. It's a pathetic wind-up, as wind-ups go, and Katie always gives him a row for it. He hears her voice in his head. *Leave him alone, Neil. What did he ever do to you?* Problem is, Pete's an easy target. He's one of those boys who just doesn't quite operate on the same level as others of his age. Slow? Autistic? No one really knows, but he's high-functioning enough to have a job and no one does anything *that* bad to him, seeing as he's Councillor Brotherstone's son. Of course there have been various stories and rumours about him over the years. Things he's meant to have done. Nothing's ever stuck. Nothing's ever been proven – probably because he's never actually *done* anything wrong – he's just one of those unfortunates in life, someone to be pitied rather than feared. He's not even that weird, as it happens. People just like to use him as a scapegoat and the butt of all jokes. On the other hand, some say there's no smoke without fire. Bollocks to that, though. Just because people are a bit odd doesn't mean they're up to no good. Neil knows he should know better, yet he can't resist it.

Pete is fiddling with something in his hands. Neil can't see what it is. He's about to ask, but the boy cuts in first.

'I don't smoke. And they're not fags, they're cigarettes. And you shouldn't smoke them because they're bad for you.

Because of the tar. It's not like the tar they put on the roads, but it's bad anyway. And everyone else is in there now and you're out here. Why are you out here? It's cold. I'm helping to fix the boiler …'

Neil ignores him and drops his phone back into his pocket. He picks up his pace again and as he rounds the corner spots the steamed-up windows of the assembly hall. Sees the outlines of bodies inside. The silhouette of 'Packety' Crisp's hair. He's another one that people are always going on about. But Christ, if having hair like a Brillo pad and being a bit too enthusiastic about the life-cycle of fruit flies is enough to make you a fucked-up paedo axe-murderer, then there's no hope for half of the school.

This is off, though. Not good. Assembly? There's never an assembly at this time. Weird. He ducks down the gap between the main building and the annexe and that's when he spots the police car sitting outside the school gates.

A strange feeling comes over him. Something squirms at the back of his mind. Dread. Fear. His heart seems to grow bigger somehow, letting him know that it's there. His breaths come out in cold puffs. Emergency assembly. Police car. Not good. Definitely not good.

He takes his phone out again. Texts Katie:

Babe, I'm outside. You in assembly? What's going on?

He knows she'll have her phone on silent, but it'll be on vibrate. She'll reply straight away. She always does. Assuming she's forgiven him, that is. He waits. Refreshes his messages.

No reply.

THREEWISEMONKEYSBLOG

Telling It Like It Is

Posted: 1st Aug 2016 by SpeakNoEvil
Status: Draft
Comments: 0

> *See, see my playmate,*
> *Come out and play with me*
> *And bring your dollies three*
> *Climb up my apple tree*
> *Holler down my rain barrel*
> *Slide down my cellar door*
> *And we'll be jolly friends*
> *Forever evermore.*

You know this one, right? Just a harmless playground rhyme, isn't it? It was always one of my favourites. The lines seem to work well for the clapping, don't they? Back and forth, you and me. Going faster and faster until one of us messes up. I always thought it was 'Cee Cee', like a girl's name, but then – thank God for the internet – turns out it's not. This is just the first verse.

There are six in total. The whole thing tells a very interesting little story. Funny how these kids' rhymes are always more sinister than they first appear. This one sounds like fun, doesn't it? Two little girls playing with dolls, climbing trees, shouting into barrels. Then there's the cellar ... what's that about? And the friends for evermore bit – that sounds good, doesn't it? Everyone wants their best friends to be their best friends forever and ever.

Bet you've become 'blood sisters' with someone, haven't you? Pricking your thumbs with a pin, making a big deal of the pain, even though it's nothing. A prick on the thumb isn't pain. Squeezing out the blood to form a shiny red orb. Rubbing it against your friend's finger, imagining your blood mingling together.

Why would you want to be sisters with someone, if you had the choice? What's that saying – you can choose your friends, you can't choose your family? I wouldn't choose my family. Not if I had a choice. A proper choice.

Families are science. You come from the same seed, spread down over the years like pollen. Friends are psychology. Chosen, or thrown together? Why do you choose your friends? Why do they choose you?

And ... what if they choose you, then they *unchoose* you? Then what?

At least your family can't 'unchoose' you – as much as they might like to. Like I said. Interesting, isn't it?

Makes you think: do you really want *anything* to be 'forever evermore'?

6

Polly

There are many reasons why people become bullies. In most cases, it's a number of factors, or a spiralling chain of events. Envy and resentment. Low self-esteem. A shitty upbringing from a parent who had a shitty upbringing, and so it goes on. The bullied becomes the bully. It's the only way they can deal with their own situation.

It's the reason that Polly became a counsellor. She tries to tell herself that what she did all those years ago doesn't really count as bullying but, studying the psychology of it all, she knows she's trying to make things sound better for herself. Of course she was a bully. OK, she never physically hurt anyone; but she made people feel inadequate. Small. She was condescending. She pitted people against each other. If that's not bullying, then what is? There are people she has to talk to. People she has to apologise to. Two people in particular, whose lives she helped to ruin. It's part of the reason she came back. To put things right. But that'll have to wait for now.

What Mandy Taylor did to *her* was something very different. Something that she's never told anyone. But that's no excuse, is it? Polly has a feeling that she's going to have to deal with this head on, and soon. Because at some stage or another she suspects she might have to talk to Katie Taylor's mother.

She glances around the wide, wood-panelled hall as Jon steps to the side and Sergeant Zucarro steps up to say a few words. 'If anyone would like to say anything about Katie … if anyone has heard anything unusual, or seen anything strange. Anything they say will be kept in strict confidence. We need to find out what happened here, and we need your help.'

Polly feels needles of dread poking at her. They aren't handling this very well. They've made it sound like something suspicious has happened to Katie. Something bad. There's barely any pretence of it being 'an accident' any more, despite what Jon has said. But what now? As soon as the kids leave the room, there's going to be chaos. Letting them out before lunchtime just isn't going to work. The parents will go nuts. These people are at work. The school can't just allow the kids to roam the streets. No, they're going to have to keep them here but let them have time to do whatever they need to do, to talk to whoever they want to. They can't expect them to be able to concentrate now, not with all the speculation that's going to come out of this.

There's a rustle of bags and a scrape of chairs as the pupils start to get to their feet after Jon's final speech.

'Head on back to your classrooms and continue your daily schedule as normal, but please talk to your teachers if you need to and if anyone needs to discuss anything in private, please come and see me, or our new guidance counsellor, Ms McAllister.'

Polly's head snaps up at the mention of her name, and she can tell from the look on Jon's face that it's not the first time he's mentioned her. He's introduced her to a room that contains the entire school and she's been too immersed in the crowd to acknowledge him. She hadn't been distracted intentionally; it was just that she was scanning the faces for signs of upset.

Trying to store their characteristics in her head so that she could access them again. It was difficult, as no one was sitting in their form class rows – they'd spilled in from various places and been told to sit down wherever there was a free seat. So that was going to make it more difficult for her to work out who anyone was. But she'd spotted one girl she wasn't likely to forget. A small girl with long red hair, as bright as a pillar box. It stood out in stark contrast to the monotonous navy of the school uniform. Polly was amazed that such a colour could exist naturally, but clearly it did as there was no way that the pupils were allowed to dye their hair. Especially not a shade as bright as that. That girl had cried all the way through the assembly, yet no one else seemed to have been bothered enough to comfort her.

Polly needs to find out who she is.

She also needs to know several other things, right now. Does Katie Taylor have any brothers or sisters at the school? Who are her friends? And most importantly, does she have a boyfriend? She also needs to know which classes she was taking, how she was doing in them, and what her plans were for June, when she finished sixth year. She wants to have everything to hand to assist the police, should they need it. She'd got off to a rocky start here, and that wasn't her intention.

Her mind drifts back to that day in her bedroom, where everything went wrong.

Claire.

She had to call Claire.

The whole point of coming here was to try to make amends.

7

Louise

'So, what do you know about this family?' Louise asks. She assumes that as Davie has spent his entire life in the town he will have heard of them at the very least. They drive down the back road and round toward the river, crossing over a humpback bridge. It's all very picturesque, the river and the quaint little pub on the edge. The fields nearby, stretching off to the low hills beyond. Louise knows there's a stately home out there somewhere. They used to do a book festival there that she'd heard about on the local radio, but apparently the owners of the house, some random Duke of something-or-other, had decided to reclaim his home for himself, so there were to be no more events, which was a shame. She catches a final glance of the pub in the passenger-side wing mirror and sighs, imagining a pleasant day there in the summer, drinking pints and not having to worry about dead teenagers.

'Surprised they've not got their sandbags out,' Davie says. 'Must be due for a flood once this snow turns to slush and the rain comes to wash it all away. Did you see how high the river was?'

She stares at him. Frowns.

'Sorry, what did you say? Oh aye. This family. The Taylors. I know them, all right.'

'Sounds ominous.'

'Oh, you know. Single mum, had her first at sixteen. Before that, in and out of the station. Usual stuff – shoplifting … criminal damage … fighting. She was a wild one, that. She works up in the professional laundry on the edge of town. Barrett's. They do all the sheets and tablecloths and all those sorts of things for the local hotels. Works nights, so probably keeps her out of trouble. And the pub. Her kids are a chip off the old block, though. Well, one of them anyway. Brooke – the middle one. What is it they say about middle children?'

'Well, they're not the leader who gets to find things out for themselves, and they're not the baby who gets spoiled rotten. They're the piggy in the middle. Left to fend for themselves. The black sheep. They might end up depressed … feel unloved. Anger is definitely an issue. Maybe they have to do more to get noticed?'

'Sounds about right. She's definitely a problem. She's as wild as hawthorn and twice as spiky. I see her most weeks in the station. I'm hoping she's going to grow out of it, but she's not really getting the support. I hear there's a new guidance counsellor starting at the school. They've had no one since Rebecca Edwards retired last year. Not sure who the replacement is, but I'm hoping she's bit less highly strung than old Mrs E. Lovely woman, but a bit crotchety. No use with those rowdy kids. Even the good ones are mouthy wee shites these days.'

'What about the father? I take it he's not on the scene.'

'Well, Brooke and Brett – that's the younger brother – their father is currently residing at Her Majesty's pleasure. Bungled bank raid. Not his first. Not sure he had much to do with any of them anyway. Katie's dad, though – well, there's one of the town's wee mysteries. There were rumours – plenty in the frame … a teacher, a shopkeeper, one of the pub landlords, a couple of the lads in the year above … a soldier that came down for the army recruitment day. Mandy refused to say who he was, and in the end no one really cared too much. She'd been in care since she was five. Neglect. No hope. It was a foregone conclusion she'd end up with a young baby and a council house after a life like that. What else could she have done, really? It's hard to pass judgement when you know the background. She had no chance in life, not really.'

'And Katie? She sounds different from her younger siblings. What about her?'

Davie pulls into the kerb on the edge of a row of terraced houses. They face out onto a field of frozen wheat. A few oaks are dotted along the boundary of the road and the field. It feels quiet. Peaceful. She was half expecting to end up in a rough estate, but then from what she knew Banktoun wasn't really like that. Sure, there was the usual divide between the rich and poor, the haves and have-nots, but overall it seemed to be quite an integrated community.

He switches off the engine and sighs. 'Katie was different. She was the only academic one of the bunch. I met her a few times, mainly when bringing her little sister back from the station. Katie would be the one to cook them their tea and keep an eye on them while Mandy was at work. Don't get me wrong – I'm sure she was no angel. But I've never had reason to see her at the station. Never cautioned her in the street. Always thought she was going to break the mould and do something with her life. Despite Mandy's brash ways, I think she'd have been proud to see one of her children do well for themselves. Have things that she couldn't give them. As for Brooke, though, she was a difficult child. I could see she resented Katie – not just for her being brighter and full of prospects, but she was better looking too. I know I shouldn't say that – but you'll see soon enough. Brooke's one that goes for the overdone make-up and the big hair, whereas Katie was more of a natural beauty – although, to be fair, she had turned a bit Goth or Emo or whatever it's called these days. She had a nice boyfriend too. If this turns out the way I think it's going to, we might have to talk to him later, although I genuinely can't imagine him being involved. Mind, I've been wrong about people in the past.'

'If someone did do something, he's going to be one of the prime suspects, Davie. Her family, too. Harsh as it is.'

'Aye. Fucker, this bit, isn't it? I'm still holding out a wee bit of hope that it was something accidental …'

They get out of the car and walk up the path to the house. There's an eerie silence on the street. She'd expected to see a few busybodies hanging around at least. She's got her finger on the doorbell when she sees the fluttering of curtains a few doors down. So they are about then. She claps her hands together, tries to rub in some warmth. Seems that rubberneckers don't like to come out in the cold.

'Ah, there you are. Get lost, did you?' Detective Inspector Malkie Reid is looking slightly less dishevelled than normal. He tends to look almost human on a Monday. Freshly laundered shirts and neatly pressed jumpers for the start of the week. By Wednesday he looks like he's rolled down a hill in them.

'Sorry, sir. I was out when DS Gray arrived. I wasn't expecting to be coming in this morning. I—'

'Morning, Malkie,' Davie says, putting a stop to any more mumbled apologies. Louise is prone to rambling on, if left unchecked.

'Davie. Right. Come upstairs, will you? Constable Benedict is with Miss Taylor in the kitchen.' He pauses. Adds, 'The mother,' as clarification.

'Should I—'

'Upstairs, DC Jennings. Come on.'

They are halfway up the stairs when Louise hears a burst

of heartbroken sobbing filtering its way upwards from the kitchen. She pauses, notices that she's the only one still wearing her shoes. She's about to sit down and take them off when she glances upstairs and sees the box of paper suits and shoe covers on the landing.

She takes a deep breath. Young girl. Just a young girl. She'd hoped that it was all a big mistake. Some awful accident. Exam stress, one too many pills. A freak medical condition gone unnoticed until now. But the quiet efficiency of the officers in the house and the forensics paraphernalia suggests that this was no accident. Anything but.

8

Polly

Polly hangs back as the crowd of children filters out towards the classrooms. There's less laughing and jostling now. A tentative calm hangs over them. Polly tries to scan their faces. To see who was a friend of the dead girl, who wasn't. *Does she have siblings?* She regrets popping out earlier. Realises she should've been reading through the registers, finding out who's who and what's what. She feels like she's been thrown in at the deep end. Feels incompetent and unprofessional. Already, Jon is disappointed in her.

So much for her fresh start.

She's standing outside her office when she spots the bright red hair again. The girl who'd been distraught during the assembly. She needs to talk to her, needs to know her relationship with Katie Taylor. A friend, surely. But she seems younger. Doesn't look like a sixth year. A dark thought swirls into her head. *Maybe she's not a friend. Maybe she knows what happened …*

Don't be ridiculous. This wasn't something a child could've done, was it? She wasn't even sure of the details of the death yet. She needed to speak to Jon. And the police.

The two police officers are at the other end of the corridor, chatting to Jon. Polly turns back to the crowd, which has thinned considerably. No sign of the redhead now.

Damn it.

She spots the teaching assistant, Lois Reibach, scuttling off along the corridor behind the last of the stragglers.

'Lois … wait …'

The younger woman turns, and Polly can see now that her eyes are red-rimmed, her face pale. Jon had said that Lois was a confidante to many of the older students. The ones struggling with their exams, the ones being plunged into making life choices they weren't ready for. Had she been friendly with Katie?

'Sorry, Polly. I need to get back to class. Mrs Cohen is off and I'm looking after her third years.'

'Sure, yeah. I just wanted to ask you a couple of things quickly. Can I walk with you?'

Lois nods. She looks away, stares straight ahead. Doesn't want to meet Polly's eye. *Interesting*.

'Do you know the girl with the red hair? I mean, of course you do. I mean, is she a friend of Katie's? Was she, I mean?' Polly stammers over her words. This is not going to plan.

'I, uh. Yes. Of course. That's Diane McBride. She's a fourth year, but her and Katie do some stuff together, they were creating a magazine or something. I think. I'm not really sure. But yes, they were friends.'

Polly frowns. Something in the younger woman's voice is off. 'Do you know where she is now? Where she's meant to be? I lost her in the crowd …'

They walk past an open area where a few of the pupils are chatting in hushed tones. She almost misses her, hidden far in the corner, obscured by taller kids huddled in front.

'Ah wait, there she is …' Polly breaks away from Lois just as a tall older boy strides through the break-out area, the crowd parting in front of him like he's Moses. People step back, staring. Whispering.

'Who's that?' Polly asks Lois, but the woman has vanished around a corner.

'Excuse me, excuse me,' Polly says, trying to push her way through the kids. They don't know her yet. They just see authority and immediately their eyes are suspicious. By the time she makes it through, the redheaded girl and the tall boy have gone.

'Damn it,' she mutters. She turns and heads back to her office. She's asked Catherine to let all the teachers know that she needs to speak to Katie's friends.

All of them.

LucasCrispIsAPaedo

🔒 Secret Group

23 Members (21 new)

Luke Crust
18h

Right, well this page speaks for itself, eh? If you've no heard already, where huv you been? Katie Taylor is dead. Dusnae take too much ov a brain to work out who dun it ...

Likes(23)   Comments(6)

Al Samson RIP Katie, poor cow.
Big Jim Nailor I always kent that bloke was dodgy as fuck. Wi a name like that?
Al Samson Who set this page up?
Big Jim Nailor Who gies a fuck?
Sally Stephens Poor Katie. I don't think this page is going to help, is it?
Big Jim Nailor Shut it, you.

9

Louise

Louise slips on the suit and shoe covers in silence. The eerie calmness to these proceedings always makes her feel a bit sick. She steps into the girl's bedroom. Outside, a tall, stringy willow is swaying in the breeze. One of the branches is tapping gently against the window. She imagines Katie lying in her bed at night, in the darkness. Listening to the rhythmic tapping of the branch.

Tap. Tap. Tap.

The girl is lying on the bed, covered with a white sheet. Next to her, a reed-thin woman she recognises as Mary Haynes, the pathologist, is writing notes into the black Moleskine notepad that she always carries in her coat pocket. She glances up as Louise enters, raises an eyebrow in greeting. She's been for a drink with Mary a few times. Enjoys her dark humour. She's quiet today though, like everyone else.

Two CSIs are busy dusting the dressing table and desk. One of them has a camera slung around his neck and Louise knows they will have photographed everything before moving it. She'd like to see the photos. It's hard to see now that things have been shuffled around, but a girl's desk and dressing table can tell you a lot about them. Her own dressing table in the flat is littered with half-empty tubes of make-up, dried-up lipsticks, nail varnishes she hasn't opened for months. There is always a neat little pile of eyeliner pencil shavings, and Louise often wonders why she doesn't sharpen straight into the bin, but there is something about the little curls of wood and the smell of the shaved wax that she likes.

Katie Taylor's dressing table is in a similar state, at first glance. Various aerosol cans – body spray, deodorant. Bottles of perfume. Tubes, sticks, packets. On the mirror fixed to the back there are an array of long necklaces, leather, beaded, some with pendants hanging on the end. Her desk is small, and she's made a neat stack of books and jotters on one side. A giant pencil sharpener-shaped container houses a variety of pens and pencils, a bobble-head pencil top wobbles gently over the side.

Malkie Reid is talking quietly to Davie in the corner of the room. There is another man with them, who Louise assumes is the GP who called it in. He looks pale. Sad. She imagines he was hoping for a different outcome, as were they all. But Mary Haynes's efficient movements suggest that he's got it right.

Louise is perusing the girl's collection of prints and framed posters that hang on the wall above her desk when Mary appears at her side.

'Bruising is new, all right. On her arms and legs. Finger shaped. Want to see?'

Something about one of the posters isn't right. She's not sure what it is.

'Right. Of course,' she says, following Mary over to the bed. She's distracted. Thinking about the poster. She'll go back to it in a minute.

Mary peels the sheet off carefully. Davie breaks away from the huddle in the corner and comes over to look. He stands close to Louise and she can feel his warmth radiating towards her. She feels her cheeks grow hot.

'Warm in here, isn't it?' No one replies.

Mary frowns. 'As I was saying. Finger-shaped bruises, here … and here.' She points to places on Katie's upper arms and just above her knees.

'Have you established cause of death?' Louise says.

'I don't know for sure yet, but the way her face is, it looks like asphyxiation. Also, I noticed that one of her pillows was under her head at an odd angle, not the way you'd put it yourself. Didn't look comfortable. I think someone put it there after she died.'

Finger marks. Bruising. Not an accident then. Someone sat on top of this girl, pressed a pillow into her face. Suffocated her. Louise feels sick, imagining the fear. The terror. Such an intimate act though, in her bedroom. On her bed. Pressing down. They'd need force. Rage. It was someone she knew, Louise was sure of it. She stands back as another team arrives.

'Ready to go, Doc?' one of them says.

Mary Haynes nods.

The room is silent as they carefully lift Katie onto a stretcher and take her away.

10

Neil

He'd been about to sneak into the back of the assembly when it became obvious that everyone in the school had somehow managed to squeeze themselves in there. They never did that. Usually the assemblies were split into year groups, or juniors and seniors. The hall is big, but it isn't big enough for the entire school of eight hundred people. Not with the partition still in place.

No. This isn't normal. And that means it isn't good.

He refreshes his phone again, just as the flashing battery light gives its last weak burst of red, then it's dead.

'Fucking phone,' he mutters. He's in the corridor, looking in through the glass. He can see Mr Poole up on the stage. Talking his usual shite, no doubt. He can't see who else is up there because the glass pane in the door is too small and he can't get the angle. A woman, though. No one he recognises.

He's still contemplating whether to go in or not when the sliding door of the partition opens fully and people start to come out. Sensing that this is not a good time to be found lurking outside the assembly hall, he turns and heads back into the main corridor.

Outside, Mr Hennessy, the janitor, is wheeling a wheelbarrow full of garden equipment towards the area near the front gate that they called 'the Students' Garden', while Pete ambles behind him, carrying nothing. The garden's a row of raised beds where various things are planted, according to registration class. The kids in years one to three plant cabbages and try to grow the biggest pumpkin. The kids in the later years are supposed to plant more exotic things, like herbs, and use them in home ec. Some of the girls plant flowers. At the moment, the whole row of beds is bare and frost-covered and he can't imagine what the two of them are planning to do there. They're not attempting to turn the soil in January, are they? Fools. He wonders, sometimes, if Hennessy just invents things for them both to do to keep themselves in jobs.

Just inside the main door of the school there is a small alcove with a couple of grey fabric chairs and a big bookcase full of stuff that looks too boring to even make it into the library. Neil slides into the space behind the edge of the bookcase and the wall, waiting for people to pass. He can still see Pete and Hennessy out in the playground. He presses himself back against the wall. Anyone outside could see him, if they looked. But on the inside he's well hidden. He tries to catch snatches of conversation as people walk past. They all seem to be talking over each other, so he's not picking out much of what they say. A few words here and there ... 'I cannae believe it', 'shocking', 'it's no true', 'that family'. He could just walk out there, grab someone and ask them what's going on. But he's been on a long run of late attendances and absences, and despite his curiosity and the feeling low in his gut that something is very wrong he's still not up for being yelled at by Poole or any of his sidekicks. The secretary, Ms Leeming, with her towering stilettos and Swedish porn-star looks, is more terrifying than the headmaster. MILF, though. Definitely. He *definitely* would. Although he'd be scared she might crush him to death between those well-sculpted thighs.

Christ, Neil, he thinks. What're you going to do? Stay here all bloody day?

He's fucked off that his phone is dead. Fucked off about Katie. Just completely fucked off, really. About everything.

He peeks his head out, just enough to see who's about. The voices have faded to a trickle. The footsteps have lessened. They've all passed.

Now's his chance.

If he can get to the senior year break-out area, he can pretend he's been there all the time. Make out he was in the bogs when the call for the assembly came. He'll manage to make something up. He always does.

He sneaks out, trying to walk on his toes so that his rubber soles don't squeak on the lino. As he rounds the corner to the break-out area, he sees that quite a few people are there, all in their little huddled groups. He spots the woman from the stage. Recognises her, now that she's up close. She's the new guidance councillor. McCabe? McKay? McAllister. That's it. She's standing at the edge of the carpeted area, looking like she's not sure who to pounce on first.

Then he spots her. Diane McBride. Cannae miss her with that hair. Some people take the piss out of her because of her English accent, but he loves it. Diane was born and bred in West London. Fuck knows what made her family want to relocate up here. Neil can't wait to get away from the place. He really likes Diane, and loves asking her about London – a place he and Katie would be moving to as soon as they got their exams out of the way. Summer jobs, then uni. That was the plan.

Avoiding Ms McAllister, Neil skirts around a row of bookcases and makes his way towards the top of the room. Diane is standing on her own, with a semi-circle of kids firing questions at her. She looks like she's been crying.

'Oi,' Neil says. 'Leave her alone.'

He pushes through the crowd and hustles the girl off around the corner.

'Neil, Neil ... oh my God, are you OK?' he hears someone say. Someone else tries to grab his arm. 'Mate ...' He shrugs it off and drags Diane into the fourth-year girls' toilets.

'Diane, what the fuck? What's going on?' She bursts into tears, throws her hands up over her face. He steps forward to embrace her, just as the door flies open and Poole's thunderous face appears.

'You're not supposed to be in here,' he says. The expression on his face changes, softens. His eyes look wet. Lois Reibach is right behind him, and she steps in and leads Diane towards the sinks.

'Splash your face with water, honey. It'll help. I promise.'

Neil tunes out the voice. Tunes out everything.

Focuses on Poole's face.

'What is it? What the fuck's happened?'

The headmaster doesn't even flinch at his swearing.

'Come on, son. I need to talk to you. Come on. Not here. We'll pop out the side door and head back around to my office. You don't need to walk past the others.'

'I don't understand,' Neil says.

Confusion is soon replaced by fear as the headmaster continues. 'I'm so sorry, Neil. This is going to be very hard.'

As the door swishes shut behind him, he can still make out the sound of Diane's racking sobs, and the sounds of the old pipes whining as water judders and splashes out of the taps.

THREEWISEMONKEYSBLOG

Telling It Like It Is

Posted: 1st Sep 2016 by SpeakNoEvil
Status: Draft
Comments: 0

> *Oh no my playmate*
> *I can't come play with you*
> *My dollies have the flu*
> *Boo hoo boo hoo*
> *Can't holler down rain barrels*
> *Or slide down a cellar door*
> *But we'll be jolly friends*
> *Forever evermore.*

I'm not sure what I think about the whole BFF thing – Best Friends Forever. Yeah, right. I used to be really jealous of those girls who were BFFs – and that's before the phrase even existed. You know the ones – same hair, same clothes, matching lip-gloss. Those vacant, pretty girls with the rugby-playing boyfriends who beat them up at the weekends.

You must know who I mean? Far be it for me to name names here, but there are some stupid, stupid girls out there who should know better. No boy should ever be able to justify giving you a black eye. You know that, don't you? Just because he's popular, and you're popular, and all your iden-tikit mates are popular – doesn't mean he can get away with doing what he likes.

I've seen those bruises, you know. That day you skived off PE and said you had your period.

Bull. Shit.

Did you see me looking? I wanted to say something to you then, but the thing is – no one ever wants to believe the bad stuff. No one ever wants to hear the truth. The only truth is that you're popular and I'm not.

But I don't have to hide my purple-tinged cheekbones under layers of pancake foundation. I've got more respect for myself than to stay with a thug just because he's popular.

You do realise he's playing around with half the girls in the school, don't you?

It's times like this I realise that I don't need to be like you.

11

Polly

Polly storms back to her office and slams her door. She's not used to being ignored quite so blatantly. She starts to wonder if any of them will ever open up. What is it with these kids? It's like they have some sort of gangster code that forbids them from talking to an adult, even if that adult tries to treat them as equals and not as kids. That's one of the main things that had worked in her last school and, Christ, that place had been in a much worse state than this.

It was tough to deal with kids who had no hopes. Not because they weren't bright, or they weren't capable, but because they came from the kind of family where generations of them had lived hand to mouth, on the dole, using petty crime to make do rather than step outside their pitiful stereotype and get a job. Polly wasn't naive. She knew it wasn't always a simple situation. Not just about being lazy and demotivated. It was about years of living in a place where the industries had shut down, where people had been uprooted and moved into new communities where no one could find a way to get along. Grandad did it, so dad did it too, so son does it as well and that's that.

But it's not like that in Banktoun. At least it hadn't been

59

when Polly was growing up. Were things really so different now? Of course there were always going to be the poorer families who had run out of choices in life. But all of these kids seemed to be acting the same. Were they always so hostile? Or was something else going on? What were they scared of? Or maybe it was a 'who' …

Polly decided to head back along to the fourth years' area. She'd asked Diane's teacher to send her down, but either the message hadn't been passed on or the girl just wasn't coming. Either way, Polly was sick of waiting. She only had thirty-minute slots and she had another student lined up for the one straight after Diane. If she didn't go and find her now, she was barely going to have time to come in and sit down before it was time for her to leave. She stands, checks her desk to make sure there's nothing on it that she needs to drop into the drawer before she leaves the room. The kids at her last school seemed to have a special knack of knowing exactly when her office was empty and exactly where to find anything that might be of value. In the end there'd been CCTV cameras all over the school. Polly wasn't against security, but the place had turned into a prison. She couldn't stay in a place like that. Still, old habits and all that. She opens the drawer and drops her phone and her engraved silver Parker pen inside. A present from her parents when she'd graduated from uni. Hardly cool enough for a student to nick, but you never know.

As she slides the drawer shut, there's a soft double rap on the door.

At last!

'Come in, then. Better late than never,' she calls to the closed door, employing her best teachery tone.

The door opens. Polly sits down, picks up a pile of papers on her desk and straightens them. She's looking down at the desk. Squaring off the edges. She doesn't see who comes in.

'Take a seat,' she says.

60

A cough.

Finally, Polly looks up. She flinches, feels heat rising up her neck, colouring her cheeks. 'Oh gosh, sorry. You must think I'm so rude! I was expecting a student ...' She lets her sentence trail off.

The man sitting in the seat in front of her shakes his head. Makes a 'no problem' gesture with his hands.

'Lucas Crisp,' he says. 'Biology.'

'Of course. I remember you from my interview. I was hoping to have a chat with you in the staff room at lunchtime. Sorry about that. Anyway. What can I do for you, Lucas? I'm sure you don't need any counselling.' Her tone is light, but she sees a dark shadow cross his eyes.

'Perhaps not, Ms McAllister ... Polly ... but. Well, there is something I'd like to discuss with you. I've been expecting the police to come and find me. Imagined someone would've said something to them already. But then again, it's early days. It's only been a few hours, hasn't it? None of us actually knows what happened, do we? I mean ...' He pauses. Sighs. Takes a handkerchief out of his pocket and dabs at his forehead. Under his eyes.

Polly takes him in. Crazy hair. Old-fashioned clothes, but given his age he's going for the hipster look rather than the eccentric. Good-looking, but geeky. Something that looks like a ketchup stain on his tie, or maybe it's the design. Hard to tell. He has no wrinkles. She can't put an age on him, but she knows he's young. Much younger than her.

He coughs, clears his throat. 'I mean – she is dead, isn't she? Christ, I can't believe I'm even saying this. Katie is ... Katie was a special girl, she ...'

Polly zones out. She doesn't hear the rest of his sentence. Special girl? What does he mean? He is visibly upset. Why?

'Polly? Did you hear what I said? I said, Katie and me, well, we were friends ...'

'Hang on. What do you mean, you were *friends*? You're her teacher, Lucas—'

'Yes, yes. I know,' he interrupts. 'Katie is one of ... Katie *was* one of my best students. Not only was she incredibly intelligent, good at all her subjects – especially science – you know she won the fifth-year science prize last year, don't you? I mean ... God, I'm sorry, why would you? You've only just arrived ... What I *mean* is, she was gifted. Brilliant. She was going to study microbiology. She was going to go on to a PhD, I know it. She had such an interest in things. It wasn't just about doing her school work and passing her exams, she ...'

He lets the sentence trail off and takes his handkerchief out of his pocket again. Carefully, he wipes his eyes, then blows his nose.

Polly takes a deep breath.

'What are you saying, Lucas?' she says. Her voice is careful, measured. She is trying to hide the feeling of shock. The creeping dread that is sweeping across her body. That sudden rush of fireside heat when you've just come in from the cold. 'What do you mean, you were *friends*?' She needs to hear it in his words. Not her own. She is already forming scenarios inside her head.

'We had ... I don't know. I'm sorry. This is so difficult. We had a relationship. I suppose that's what you'd call it ...'

He is stopped from saying more by a thump on the door. Polly jumps.

'Who's that?' He spins around in the seat, but Polly is already on her feet. She yanks the door open, looks up and down the corridor.

'Hello?' she says. Her heart is thumping now. The heat rash has vanished, leaving an icy chill. 'Did someone just knock on my door?'

'Who was it?' Lucas says, his voice cracking with the pain. Fear. 'Do you think they ...'

Polly steps back inside the office and closes the door with a quiet click.

'I'm sorry, Lucas,' she says. 'Whoever it was, there's a good chance they heard our conversation. And whoever it was, they're not there now.'

12

Louise

'We're going down to talk to Katie's mother.'

She nods at Davie. 'Sure. I'd like a few more minutes up here, if that's OK? I just want to have a look around.'

'Mind and not disturb anything then, there are people here doing their jobs.' Malkie's voice is dripping with sarcasm. He has a thinly veiled disdain for the CSI technicians and their meticulous nature. Louise knows that Malkie's been told off one too many times for buggering up a crime scene through his impatience. He might be a good detective, but he's a bit of a dinosaur when it comes to modern procedure. Which makes Davie all the more interesting – because the men are the same age, and Davie has only been a detective for a few months. When she'd first found out he was moving across from uniform, she was expecting a slightly less competent Malkie clone – someone set in their ways with no desire to change. She was pleasantly surprised to find that he had a keen eye and a willingness to learn. His years in local policing were serving him in good stead for the new role he'd taken on.

She wasn't sure exactly when it was that she had started to fall in love with him.

After Malkie and Davie leave, the room becomes quieter still. Mary follows the men down the stairs, whispering to the GP as they leave the room. She gestures to Louise – a flickering of her fingers behind her – that Louise knows means see you later, I'll fill you in, call me. They know each other well enough to know how to interpret hand signals like this. The usual one, normally spotted in the corridors of the station at about 5 p.m., was a cupped hand lifted towards the mouth, twice, quickly. It meant quick drink, but it usually ended up being two bottles and a morning with a battering headache.

'OK if I have a look around?'

'Aye. If you can manage to keep your hands in your pockets. You lot are all the same.' She doesn't recognise the man who says this, but she recognises the tone – he's obviously encountered Malkie before.

'I'll try to be good,' Louise says. She turns slowly, surveying the room.

'Seriously, though – we're just about finished,' the tech says. 'Feel free.'

She smiles. Nods a 'thanks'. They're zipping up a couple of plastic bags, noting things down in their log. She walks over to the other side of the room towards the dressing table, and the desk that sits next to it. There's only one chair – a red fabric office chair on wheels, with armrests and a decent-looking back support. It looks expensive, and Louise takes this to mean that Katie was someone who took her studying seriously. Someone who knew she had to sit for long periods of time and was astute enough to know that this wasn't healthy.

It's funny, all these things people do now that would never have crossed her mind when Louise was young. People are always complaining now that kids don't do enough exercise. Louise can't remember a time when she wasn't outside as a kid, playing games, running around. Some of these kids today don't even walk to school – stranger danger has become an obsession; parents are convinced that paedophiles are lurking on every corner – so they drive their kids to school and nanny them through life until they leave school and don't know what the hell to do with themselves. Louise was cooking, washing and ironing when she was thirteen.

What about Katie? Was she someone who was self-sufficient?

Louise takes in the bottles and cans on the dressing table. Mixed in among the cosmetics is a distinctive leaf-patterned water bottle. She recognises the Orla Kiely design. Again – something nice, something expensive. Water. No one drank water when Louise was at school. You had a cup of tea at breakfast, maybe a juice at playtime and again at lunch, then nothing until you got home at half-past three. Bottled water was only for holidays in France and Spain when people were paranoid that cleaning their teeth with the tap water would give them the scoots.

She sits down on Katie's chair. Rolls across towards the desk. A sudden wave of sadness hits her, imagining Katie doing this. Imagining Katie making plans for the future. The final exams were only a couple of months away. She must've had plans. The thought of this young life being snuffed out too soon makes her both tearful and angry.

'Someone did this to you, Katie. I'm sorry that they did. But I'm going to do what I can to find them, OK? But I need your help. What am I looking for? Who would've wanted to hurt you, Katie?'

There is a small sound, like a tiny piece of metal hitting another piece of metal. Louise flinches in the seat. She is easily spooked, and the quiet of the room means that everything is magnified. Something has been disturbed. She glances across at the window, where the mournful tree is swaying. She'd thought it sounded like maybe a window key falling down, but she can't see anything out of place.

She turns back to the desk, looks around, across to the

66

dressing table. There is a string of coloured paperclips hanging over the mirror. She hadn't noticed them at first, had thought they were all necklaces. She moves a few of the bits and pieces, expecting to find a stray paperclip that has dropped off the chain, but there are none. She frowns. Not that then.

Her eyes scan the rest of the desk, back to the dressing table. Nothing. She's not sure why, but the sound has caused an alert to trigger somewhere inside her. There is a clue here. Something she needs to find. What the hell is it?

'Lou, you coming down here? Kettle's on ...' Davie's voice comes up the stairs, breaking the silence, breaking her concentration.

'Two minutes,' she calls back, trying to keep the annoyance from her voice.

She scans the surfaces again. Looks around the pencil sharpener pen holder. Nothing. Her eyes go up.

It's obvious, really. She doesn't know why she hasn't seen it before.

There is a framed photograph hanging on the wall above her head. It's a collage – lots of smiling faces. Lots of smiling Katies. She stands up, lifts it down. There are specks of something beige that have dried onto the glass. She knows what they are. Make-up. Foundation. Spattered on when she'd squeezed it from the tube and left there to dry out like freckles.

This is stuff only a female would spot.

The make-up is on the frame, because the photo collage is normally standing on the dressing table, in the gap between the cans and bottles and the smaller make-up that sits in front of it. She runs her hand across the dressing table. It's covered with fingerprint powder, so she can't be sure. But they will have photographed it. There will be a gap, where this photo collage frame is meant to sit.

On the empty expanse of wall, there is a rectangular space, defined by the slight discoloration you get when something has been hanging there for a long time. If she was to lift any of the other things off the wall, the lighter colour would be behind them, and the space would fit what it was she lifted off. The photo collage is too small for the lighter-coloured rectangle on the wall. Someone has taken something off the wall and put this photo in its place.

She stares at the photo. Katie with her arms around a teenage boy who has a scowl on his face but a smile in his eyes. Katie with a little boy on her knee – her little brother, Brett? There are none of anyone who looks like she might be Katie's sister. There's another one of Katie, her arms wrapped around a slightly younger-looking girl with flame-coloured hair and pink shiny lip-gloss.

Louise flips out the little stand on the back of the frame and stands the collage back on the dressing table.

She leans over to the wall, runs her hand over the pale rectangle. What was here?

Where is it?

The other things on this section of wall are framed nature posters. One has a selection of butterflies, a huge one in the centre that Louise recognises as a red admiral – it's the only one she knows. It's an unusual print. Reminds her of something but she can't think what. One of the others is of a clear, still pond surrounded by beautifully coloured trees and bushes. Hazy pinks and bright oranges. All shades of green. 'Exbury Gardens' it says. New Forest National Park. Somewhere that Katie had visited? Had hoped to visit? The other poster is the periodic table, except instead of the elements it's got horror movies categorised into 'slashers', 'creepy kids', 'psychopaths' and so on. 'Ex' for *The Exorcist*, 'Om' for *The Omen*. So Katie loved nature, science and horror movies – but she had a sense of humour too. And good friends, according to the photo.

On a whim, Louise hunkers down and looks on the floor behind the desk. There's a radiator there. She touches it and finds it cool, despite the heat of the room. Some houses are just warm like that. But it's unusual, as Louise usually finds herself freezing at scenes like this. She still feels a chill going through her, but there's a warmth. It reminds her of that game when you have to guess where something is, and as you get closer, your friends shout 'getting warmer, warmer, hot' and when you're way off target it's 'cooler, colder, cold'.

She crawls under the desk towards the radiator. Although it hadn't felt too hot to the touch, she suddenly feels like she's about to roast. Like being in a sauna when someone's tipped a bucket of water over the coals.

Warmer ... warmer ... hot ... HOT.

It's under the radiator. She was right about the noise. A small piece of metal hitting metal. It's a long metal pin. Like a haberdashery pin, but longer, thinner maybe. She wouldn't have seen it if it hadn't been for what it was attached to.

A bright turquoise so delicate it looks like it would crumble if you touched it. An insect of some sort, with a pin stuck through the body. She crawls closer.

Two larger wings, two smaller. She reaches out, longing to touch it. What is it? Why has it got a pin through its body?

She slides back out. Sits down, cross-legged, as she pulls an evidence bag out of her coat pocket. Frowns, wondering if she's going to be able to pick this thing up without damaging it. She closes her eyes. Opens them. And she is drawn back to the print of the butterflies. She knows what it reminds her of now ...

'You weren't the average seventeen-year-old, were you, Katie?' Louise says to the empty room. There is no one there to reply. Nothing left in the room now but a heavy mist of sadness.

13

Polly

The bell rings for lunch, but both Polly and Lucas ignore it. He's crying now. Sobbing into his handkerchief. She wants to comfort him, but first she needs to know all the facts.

'Lucas, I know this is difficult, but I need to know everything. Everything about you and Katie. Maybe I should make us some tea? It always helps.' She smiles, but he doesn't look up.

There is a kettle and some cups on top of the filing cabinet. She hasn't had a chance to use it yet, but presumably it's all in working order. She had filled it up with water from the bathroom down the hall when she'd arrived that morning, but before she'd even switched it on she'd become engrossed in the student lists, then she'd popped out to the post office.

And then all hell had broken loose.

'I've got some herbal, if you don't drink normal tea. What do you drink? Would you like some?' She starts fumbling in her oversized handbag for the box of mixed fruit infusions she'd thrown in there this morning. Simon always berated her for buying it and never drinking it. She could buy what she wanted now. Throw it all straight in the bin if she felt like it. Bringing it to school was supposed to be a way for her to reduce her caffeine intake and be a bit more healthy. It wasn't just herself she had to think about now.

She's babbling. Stalling. Too scared to let Lucas speak.

'Whatever you're having is fine.' His voice is thick, muffled behind the handkerchief. Polly hasn't seen anyone use a cotton handkerchief since her grandad died. She's always thought there was something vaguely revolting about having to boil-wash your own mucus. She stands up and flicks on the kettle, drops two raspberry zingers into pale blue mugs. They wait in silence, the sound of the boiling kettle filling the air.

'It's not what you think,' he says, eventually.

She hands him a mug and sits back down. The smell coming from the tea is fruity and warming, but it's far too hot to drink.

'Go on.'

'I suppose maybe *relationship* was the wrong word. It was a friendship. Nothing more.'

'So you saw her outside of school?'

'Yes. Not at first. At first it was about extra study. Stuff that wasn't on the curriculum. Like I said – she was a bright girl. Very bright. And that's despite the family life she has … had. I don't know if you know much about that yet? I realise this is all new to you. You've been thrown right in at the deep end, as it were.'

She nods. That's an understatement. 'Some of it,' she says. She's not keen on showing her hand this early. She blows on her tea. 'Why don't you tell me what *you* know?' She takes a tentative sip, but the liquid is still lip-burningly hot.

'Her mother had her young. I mean, way before my time. She might be about your age, I imagine. She would've started here in 1992.'

Polly nods. Her skin prickles. 'Yeah. That was my year.' She really didn't want to go there, but she's been drawn in and there's nothing she can do about it.

'So you knew her? Mandy Taylor? From what Jon's told

71

me, she was a handful. Not stupid by any means, but easily distracted. Not really interested in working hard. Jon told me he always thought she was trying to conform to a stereotype, if that makes sense. Her friends were wasters and losers who would never go anywhere – I know we're not meant to say that, but sometimes it's just the way it is ...' He pauses, waits for Polly to say something, to contradict him maybe. And when she doesn't, he carries on. 'It was as if she didn't really want to do well because then what would she do? She had a rough home life, by all accounts. No dad on the scene, mother working two jobs to make ends meet and no time to bring up her daughter properly. No time to encourage her to break away, you know?'

Polly nods again. Her insides are squirming, but she tries not to show any recognition. Any knowledge. It's all going to come back to bite her, eventually. She was the one who thought coming back *home* was a good idea.

'She got pregnant at fifteen. Refused to name the father. Never has, as far as I'm aware. Katie never knew her dad. There were rumours. All sorts. Rumours that she'd been abused by someone. That it might've been a teacher.'

He blinks slowly, as if trying to erase the irony of his words.

'Anyway, that was her. And sadly it's a case of history repeating itself. Mandy works hard, tries her best. She had two more kids, but their dad isn't around either – in and out of prison. I don't really know the details. Anyway, Mandy never encouraged any of the kids to do well. I think she's got an inbuilt fear of breaking the mould. She wanted to fit it, so she kept herself off the academic radar. What if she'd done well? She wasn't the same as those proper studious kids – the geeks and the swots – their words, not mine.'

Polly gives him a rueful smile. 'I'm afraid I can relate all too well. I was one of the *swots*, as you call them. I thought the kids might've moved on from that phrase, but they haven't, have they? People like Mandy liked to make my life hell.'

Lucas sits up straight. 'So you *did* know her?'

'Yes,' Polly sighs. She'd love to tell Lucas all about Mandy, but it wasn't the time. 'I knew her. Haven't seen her since she left school. She left to have the baby, I suppose. I didn't even know she was pregnant. I do remember her wearing baggy jumpers, but then so did half the girls at school back then. I wasn't part of her crowd. I was never around the places she was. Too busy being a swot.' She tries for a rueful smile. 'Then I left to go to uni, my parents split up, moved away. I've barely been back here since.'

He stops sniffing, finally. 'So, why now?' he says. 'What made you come back?'

She takes a breath, stares up at the ceiling. 'The job? A fresh start.' She can't tell him the main reason. No one knows that. 'Maybe, I don't know. Maybe I wanted to face some of my demons.'

Fuck, Polly thinks. What am I doing? This isn't about me. She takes a drink and puts the mug down on the desk a little too forcefully.

'I'm sorry,' Lucas says, reading her mind. 'Another time, maybe. You want to know about Katie. Well, I figured it was best for me to come and tell you everything now. I expect I'll have the police wanting to talk to me soon enough. I wanted to tell you first—'

'It wasn't a secret, then?'

'Not really, no. She used to get called my little lab rat – but she just laughed.' He sighs and leans back in the chair. 'The first time we met outside school, it was a Saturday morning trip to the National Museum, you know, the one on Chambers Street? She wanted me to show her the fossils. Explain them to her. The insects, in particular. She was fascinated. I told her that it wasn't a good idea, but she insisted. We travelled up separately. Met inside. Just a coincidence, should anyone see us. I go there most weekends anyway. I don't have many friends here. I like going to the museum. There's nothing wrong with that.'

'Of course not. But then what? Did this become a regular thing?'

'Yes,' he says. He pauses, takes a gulp of his tea. Grimaces. 'But not just there. After a while, she started coming to my house.'

14

Louise

The kitchen is even hotter than the bedroom. The air is dry, slightly stale. It smells of dirty tea towels and too many cigarettes. Louise notices the small blow-heater that's fitted under the kitchen units. Katie's mother – Mandy Taylor – is sitting at the kitchen table. A cigarette is burning out in a blue glass ashtray in front of her, a smoky grey snake more than an inch long lies curled on the bottom, creating a dark brown stain. She's holding a mug with both hands. Through the gaps between her fingers, Louise can just about make out the letters that are printed on it, with an oversized red heart in between them.

I 'heart' Mum.

The mug is chipped on the top, the writing faded from too many washes. It's the kind of mug a young child buys their mum for Mother's Day. By the looks of it, it's not something they've felt the need to update. Or maybe she's just sentimental about this one.

Or maybe it's all for show.

Louise hates it when her cynical, suspicious side kicks in, but this is a murder inquiry and in most murders the killer is known to the victim. Most are domestic in nature and, appearances aside, killing your kids is not that uncommon. Sadly, Mandy Taylor will remain one of their key suspects until they've got reason to believe otherwise. Louise hopes, for everyone's sake, that it's not her. She recalls a heart-breaking case a few years ago: a woman beat and killed her little boy, rolled him in a carpet and drove thirty miles to bury him in a garden, all the while helping the police search for her missing son, getting the whole community involved. When they finally found him, the truth was enough to make you sick. Poor little mite had died from repeated physical abuse and neglect. She'd tried to cover it up, saying he was ill, and people wanted to believe her because who wants to believe the truth when it's something as awful as that? She's in prison now, but Louise will never understand how that woman could do such things. All these sorts of people. The things they do. Terrifying.

The other possibility, of course, is not Katie's mother but her father. Long-kept secrets aside, this might be something that Mandy is going to have to share after all …

Then there are the other obvious options – boyfriends, other friends. Siblings. But they're both younger. Doesn't rule them out, obviously. There have been too many horrible cases of kids killing kids. But not like this. This doesn't feel like that.

Louise's instinct says that someone else is involved. And this insect is the key to it all.

'Davie,' she whispers, trying not to draw too much attention to herself – Malkie is sitting with Mandy, trying to get her to talk. The FLO, PC Steph Benedict, is making tea. He turns, eyes questioning. 'I need a hand with something.' She wants him to come upstairs, to help her pick up the insect. She's considered using tweezers, but she's terrified of damaging it. She wants him to come and have a look first.

'I found something …'

He doesn't say anything. Clearly her eyes have given her

away, or else they've got a telepathic bond forming. She hopes so. She knows she wants to get to know this man. Something about him draws her in. He is a good man. Not without his flaws, like anyone. But fundamentally good. She walks carefully back up the stairs, hears the slight creak as he steps on the bottom stair, following her up.

Back in Katie's room, the air seems changed. Malkie and Steph have done a good job of keeping Mandy distracted while her daughter was brought down the stairs and into the waiting ambulance. The uniforms outside have done a decent job of keeping the enquiring crowd at bay, as much as is possible. The rumours will have started already, though. Two police cars, an ambulance, various other vehicles – small place like this. People aren't stupid.

'Well?' Davie says. His voice is more clipped than usual, and when Louise looks at him she can see the pain in his eyes. A child. A dead child. She's guessing that this isn't something he's had to deal with before.

'Are you OK, Davie? I know it's not been long since you joined the team … it's … er. It can be a challenge, the first time.'

He opens his mouth to speak, shuts it again. Exhales. 'It's not my first time,' he says, quietly.

'I know it's not. Not your first … I mean, a child though …'

'Like I said. Not my first time.'

Louise had forgotten that Davie had been in the force a long time. He may not have been a detective for very long – a few months of secondment before doing his exams and taking up the position full time – but he'd been in local policing long enough to have seen more than she could imagine. Even in a small town. *Especially* in a small town. People do bad things. One day she might ask him about his old cases – the ones before she got to know him. Know *of* him. But not now.

She coughs. Turns away. 'I found this.' She kneels down on

the carpet next to the radiator, looks up at him, gesturing him over with a nod of her head.

'I can't imagine the CSIs would've missed anything important,' he says. 'They know what they're doing. I saw them picking up and bagging the tiniest bits of fluff and hair, just in case—'

She interrupts. 'They wouldn't have seen this. It's down behind here. It was sheer luck I was still poking around when I heard it slide down. I heard the pin rattle against the metal of the radiator. I don't know why it happened when it did – maybe just 'cause there was so much activity, plenty of moving air, then it stopped. The house resettled. You know? Anyway, it slid down. Here. Take a look.'

He kneels down and shuffles towards her, casting a shadow over the radiator. A dark cloud has passed over, blocking much of the light through the window. He peers in, then sits back on his haunches, fumbles with something in his pocket.

She smiles when she sees it. 'I had a feeling you were a good Boy Scout.'

'You should never be without a Mini Maglite, Jennings. Have you never seen *CSI Miami*?'

He shines the torchlight down the front of the radiator and the insect is bathed in an orange, circular glow. It's about three centimetres long, with its wings spread out to the sides, as if immortalised in flight. A long silver pin protrudes from the back of its tiny body, as if it has been speared.

'What is it?'

'No idea. But I know where it came from.'

'Oh?'

'Well, I don't *know*. It's just a theory at this point – I need to ask Katie's mum about it. I could be bang off track. Have you got any other handy tools in your pocket? We need to get this bagged, but I'm scared to touch it – it looks so fragile.'

Davie takes a handful of clear plastic bags out of his pocket.

Glances around the room. 'Don't suppose you've found any tweezers on that dressing table?'

Louise brandishes the small metal pincers like a trophy. 'Mine – they were in my bag. Should we photograph it first?'

Davie nods and takes out his phone. He hands the torch to Louise and she keeps it directed at the insect while Davie snaps a couple of photos with his police-issue Blackberry. He slips the phone back into his pocket. Stands up, surveys the dressing table again.

'How about this?' He picks up a small eye-shadow palette with a clear plastic lid. If the CSIs hadn't take this, then Davie knows it's fine to touch. He lifts the lid and it comes right off – the plastic hinges at the back have already snapped; one of the small plastic lugs is missing. He takes a tissue from a box that has a picture of a black Labrador puppy on the side. Wipes the inside of the lid. 'If we lay it out on this, then we can wrap it up in a bag. Might stop it getting crushed.'

Resourceful, Louise thinks. She's impressed. 'Shall I?'

He shrugs.

She leans forward and grips the top end of the pin with the jaws of the tweezers. Davie kneels back down, holds the plastic lid as close to the insect as he can without getting in her way. Louise lifts the insect, hoping that the thing isn't going to crumble to pieces when she removes it from the carpet. It doesn't. She has no idea what's been used to preserve it, but clearly the thing is stronger than it looks and it survives intact.

With the insect safely on the plastic lid, Davie stands up and takes it from her. She stands next to him, looking at it. She's standing so close she can feel his warm breath on the side of her face.

'It's not a butterfly. It's more like a dragonfly, but it's not something I've seen before. I don't think so, anyway.'

'Can I?' Louise puts out her hand to take hold of the lid. He hands it to her, starts rubbing a plastic bag between his hands, trying to unstick it from itself. 'I've seen one of these before. Two sets of wings. Look at these markings. They're so unusual. Sort of thistle-shaped. Beautiful, isn't it?'

'It was probably happier before someone stuck a pin in it.'

'It's like the poster – look.'

He looks. 'Victorian butterflies. Ah. Right. Yes. They'd catch them in nets, then they'd squeeze their bodies to kill them before drying them out in little boxes and pinning them onto mounting boards. I watched a documentary about it once. Bit weird, but each to their own, eh? Don't think anyone does that now, do they? Animal rights and all that.'

She glances at him and sees the smirk on his lips. He's trying to lighten things. As it is, she'd almost forgotten where she was and what she was doing – so focused was she on the task of getting the insect up from the floor without breaking it. She tilts the plastic case back and forth, uses the tweezers to move the pin, getting a good look at it. Its wings are a distinctive turquoise colour, its body patterned with black markings. She turns it around, notices the green eyes. It looks familiar. She'd visited Edinburgh Butterfly and Insect World a few months ago. Remembers the corny strapline 'It's a jungle in there'. It was, actually. Her nephew had been fascinated by the spiders. Wanted a pet tarantula. But luckily his mother wasn't having it. While he'd spent far too long in there, letting things with bodies like fat pin cushions and legs like pipe cleaners crawl over his hands, Louise had gone into the *odonata* section – carnivorous winged insects, which were mainly dragonflies, and things like this one, that she'd never heard of before, the damselfly. She'd looked them up afterwards, found that some of them were quite rare. Some were protected species. This one … this one was beautiful.

A rare find, then, for someone who liked to collect things.

Was it significant that this insect had been left behind, and the others snatched away? Louise wasn't sure that she believed in coincidences, but there's no doubt in her mind that she remembers this one. It was as if it was meant to be imprinted in her brain somehow, so that she would recognise it when the time was right. Her body tingles, thinking about it. A sense of unease slithers through her. Was it fate that she'd found this thing? She'd noticed a heightened awareness lately. The occasional panicked fluttering in her chest. Something bubbling under the surface. Something not right. A horrible feeling that bad things were about to happen.

She shakes her head, trying to dislodge the thoughts. 'Stupid,' she mutters.

Davie turns to look at her, his face is questioning. 'What?'

'Nothing.' She smiles. 'Nothing at all.'

15

Neil

He runs all the way. He's not really the sporty type, but somehow adrenaline pushes him along. How far is it? Half an hour's walk, maybe? If he runs, and he doesn't stop and he doesn't slow and he doesn't get hit by a car, or if someone else doesn't run into him, he can make it in fifteen. Maybe. He runs past people pushing prams, people gossiping over fences. People out and about, doing their daily things. Living their lives.

Living.

Fuck.

He hasn't cried yet. The shock hasn't hit him. There's that instant wave of denial when someone tells you that someone has died. No. It's not true. Of course it's not true. He only saw her last night. They were on the verge of shagging when he said something stupid and she told him to fuck off, and so he did. If he hadn't said that, if he'd listened to her, if he hadn't been such a stupid fucking *bloke* about it, then maybe she'd still be alive.

She *is* still alive. Of course she is. There's been a mistake. One big monumental fucking mistake.

The last stretch is uphill, and it's only now that he starts to wonder if he can actually do it. And if he does do it, what's he going to find when he gets there? He slows down to a jog. Tries to slow his breathing to match the pace.

'You OK, son? Terrible, isn't it?'

He recognises the woman who has spoken to him from her garden. She is scraping bits of ice and snow off her garden ornaments. What's her name? Mrs Delgado? Mrs Delahunty? Something like that. She's someone's granny. He's seen her picking up a kid at school. Younger than him. A few years below? Brett's age? Fuck. He knows the kid, but now all he can see is a face. His mind has gone. He says nothing, just nods. Slows to walk once he's well past her house, makes it to the top of the hill and finally stops, just for a moment.

Sweat is running down his back, and his face burns – all the exertion against the cold air. His heart rate is off the scale. He wonders if it's possible for the thing to explode right there and then. Burst out of him, all blood and stringy bits and tubes that keep it all attached properly inside his chest. That'd be two of them gone, like something out of *Romeo and Juliet*, except neither of them planned it. Not their style. He hears her voice: *No games, Neil.*

It's not happening. He's still asleep. It's one of those fucked-up dreams that you can't seem to wake yourself out of, even though what's happening clearly isn't real. Panic. Don't panic. It's not real. Stay calm.

He rounds the corner onto Katie's street and a sudden wave of nausea hits him. Not from the running. Or maybe that. But mostly it's because he can see a police car down the road, right outside her house. He can see the blue-and-white crime scene tape stretched across from lamp post to tree, a couple of hundred metres down. He's always thought crime scene tape was yellow and black. But that's in America, isn't it? Shows you what you notice.

He swallows great big gulps of air. It's cold, so cold, yet it burns inside him. Inside his overworked lungs. He's not going to be sick. He's never sick. Not even after ten cans of Strongbow. Not like Katie. Katie's a lightweight. Three-can Katie, he called her. Five cans and she'd be throwing up in your face. She'd actually done that, once.

He feels tears pricking at the corners of his eyes. No. Fucksake. Don't cry. Don't be sick. It's not real, remember? It's a dream. It's a nightmare. He keeps walking. There's a uniformed policeman standing next to the tape. Young. Dark-skinned. Indian or something.

'Sorry, son. Can't go through, I'm afraid. Police investigation.'

It's not real, remember? He walks past. The policeman tries to grab him but he shrugs him off.

'Oi!'

There's a woman walking towards him. Slim, dark hair tied up in a pony-tail. In her thirties, maybe? He's never seen her before. No idea who she is. No idea what she's doing. Just some other character inside his fucked-up nightmare. He'll wake up soon. He has to wake up soon. This is his punishment for last night. The stupid argument. What he did afterwards. His behaviour. Idiot. You're a fucking idiot.

'Are you Neil Price?' the woman says. Up close, he realises that she's quite nice looking for an old bird. That's his phrase. Katie always tells him off. Doesn't matter what age she is if she's nice looking, does it? That's not what he means, though. Just means she's too old for him. He's not even eighteen. He's not ready for an older woman. Not yet. The idea scares the shit out of him. Still, she's fit. Nice athletic body. Clean, shiny hair. He'd ask how she knew his name, but there's no point. She's in his dream, of *course* she knows his name. Anyway, the uniform hasn't bothered to chase after him. Has to stay at his cordon. That's his job. *In my dream.*

'Yeah, that's me,' he says anyway. Just confirming.

Her face changes. She had a bit of a smile before, but it slides off her face like that last bit of ice lolly when the heat finally shoves it off the stick. Ice lollies. Katie loves ice lollies. *Loved.*

He feels his legs go from under him, but she's there in a flash. The uniform too. He must've been watching all along.

'No ...' he says, and it comes out as a bit of a wail. 'This isn't real.'

'Help me get him inside, Rav,' the woman says. They're both holding him. He's walking, but he can't feel his legs. Can't feel anything. Just letting them guide him. Katie's front door is standing wide open. Her mum'll be doing her nut. She's always yelling at them for leaving the door open. Brooke does it on purpose. Katie only does it to wind her up.

Does it.

Did it.

There's a man standing in the doorway. He's not in uniform, but Neil recognises him. Davie Gray. Sergeant Davie Gray. His face is what does it. It's Davie's face that wakes him up.

'This is real, isn't it? It is, isn't it? I'm not asleep, am I?' Neil says, his words coming out in a jumbled gush.

Davie frowns. Takes a step outside. Nods at the guy in uniform and takes his place. Davie and the woman help him inside the house, and from the kitchen Neil can hear a sound, a horrible animal sound. A roaring. A cry. Like a bear caught in trap.

Neil's voice cracks as he speaks. 'I'm not asleep, am I, Sergeant Gray?'

Davie pushes the door shut behind them. 'No, son. You're not.'

THREEWISEMONKEYSBLOG

Telling It Like It Is

Posted: 1st Oct 2016 by SpeakNoEvil
Status: Draft
Comments: 0

> *Say, say, my playmate*
> *Don't come and play with me*
> *Don't bring your dollies three*
> *Cut down my apple tree*
> *Fall off my rainbow,*
> *Into my cellar door*
> *And we'll be enemies*
> *Forever evermore.*

I'm not the type to bear grudges, you know? Life's too short and all that. If someone doesn't want to be around you any more, then that's down to them, not you. If someone is truly a friend, then they will talk to you and tell you what their problem is with you. You're meant to be friends. You're meant to have arguments and fall out over stupid things – but then you're meant to talk about it and sort them out – and then you're meant to be friends again.

Of course there are lots of reason why friends fall out. Sometimes it's something really bad and really shit and no matter how much you talked about it, you'd never be able to fix it. But sometimes it's not that. Sometimes it's about one person being stupid and petty and having the wrong fucking end of the stick. Right?

What are you supposed to do then? You tell me, Webfreaks. Cause I sure as hell don't know.

Say, for example, you told a friend something really important. And then that friend laughed at you, and then made it into something else. And then told someone else. And then that someone else, who, by the way, was already a fucking bitch, decided to make your life even harder?

What do you do then? Can you talk it out? Can you be friends again? I'm guessing not. I'm guessing this is the time when you turn into enemies.

This is when you fall off the fucking rainbow.

Right?

16

Polly

'I think we need to get Jon in here, don't you?'

Lucas nods.

Polly goes out into the corridor. She wants to scream. *This.* On her first day? This is madness. Whatever's gone on between Lucas and Katie has got him worried enough to come and talk to her before the police talk to him. Where are they, anyway? Probably still at the scene, she thinks. But wouldn't they send some different ones here? They can't do everything. Surely they can send some here to make some enquiries while the others are at the house. Or does it have to be the same officers, the same team as the one doing the murder investigation? If that's what it is – a murder. No one has actually said that yet, not officially, but it's coming. She's sure of it. If the girl had just died of something weird, some natural cause – you hear about it, those weird undiagnosed medical conditions. But no, this is not that. This is something bad. And Lucas is involved. Somehow he is involved.

She knocks on Jon's door, even though it's not fully closed. Force of habit.

'Polly,' he says. He's sitting behind his desk. Catherine, his secretary, is sitting in the chair opposite. She's been crying.

'Jon, I'm sorry to interrupt. I'm not sure what time the police are due, but something's come up. Can you come through to my office?'

Catherine says, 'Do you want me to come, too? I could take notes or something?' She sniffs, takes a hanky from up her cardigan sleeve and blows her nose noisily.

Polly knows she's only trying to be helpful, trying to keep herself busy, but she also detects a hint of nosiness and she's not ready for that, not yet.

'No, that's fine, thanks Catherine. Just Jon for now. You should probably be at your desk, in case the police come. Or if they ring. I don't know what the protocol is—'

'No, you're right. Thanks, Polly. Cath, do you mind? I'm sorry. I'll fill you in once I know what's going on.'

She walks back to her office in silence, Jon close behind. He has the grace not to ask her anything else. She hopes that he can sense from her tone that she wants him to wait. That whatever it is she wants him to hear will come from someone else, not her. This is not her story to tell.

Back in Polly's office, Lucas is slumped forward, his head in his hands.

'Lucas!' Jon's voice is filled with alarm. Clearly this is not who he was expecting to see in here.

Lucas sits up. His eyes are red and his face blotchy. Polly hopes he won't clam up now. Hopes he'll tell her the rest, with Jon here. If they need to provide him with support, he's going to have to tell them all he knows. The police aren't likely to be so sympathetic. Not if they think … Polly pushes the thought away. Don't jump to conclusions. Although it's hard not to.

'I'm sorry,' Lucas says. 'I'm so sorry.'

Jon sits on the spare chair at the side of the desk. 'What's this about, Polly? Lucas? Is this something to do with Katie?'

Lucas looks like he's going to be sick.

'Jon, Lucas came to me to discuss what's been going on with Katie. He thought it would be useful to put us in the picture before the police arrive. They'll want to question everyone, including me, although I can't think I'll have much to contribute. You two knew Katie. They'll be expecting your help.'

Jon sighs. 'Is this about your tutoring, Lucas?' Something in his voice gives him away. He knows, Polly thinks. He already knows about this.

'Tutoring?' Polly says. 'From what I can gather, it's a bit more than that.'

Lucas addresses Jon. 'You know I was helping her out with stuff. Her uni applications. Extra work. You know she used to come round to my house sometimes. I told you this before. It was hard to find somewhere to chat properly. The school is closed in the evenings, except for Wednesday's after-school club, and, well, I didn't see the harm. I mean, maybe I spent too much time with her, I don't know, it's just ...' He lets the sentence trail off, blows his nose again. That hanky must be sodden, Polly thinks. She pushes a box of tissues at him from the other side of the desk.

'Lucas was telling me how he met Katie in Edinburgh sometimes, at the museum. He was teaching her about fossils and things, is that right?'

'Not just that. Insects. Entomology. She was interested in microbiology initially, but then it led to more. She was keen to study forensics. She loved *Silence of the Lambs*. The guys in the lab who analyse the moths. Stuff like that fascinates her.'

Polly notices that he is still talking about her in the present tense, but she knows that's normal. She doesn't correct him.

Jon moves his chair closer. 'Lucas. I know about this. I know about you meeting her at your house. We discussed it, didn't we? I told you it was OK as long as that's all it was. Teaching. Tutoring. That's all. You're not telling me now that there was any more to it? She was barely seventeen, Lucas. You never forgot that, did you?'

'No. No! Jesus. That's why I'm here. Of course. Of course.' He takes another tissue from the box and rubs at his face until the tissue breaks into pieces.

Jon and Polly exchange a glance.

'What are you so worried about, Lucas? If that's all it was? I see what you mean now about your friendship, but I'm not sure it was even that, was it? Not if it was all schoolwork—'

'It wasn't just schoolwork,' Lucas says quietly.

Jon lets out a long, slow breath.

'Spit it out, man. What's been going on?'

Lucas sighs. 'We *were* friends. She told me stuff. About her family. About her boyfriend, about—'

Fear slides through her veins. 'Told you what? What kinds of things?'

'She told me about things they did with each other. She wanted me to tell her it was OK. She wanted a male opinion, I suppose. I mean, her dad's not around. Her mum doesn't seem to have anyone regular in her life. And she told me about her sister and her brother and her mother, and everything. She told me everything. She told me about her friends, and the ones she'd fallen out with. She wanted ...' He pauses, unsure. 'She wanted to know if I found her attractive.'

'She what?' Jon's face has gone a deep red. He is trying, and failing, to keep his anger in check. 'And you didn't think to nip this in the bud? Didn't think it was inappropriate?'

Lucas sighs. 'I'm twenty-five, Jon. I'm not that much older than her. It's perfectly feasible that she could have friends of my age. She's very mature for her age, she wasn't like the other girls in her year, she—'

'That's enough, Lucas. I think maybe we should leave this for the police to deal with, don't you? Polly, what do you think?'

Polly wants to say she's shocked, but she isn't. She can relate to Katie, even though she never even met the girl. She'd always had older friends. When she started going to the pubs at eighteen, most of her friends were in their mid to late twenties. She'd looked up to them, admired them, wanted affirmation from them that she was doing OK.

But that's not the issue here.

The issue is that Katie was seventeen, and that Lucas was her teacher. And if these things were being said – Katie flirting, sounding him out – then he should've put a stop to it. Discouraged her. Told her she needed to talk to someone else about her feelings – that their meetings should be about school and nothing else. But it wasn't as simple as that. Nothing was cut and dried. It never was when teenagers and hormones were involved.

'I think we should keep this to ourselves, just for a bit,' Polly says. 'I understand why Lucas is upset, and I understand why he's worried – but flagging this up as an issue isn't going to help right now. It might send the police off on the wrong track. It's not as if Lucas knows anything about Katie's death, is it?'

She looks at Lucas, who barely nods. He looks away.

'*Do* you know something?' Jon says.

'Of course not. It's not that. Of course I don't. It's just that, well, she died early this morning, didn't she? The police will want to talk to whoever saw her last ...'

An icy tingle runs down Polly's spine. 'When did you last see her, Lucas?' She wants him to say Friday, leads him there. 'Was it Friday? After school?'

Lucas lets out a strangled sob. 'No,' he says. 'I saw her last night. I was in her bedroom.'

LucasCrispIsAPaedo

🔒 Secret Group

168 Members (100 new)

Luke Crust

12h

Good to see you're all sharing this and getting the word out there. We cannae let him get away with this …

Likes(65) Comments(8)

Sally Stephens Do we know who set this page up? I don't think it's a very good idea when we don't know all the facts yet, is it?
Big Jim Nailor Fuck off, *Sally Stephens.*
Al Samson Maybe somebody could tell us all the facts, eh? It's only rumours so far.
Big Jim Nailor What facts do you need, you numpty? The girl's deid. That dodgy teacher has been trying to get into her pants. Or he wiz in them …
Al Samson See what I mean? You dinnae even ken!
Luke Crust Fucksake. I'll post details in a separate thread.
Joe Crow Ooh, this is a bit exciting!
Leanne Keddie Yous are all sick.

Luke Crust

10h

Here's the facts as we know them:

1. On Monday morning, Katie Taylor was found dead at home, in her bed, by her mother

2. On Monday afternoon, Lucas Crisp had a private

93

meeting with the new school counsellor and the headmaster

3. It has been reported that Katie was seen with Crisp outside school hours, not on school property

4. It has been reported that Crisp has sent inappropriate letters to female pupils at the school, pupils who are under 16

5. It has been reported that Crisp has commented on what some of the female pupils wear to school

6. It has been reported that several girls at the school have felt uneasy in Crisp's presence

7. [edited to add] It is known that Crisp has in the past helped Katie with extra-curricular activities

Likes(110) Comments(18)

Sally Stephens According to whom? Is this from the police?

Big Jim Nailor Fuck off, *Sally Stephens*.

Al Samson Who's goin round to see this prick, then?

Big Jim Nailor Now, now, *Al Samson* *wink* We've no got any 'evidence' apparently …

Joe Crow Can I come?

Leanne Keddie You're all joking, right? No one is really going to do anything, are they? We don't know anything yet. This is mad!

Al Samson Fuck off, *Leanne Keddie*.

Luke Crust Are there not enough facts in the list above? Jesus, what's it going to take to get yous lot to do something?

Sally Stephens Please … I agree with *Leanne Keddie* … this isn't right.

Leanne Keddie Thanks, *Sally Stephens* – maybe we

should report the page?

Al Samson Are you two fucking radge? Want us to come round yours when we're done?

Big Jim Nailor Ignore them *Al Samson*. Two stupid bints. We'll get plenty more support from people who know what we need to do about this shite.

Lou Peters I'm up for a rumble.

Gary Niven Me tae.

Pete Reed Count me in, boys.

Joe Crow What time?

Sally Stephens Right, that's it. I'm reporting this page.

Big Jim Nailor I ken where you live, *Sally Stephens* ... You'd better make sure your doors are locked the night, ken what I mean?

17

Louise

Louise is struggling to breathe in the kitchen, with the amount of tobacco smoke hanging in the air. If it was summer, the back door might be open, letting it disperse. Some of it, at least. But it's four degrees out there and there's no way that Mandy Taylor is letting anyone leave the back door standing open. She's already shouted at anyone who's made the mistake of leaving the front door open, even for a couple of minutes. Louise coughs, she can't help it.

'Sorry, doll,' Mandy says. Her voice is hoarse from the crying and the endless cigarettes she's smoked since they arrived. Before, in fact. The ashtray is full to the brim. 'I'm sick of telling people to shut the bloody doors in this house, ken what I mean? And it's bloody Baltic out there too.'

Louise sits down. 'Is that a regular occurrence, then?'

'Is what a regular occurrence?'

'Someone leaving the door open. Do you mean both, or just the back?'

Mandy looks at her like she's grown horns. 'The front, hen. Did you not hear me shouting at your pal out there? Honestly, I don't know what's wrong with folk.'

Louise inhales and has to try hard not to sigh it back out. 'Who leaves the front door open, Mrs Taylor?'

'Fucksake. It's *miss*. And I told you to call me Mandy. Mrs Taylor was my mother. The old bat. God rest her soul. She'd know what to do about all this ...' She waves the hand that is holding the cigarette and ash flies around the kitchen like embers off a bonfire. 'This. This *shite*. Our Katie. Jesus Christ. Can someone make me another tea, please? I'm bloody gasping here.'

Malkie stands up. 'I'll get it. Steph's gone out to wait for Neil. School called. The headmaster has told him. Thinks he's on his way up here.'

'I'll go and see what's happening,' Davie says.

Louise tries again. 'Do the kids leave the door open a lot, Mandy? Only, I'm just trying to find out if there's a chance that someone could've come in this morning without anyone hearing. Do you lock the door at night?'

Mandy rolls her eyes. 'Yes. But like I said to the other officer earlier – I'd already gone out to work before Katie came home last night. I was working a seven-seven. Katie was to make their tea. I don't know what any of them were up to after that. I didn't get home until half eight this morning, and when I got here the house was empty. Well, at least I thought it was. Until I went upstairs to collect the sheets. I always wash their sheets on a Monday. Brett and Brooke had dumped theirs on the floor next to the machine – look. See? They're still there. Only I knew Katie's weren't there because her sheets are yellow, and all the sheets in that pile are white.' She pauses and takes a heavy drag on her cigarette. 'It wasn't like her. She's always the first to do what she's told.' She looks away. Louise can see she is trying to hold it together, but she's shaking. Little angry sobs are escaping with each exhale of smoke.

Louise hadn't even noticed the kettle boiling until Malkie laid the cups down in front of them both. She picks hers up and lets the warmth of the mug heat her hands. She gives Malkie a grateful smile.

He says, 'What we were discussing a wee while ago, before you came down, Louise, was who were the usual people, other than the family, that might be round here regularly, you know? Friends, boyfriends. Whoever. And whether anyone else had a key.'

'You know, it was probably Brooke. In fact, I'd say it was definitely Brooke. It's just like her. Especially with me being away.'

Louise isn't sure she's heard this right. 'Sorry. What was probably Brooke? Are you saying—'

'I'm saying she'll have left the door open. She's a little bugger for it. I think she gets her kicks from it. Likes the sound of me yelling at her to shut the damn thing.'

Louise lets out a relieved breath. For a minute there she thought the woman was accusing her younger daughter of killing her eldest. Not that it wasn't a valid possibility. They didn't know much about Brooke yet, and what they did know didn't paint a particularly pretty picture. 'Did Katie and Brooke get on? I used to fight with my younger sister all the time when we were younger, but we're good friends now.'

Mandy snorts. She stubs her cigarette out and pulls another one from the packet. 'Those two are a bloody nightmare.' She lights another cigarette and takes a drag. 'Can't stand the sight of each other. There were plenty of times I came home from working a backshift – you know, four till ten – and found them screaming and pulling each other's hair in the kitchen. Place covered in spaghetti hoops and trampled toast. I often thought, Jesus Christ, one of these days they're going to kill each other.' She stops abruptly and sucks in a sharp breath, which leads to a coughing fit. 'Oh no. Oh no. I didn't mean that, I ...'

'Where is Brooke at the moment, Mandy?' Malkie pulls out

a chair and sits down next to her. He throws Louise a look that says 'find her'.

'She's ... she's ... I don't know where she is. I texted her, told her to come home. Told her to bring Brett – he follows her around like a lost puppy. They're too alike. They even sound the bloody same. She didn't reply. I assumed they'd have told them at school, brought them back.' She lets out a long, low wail.

Louise feels a sudden lurch in her stomach. 'You mean you don't know where they are, Mandy? Either of them?'

Mandy shakes her head violently. She tries to light another cigarette off the butt of the last, but her hands are shaking too much. 'No ... no,' she says.

Louise feels a blast of cold air from behind her. The front door is open again. She wonders if Mandy is going to lose it completely, or has the realisation that she has one dead child and two missing knocked out all other thoughts from her head? What the hell is going on here? Louise knows they weren't at school. The headmaster had called earlier, after checking the place thoroughly. No one has seen them. They weren't in registration. They hadn't turned up late, or if they had they'd disappeared again before anyone knew. They could be anywhere. Maybe they'd heard the news and were too scared to come home. Any other option didn't bear thinking about. Could someone really have walked into this house, killed one child and abducted the other two? For a start, it didn't make any sense.

'Mandy, I know it's difficult for you. But we need to know of everyone who might've had reason to come round here,' Malkie says.

'I'll tell you. I will. Just ... God. I can't believe this is happening. My baby. She was such a good girl. Such a good girl. She was going to university, you know. To study all these scientific things that I've never even heard of. I don't know where she gets it from. All of my lot are thick as two short planks. Her dad, though ... Christ.'

99

'Mandy, I wanted to ask you something about the university stuff. She was interested in insects, is that right? I noticed the print on her wall – the butterflies. Did she have anything else like that? Maybe something more *real*? The print was of the type of boards the Victorians were fond of. I don't suppose she had a real one of her own? A board of mounted insects?'

Mandy looks at her and frowns. 'Well, aye. You must've seen it. It's up on the wall, next to the butterflies print. She cracked the frame last time she cleaned it, so all the wee beasties are out on display. Makes me shudder. I told her I wasn't going in there to dust and hoover until she put the glass back on the front. Creepy thing, isn't it?'

'Well, that's the thing. It's not there. I had a feeling there was meant to be one, but someone had taken a photo off her dressing table and hung it up in its place. I found this, though.' She holds out the plastic bag, with the damselfly sitting on the lid of the eye-shadow case.

Mandy reaches out, but doesn't touch it. 'The damselfly. That was her favourite one. She told me about them. Endangered species. She got this one when they went on a field trip down to the New Forest. She never said how she caught it. I don't think they were meant to bring anything back with them. Wee bugger. They're pretty wee things, but they creep me out. The buggy eyes are the worst. Where did you find that? Where's the rest of them?'

'I found this one down the back of the radiator, but the board isn't there. Maybe she lent it to someone? Maybe she'd taken it away to get a new piece of glass?'

Mandy starts shaking again. And crying. And that wail. That awful, awful wail. 'She'd never let that thing out of her sight. Her friend Lucas helped her make it. It was her pride and joy. She caught all of the insects herself. Dried them and positioned them – *relaxing*, they call it. She learned how to preserve them. Pinned them on that velvet backing. Fiddly wee things, some of them. Can't say it's my cup of tea. Like I said, I found it all a bit creepy. But she was so proud of that thing.'

'Who's Lucas,' Malkie says. 'I thought her boyfriend was called Neil.'

'He is. Neil Price. Nice laddie. But she had other friends too. Not many. I think she had a falling out with some of them last summer. I don't know what it was about. But Lucas was a good friend, although—' She pauses, looks up, as if trying to remember. 'I don't think I ever met him.'

'So he's never been round here?'

'Not that I know of. But then I'm out a lot. My shifts are all over the place. Any old Tom, Dick or Harry could be coming in and out of this place.'

'So anyone could've come in here this morning?'

'Yes,' she says; it's practically a whisper. 'Yes.'

Louise hears the front door close, hears shuffling footsteps. Three voices.

Mandy's wail peters out to a whimper. 'Who's that?' she says. 'Is it Brooke? Brett?'

Davie and Steph come into the kitchen, half-supporting, half-dragging a teenage boy between them. His eyes look glazed, as if he's not quite sure where he is.

'Mandy?' he says. 'What's going on? Please ... I don't understand. Where's Katie? Mr Poole said she was ... said she was ... '

Mandy stubs out her cigarette and stands up. She's shaking as she walks around the table. Takes the hands of the police off the boy and pulls him tight towards her. Soon, the sound of their combined cries fills the air. Louise has to leave the room to stop herself from joining in.

18

Polly

Jon closes his eyes and lets out a long, slow sigh. Polly can see that he's angry, but he's trying hard to keep it in.

'What were you doing at her house?' Jon says.

Lucas opens his mouth to speak, but before he can answer Polly interrupts. 'Does anyone else know about this?'

'Yes. I mean, I'm pretty sure. Not from me, I mean. I didn't *not* tell anyone on purpose. I thought it was OK. I mean, no, I knew it wasn't OK. Not really. But I thought I had a handle on it. Thought I knew what I was doing. I didn't do anything to encourage her, I swear.' Lucas looks away.

'Who knows?' Jon is pacing up and down the small office. The air has become thick with fear. 'Who knows, Lucas?'

'I think … well, she told her boyfriend. See, that's why I thought it was OK. He spoke to me one day. Asked me about it. I told him it was extra study, that's all. He didn't seem too bothered.'

'Neil's a pretty relaxed kid,' Jon says. 'I'm sure he didn't assume anything untoward was going on. If he had, I imagine he'd have said something.'

'Yes, well. Right. And nothing was going on, but—'

'Who else knows, Lucas?' Polly is getting sick of his dithering now. She understands that he's upset, but they need to get to the bottom of all this before it goes any further. They need to make sure they've no case to answer when the police start asking questions. It's a mess, of course it is. But if nothing sexual happened, then maybe it's OK. Maybe it's nothing.

'She told her friend, Hayley. It didn't go as expected. I'm not entirely sure what she said to the girl, but Hayley started giving me sly looks in the corridor. She thought there was something going on, something—'

'Something sexual?' Jon says, his face wrinkled with distaste.

'Yes, and I swear it wasn't like that. We were *friends*.'

'So you keep saying, Lucas,' Polly says. 'Why was Hayley so suspicious? What happened?'

Lucas sighs and rubs at his face. The tears have gone now. The reality of the situation is sinking in.

'I don't know. Honestly I don't know.'

'Does anyone else know?'

'I think Hayley told Brooke.'

'Katie's sister, Brooke?'

'Yes. Because I'm pretty certain that Katie wouldn't have told her. She'd never have spoken to her sister about anything like that. Anything she saw as important. Anyway, I know that Brooke knew, because she started doing stuff.'

Polly glances at Jon. His face has gone from deep red to purple.

'What stuff?'

'Leaving me notes. I wasn't sure at first. I thought it was Katie having a laugh. But then, it wasn't her style. And it wasn't her writing – although whoever had written the notes had tried to mimic her handwriting. Not very well, but at first glance, with nothing to compare to ... I didn't do anything at first. I cancelled a couple of meetings with Katie, told her I was too busy with marking and class prep. She understood.

Never questioned it. That's when I knew for sure. I checked the notes against one of Katie's essays, and I knew that she hadn't written them.'

'What did they say?' Jon says.

'The first one—'

'Have you still got them?' Polly says. Her voice is hopeful. If he has the letters, and they can show that they weren't from Katie, it might help.

'No. I burned them in my fireplace at home. I clean it out once a week. There's no way there's any trace. Anyway, the first one – it was odd, because it sounded like Katie. Like the kind of thing she would say. But I didn't understand why she'd leave me a note in my desk, I mean – I saw her often enough. She could've left me a letter at home if she thought she couldn't say it to me to my face. But it wasn't really her style. She was pretty forthright.' He pauses and takes a drink from his mug. The tea must be stone cold by now, but he doesn't comment. 'The first one said: *I can't stop thinking about you. It's not enough any more.*'

Polly picks up a pen and starts rolling it back and forth in her hand. 'And you didn't react to this? You didn't say anything to Katie?'

'No. Like I said, I cancelled the next meeting we had planned. Then the next. And then I got another note.'

'And?'

'It said: *I've been fantasising about you. I've been thinking about your beautiful hands. Thinking about what they could do …*'

'For Christ's sake,' Jon spits, 'tell me you spoke to Katie then?'

Lucas shakes his head. 'She came round one night. It was unplanned. She was working on a project, said she needed my help. I was paranoid the whole time, trying to work out a way to bring it up. There was no indication in her behaviour that she was expecting me to react to the note, so then I started to

104

doubt it. I asked her if she had told anyone about our friendship, and she got upset, told me about Hayley and how Hayley had said she was a filthy bitch. So I didn't say anything. I started to wonder if maybe Hayley was writing the notes. Next morning at school, I had another one: *I miss you so much. I want to do things with you. Please, I know you want me too.* That's when I knew they weren't from her. She'd only just seen me. Why would she leave that note at lunchtime the next day? That's when I checked the handwriting. I checked it against Katie's, then Hayley's. But neither matched. So that afternoon I told Katie – I asked her to stay behind after a biology class. This wasn't unusual. I did that with lots of kids. Anyway, I didn't say anything. Just showed her the notes.'

Polly clicks the lid of the pen and drops it into a drawer. 'What did she say?'

'One word: *Brooke.*'

Jon stops pacing and sits down hard. 'OK. So her little sister was stirring things up. Causing trouble. Did you ask Katie to talk to her?'

'Yes, but I knew she wouldn't want to. Hers and Brooke's fights often got physical, and I knew she was trying hard to keep away from her, keep things calm. Their mother expected Katie to look after Brooke and Brett when she was at work, and despite her frustrations she loved her mum. She wouldn't have wanted to make things more stressful for her.'

'OK, OK,' Jon says. He holds his hands up in surrender. 'This is a mess. A real mess. But I'm not sure it's got any bearing on her death, has it? Unless there's something you're not telling us.'

Lucas looks down. He is clenching and unclenching his fists.

'Katie called me last night. Asked me to come round. She said that she had confronted Brooke about the letters and that Brooke was furious, was planning to spread more rumours about us. Said she was going to try and get me sacked.'

'Hang on, so this is all recent? The letters? And why would she want you sacked?'

'Just for kicks, I suppose. I'm not even sure that Brooke cared what her sister got up to. She certainly didn't care about me. Brooke is one of those kids who is always on the lookout for trouble. And yes, it's recent. The third letter only came last week. I think Brooke was pissed off that her little game had been sussed out so quickly.'

The same thought hits Polly and Jon at the same time.

'You don't think ...'

'You don't mean ...'

'I don't know what I think or what I mean,' Lucas says. 'But that girl is out of control. Katie was so upset last night. She wanted me to speak to Brooke, but she'd already gone out after their argument. I didn't want to hang around. Their mother was still at work. What was she going to think if she came round and found me in the house at half ten at night?'

'Hang on,' Polly says, 'if Katie had an argument with Brooke, why didn't she call Neil, her boyfriend – get him round?'

Lucas sighs. 'They'd had an argument of their own, earlier in the day. She was ignoring his messages. She was scared about what Brooke was going to do. Scared it was going to get me in trouble. She didn't care about herself. She knew she hadn't done anything wrong. Not really. But she knew it wouldn't look good for me. People think what they want to think, don't they? No one would believe me if I said we were just friends. And what am I supposed to do now? It's only going to get worse, when Katie isn't here to defend me—'

'Defend you? The poor girl's dead! Murdered, in her own home.'

'I'm sorry, I didn't mean it to sound like I didn't care. Of course I bloody care. Jesus. I know you think it's wrong, but she was my friend. She really was.'

'I think we should get the police in here to see you. I mean, they mentioned that there would be some detectives coming in later, but—'

'No, please. I'm a mess. They'll think I'm trying to hide something. Please, let me go home. It's nearly time anyway. I think it'd be better for all of us.'

Polly has a sudden thought. 'You're not … you're not going to do anything stupid, are you, Lucas?'

'Christ, no! Look, I'm going to get grilled once the police get hold of this. I've no doubt that Brooke will be making me their prime suspect as we speak. Let me go home. I'm probably going to have to go down the station. They might want to keep me there. Please. I need to sort out stuff at home first.'

Jon looks at Polly. Polly shrugs. It's not right. They both know that. But he's their colleague and they need to support him as much as they can.

'OK,' Jon says. 'Go home now. Don't talk to anyone else. When the rest of the police arrive, I'll give them the gist of it. Make sure they get the right end of the stick before they go round to yours. It's all I can do. You've been stupid, Lucas. We'll have to discuss this further. But for now, get yourself home. If anyone asks, we'll say you've gone home with a migraine.'

'Well, that's not too far from the truth, to be fair. I can already see the aura. It's best that I drive home before my vision goes.' Lucas gets up and gives them both a small smile before he disappears out of the room.

Polly rubs at the back of her neck. She's been tensing it for what seems like hours. The bell will go soon. The kids will go home. The detectives will come to talk to her and the other staff. Tomorrow, she'll have to talk to the kids – the police will want to question Katie's friends, and she'll need to be their responsible adult. Or maybe they'll want her to talk to the kids? Lead the discussions, as their counsellor. Either way, tomorrow is going to be a shitty day, as if today wasn't bad enough. Poor Katie. And poor Lucas. He's got himself mixed up in something that he could never have foreseen.

But that's not her biggest worry. What she's heard about Katie's sister is her main concern. Polly is uneasy about Brooke. Surely she couldn't have. Surely she wouldn't have. She hasn't done anything to hurt her own sister – has she?

19

Louise

Louise needs air. She leaves Mandy, who is comforting Neil in the kitchen; watches as Malkie discreetly takes himself out the back door. Officers have already searched out there, but he'll be taking the time to have a look round himself. The uniforms on door-to-door will be back soon, and while there's clearly no chance to speak to either Mandy or Neil, it's as good a time as any for a break.

She takes her handbag from the back of the chair and walks out the front. They've managed to keep the press hounds to the end of the street at the cordon and the residents have been asked to stay inside. There are a few lurking around on the empty street, smoking, casting glances down the road. Louise catches the eye of a man dressed in what looks like pyjamas, with a long, thick coat over the top, and he looks away.

She takes a packet of cigarettes and a lighter from her bag. She's only taken the first drag when Davie appears. He's been down the side of the house next door. It's one of those terraces joined by small arched alleys that lead to shared back gardens.

He nods at the cigarette. 'Didn't know you smoked, Lou? Thought you were on a health-kick?'

'I am. I *was*. Well, I always have a packet in my bag for emergencies. I wasn't going to have one today, but I figured I've already passively smoked a ten deck in the kitchen – what's the harm in another?'

He reaches out. 'Give us one, then.'

'Hang on, since when do *you* smoke? You're the proper fitness freak around here. You know they call you the karate kid back at the station.'

'Aye. Well, they might take the piss, but they've asked me to start some self-defence classes up there, you know. For the staff, I mean, not the public.' He lights the cigarette and takes a long drag. Closes his eyes. 'Christ, it's been a while. Anyway, yeah – a few of the lads were saying they could benefit from a bit more than the usual mandatory training. The super thinks it's a goer. If it works, might be something I'll do elsewhere.'

'Other stations, you mean?'

'Yeah. Could be a wee sideline. Or maybe more ...' He gives her a look.

'What? You're not leaving CID already? You've only just got your warrant card reprinted.'

'Ha! Well, you know. It was all fine when I was doing it to help out. I was never really sure about it being a thing. I mean, it's things like this today ... I'm not sure I'm cut out for it.'

Louise takes another drag. 'I know what you mean, Davie. It's days like today that make you want to start searching the job ads in Tesco's. Don't get me wrong, I love my job. I love the problem-solving bit, especially – finding the clues, putting them together. But when you see that ...' She gestures towards the house. 'Two people in there, breaking their hearts.'

'Yep. Although ...'

'Although what?'

'What do you think about Mum?'

'I think she's someone who's struggling to take in the fact

that she's just lost her eldest kid, and she's realising that she's no control over the others.'

'All real though, you think? She's shaking constantly. Never seems to meet anyone's eye.'

'You're not saying—'

'I don't know what I'm saying, Lou. I'm just saying we can't rule anything out. Most of these things are domestic, you know that. I'd be very surprised if Katie didn't know her killer.'

Davie takes a final long draw on the cigarette and flicks the butt towards the drain. It bounces once and falls neatly into one of the holes between the metal slats.

'Still got it,' Louise says, and immediately feels stupid.

Davie gives her a small smile, but it fades before it reaches his eyes. 'Look sharp, Lou. We've got company.'

Louise follows Davie's gaze towards the cordon, to where a teenage girl and a younger boy, both in school uniform and thick parkas, are running down the pavement towards them.

Shit.

'Woah! Woah,' Davie says, putting his hands out to stop them from barrelling into the house.

'What's happened to our Katie?' the girl says.

'Is it true?' says the boy.

They're like two peas in a pod, Louise thinks. If she didn't know otherwise, she'd think they were twins, but clearly Brett is just tall for his age and his voice hasn't broken yet, hence the similarities with his sister. It is a bit unnerving.

'Come on,' Louise says. 'I'll take you in to your mum.'

20

Neil

Neil hears the sound of raised voices coming through from the hall. He pulls back from Mandy's embrace. She'd had him in a tight grip, almost smothering him; he can't recall her ever showing such emotion before, but then it's not every day that your daughter is found dead, is it? His face is wet, and he's not sure if they are her tears or his, or both of theirs mixed together.

'Brooke,' Mandy says. She moves towards the kitchen door, but before she reaches the handle, it bursts open.

'Mum! Mum, is it true?' Brooke is bright red, her breath is coming out in small panting bursts.

Brett stands behind her, his face ashen. At some point, the other policeman – Neil didn't catch his name – has come in from the back garden. He's standing next to the kettle, observing. The kitchen is too crowded now, with Gray and the two female police officers in there too, and all the kids. And Mandy. And the grief. The grief is taking up most of the space, sucking all the air from the room. Neil leans on a chair, worried he might collapse.

'Oh, Brooke ...' Mandy steps forward and embraces her

daughter. Grabs out with her free hand, beckoning for Brett too, her son. Neil casts a glance over at the police, who seem to be leaving them all to it. They're watching, though. Neil knows they're taking it all in. Despite their kind words and their endless cups of tea, they are watching.

They're all suspects, aren't they?

Neil knows he didn't do it. Well, of course he's going to say that, if they ask. Which they haven't. Not yet. But they will. He's sure that they will. Once they start digging around. Once they find out about ...

'Brooke. Brett. I know this is a huge shock. Would you mind just answering a couple of questions for us?' It's the policeman who took on the tea duty. Fucking great timing, that one, Neil thinks. Yeah, he's only doing his job, but the two of them have only just arrived. Let their mum have a few minutes, at least. To be fair, he's also quite interested in where the two of them have been – but it can wait five minutes, can't it?

'You OK, Neil?' The nice-looking copper has clocked him staring. Fuck. He doesn't want to attract any attention. Not now. Not with the others here.

'Sure. Jesus. It's all just a bit of a shock. I can't really take it in.'

Out of the corner of his eye, he spots Brooke lifting her head off her mother's shoulder, just enough so she can see him. And he can see her. He can only see her eyes, and he can't read them. Brooke's a cold bitch at the best of times, and even now it's hard to imagine she's as upset as she's making out. He wants to talk to her on her own. Find out if she saw Katie last night. After he did. After their stupid argument. Fuck.

Fuck this shit.

'Maybe I'll just get some air.' He walks past the stares, outside into the cold afternoon. The blonde one follows him, closes the door behind them, almost, not the whole way. Leaves it open a crack. She still wants to hear what's going on in the kitchen. Good. So does he. He's no idea what to say to her. Tell her everything, right now? Or wait till he's asked? Maybe it won't come up. Maybe he can keep it to himself. Some of it, at least. The worst bit, anyway. He hopes.

Back in the kitchen, someone is crying. Brooke? Brett? Trying to say something but no one can make it out through the sobs. It sounds a lot like 'sorry' but maybe that's just because that's what Neil wants it to be.

THREEWISEMONKEYSBLOG

Telling It Like It Is

Posted: 1st Nov 2016 by SpeakNoEvil
Status: Draft
Comments: 0

> *Say, say my enemy.*
> *Come out and fight with me.*
> *And bring your Bulldogs three.*
> *Climb up my sticker tree.*
> *Slide down my lightning.*
> *Into my dungeon door*
> *And we'll be jolly enemies*
> *Forever evermore.*

OK. I get it. We aren't friends any more. That's fine. No biggie. I mean, if you're not prepared to listen to what I have to say about things ... if you'd rather start spreading rumours – about things you have clearly misunderstood – well, that's up to you. Nothing I can do, is there? I could plead with you, try to make you understand. But what's the point?

Things aren't always cut and dried, black and white. Things aren't always seedy and sordid just because you want them to be.

Maybe you're jealous. Is that it? Because you just want things to be about one thing only, and you don't get the bigger picture. You don't get that males and females can be *just friends*. Because that's not how you see things any more, is it? Boys exist to be your playthings. Is that it? Is that really all you're about?

I used to imagine us growing old, having families, going on holiday together with our kids. I imagined us both moving away, to bigger and better things. Great jobs, great lives. Away from all this small town crap that we've had to grow up with.

It's sad.

I'm sad. I'm sad that you don't understand, and I'm sad that there's nothing I can do to change that.

But you didn't have to tell *her*.

Do you know what you've done?

Have you got ANY IDEA what you've done? As if my life wasn't difficult enough already. You had to do that. You had to go there. Jesus, if only I'd realised what a vacuous piece of shit you'd turned into, I'd never have opened my fucking mouth.

116

21

Polly

Polly stands by the window near the front door and watches as the kids file out of the front door. The mood is subdued, sombre. There is none of the usual pushing and name-calling that she's used to seeing. She wonders how many of them will go home and talk to their parents about it all. Wonders how many will sit in silence, keeping it in, too scared to show emotion in case it leads to something more. Polly dealt with a lot of kids like that back in her old school. The ones with parents who left them to themselves, except when they were shouting at them or demanding something from them. The ones who ridiculed their kids for trying to do well in case they got too big for their boots and – God forbid – made something of their miserable lives. Those parents were prone to extreme reactions – and most of those reactions were not good.

Those are the kinds of parents that would go after Lucas. If they were to hear that he'd got too close, they wouldn't care about the facts, the details. Things like the truth. Because Polly is sure that Lucas is telling the truth. He's been naive, sure. But nothing more. She rubs her eyes.

She's only been back for three days, yet already she's

regretting it. Not the job. Not this – this thing that's happened – as awful as it is; she wants to help. Feels like she owes it. She'd come here for a new start, and Simon couldn't even be arsed to send her a quick 'good luck' text for her first day at work. She realises now that Simon doesn't care about anything at all, certainly not her. So, in many ways, it's just as well that the baby that's currently growing inside her isn't his. It's just as well that she's left him.

'Polly, there you are!' Jon interrupts her. She blinks, realising that the playground is empty now, the last of the bright rucksacks just disappearing out of view outside the gate. 'The detectives have arrived.'

'I didn't see them come in. I've been here for ages.'

'They came round to the side gate. The uniformed officers have gone for now. I didn't want to upset the children any more. Come on, everyone's through in the staff room.'

She follows him along the corridor. 'Jon, I'm starting to think we've made a mistake …'

'What do you mean?' he snaps at her, then frowns. The strain is getting to him. He knows.

'Letting Lucas go home. Maybe someone should go round there, make sure he's OK. I mean, we're telling the police, aren't we?'

Jon squeezes her upper arm, pulls her back. She stops. 'Let's not be too hasty here, Polly. Lucas is a good teacher. I don't want to do anything to jeopardise things for him. Let's wait it out a bit.'

'Jeopardise what? If he's done nothing wrong, then there's nothing to be concerned about, is there? The police are going to need to talk to him. I don't want to lie.'

'No one's going to lie. We're just going to explain that he's gone home early as he was feeling unwell. He does get those hideous migraines, you know. He's off at least once a month with the things. I've told him to go back to the doctor—'

Before Polly has a chance to respond, a voice cuts in. 'Who needs to go back to the doctor?' he says.

Polly recognises the voice straight away. He's standing just inside the door of the staff room, leaning against the wall. He's dressed smartly in a well-fitting navy suit with a pale blue shirt. No tie. He smiles at her. His eyes tell her that he's been waiting for her to make an appearance.

'Sergeant Gray—'

'It's Detective Sergeant Gray now.' A woman who looks about her age is sitting on the couch on the other side of the room, next to Marnie Cohen, the head of English, who is sniffing into a shredded hankie; small pieces of white tissue-fluff are dusted across her grey-skirted lap.

The woman stands up. 'DC Jennings. Louise.' She offers a hand. 'You must be Polly?'

Polly glances back at Davie, who gives her a small nod. They've been talking about her? Or just noting that she wasn't there? Everyone else is crammed into the room. Sitting upright on the chairs and the sofas. Leaning against walls. Some are on the hard wooden chairs that are usually kept in the hall outside Jon's office. Every member of staff who was working today is in this room, including the dinner ladies and their janitor, Mr Hennessy, and his assistant, Pete.

'Hello, Polly,' Davie says. Glancing across at Jon, he says, 'Is that everyone now?' Jon's eyes flit to Polly, just for a second. Davie is looking at a list of names on a clipboard in front of him, but DC Jennings is fully alert. She catches Polly's eye, and Polly looks away.

'Yes,' she says, addressing Davie. 'That's all of us.'

'Where's Lucas?' Catherine, the school secretary, says. 'Is he OK?'

'He's gone home,' Jon says. 'One of his migraines. I thought it was best if he got back and took his medication. I told him I'd get the police to pop in and see him later.' He

119

pauses, looks at Davie, then Louise. 'That's OK, isn't it?'

Louise frowns. 'Would've been easier if he'd stayed here. Lucas ...'

'Crisp,' Davie says. 'It's fine, we've got plenty to be getting on with here. We'll go and see him when we're finished up. Hopefully he'll be feeling a bit better by then.'

Polly bites her lip and looks away. She can feel Louise staring at her.

'Brian, you and Pete can go now, if you like.' Davie addresses the janitor and his assistant, who they have already questioned. 'We'll follow up with you later if there's anything we've missed.'

'Grand. Not a bother,' Hennessy says. 'Come on now, lad.' His voice has a gentle Irish lilt, and he has huge brown eyes, like a puppy. A sad puppy. Polly doesn't know him at all. Doesn't remember him from before, but there's no reason she would. There will be lots of new people here since she last lived in the town. She doesn't know Pete, either. But she remembers something Jon told her about him being the local councillor's son. Martin someone. Brotherstone, that's it. He's a lumbering lad of about twenty, with a quirky way about him that Polly can't quite put her finger on. He's staring straight ahead, but she can't tell if he's deliberately trying not to make eye contact with anyone or if he's just zoning out of the situation. Anyway, he clearly doesn't know anything – not if Davie is telling him and his boss they can go.

'Eva, Anya, Gillian – you can go, too. We'll be in touch if we need you.'

Polly watches as the three dinner ladies make their way out of the room. Two older women, one young. The younger one has a streak of blue hair escaping from her regulation hair net.

Polly sits down on the sofa, in the space left by the janitor.

'Bit of a shock this, on your first day,' Louise says, sitting down beside her. 'Hardly had a minute to settle and you've been thrown into this. You know, it's a good job that you're here. We'll need you when we start questioning the kids. The fact that you don't know any of them might work to our advantage. They might be more likely to talk to a stranger, don't you think? Rather than someone who knows all their dark deeds?'

'I'm not sure,' Polly says. 'In my experience, kids open up more when they're dealing with an adult they can trust. It can take a long time to build that trust. I'm hoping they might talk to me when I tell them I went to this school, that ...' She glances over at Davie. 'That I've been questioned by the police myself. You know, when that terrible accident happened down at the burn. I was only a child myself ...'

She lets her sentence trail off. Why did she bring *that* up, of all things? Polly catches another glance passing between Louise and Davie.

'Jon,' Davie says, 'why don't we start with you? Shall we pop through to your office? Polly can look after the others in here. Maybe get a bit of insight into which kids we might need to speak to. Polly?'

'Sure. Sure. That'd be fine,' she says.

Fuck, she thinks. They're talking to Jon on his own. What's he going to say about Lucas? More and more, Polly wishes that she hadn't let the man go home.

She has a horrible, horrible feeling about it, but right now there's absolutely nothing she can do.

121

22

Louise

Louise takes the seat opposite the headmaster. 'So, Mr Poole—'

He cuts her off. 'Jon. Please.'

'Jon, any ideas what's going on? Anyone you think we need to be speaking to?'

'Did Katie have any enemies?' Davie says. He is looking at the certificates on Jon Poole's walls. Louise knows he's leaving her in the hot seat, as it were. Hoping she might be able to get something more out of Jon, making it look like she's just having some general chat when really she is observing everything he says and does.

Jon rubs a hand over his face. Sighs. 'She was a good student. Very good. It's not very PC of me to say this, but her family aren't the best. Her younger sister is a troublemaker. The brother is a bit – how can I say? – lost. I'm not sure their mother has much to do with them, to be honest. Katie seemed to bear the brunt of bringing them up.' He stares down at the pile of papers that are neatly stacked in the middle of his desk. He picks up a pen and places it back down, parallel to the stack of papers.

'What about her friends?' Louise says. She glances at Davie and he gives her a look that says *push it*. 'Have you been made aware of any fallings out recently? It's not a huge school – if Katie was well known, I imagine these things would be noticed ...'

Jon sits up straight. 'I don't really take too much notice of that sort of thing. You'd be better asking some of her teachers, maybe—' There's a sharp knock on the door and he stops talking. 'Come in!'

Polly, the brand-spanking-new guidance counsellor, sticks her head round the door. 'Jon, sorry to interrupt. The others are wondering if you still need them, or if they can go? People are tired. They need to absorb all this. Might be best if we talk more in the morning?'

Davie clears his throat. 'Good idea, Polly. Why don't you all get off? We'll finish up here. Talk to you all again tomorrow. Maybe you could have a look at the student lists tonight, then tomorrow we can start to chat to the classes too?'

Polly nods, gives them a small smile. She retreats back through the gap and closes the door behind her.

Jon lets out a long, slow sigh.

'Difficult day ...' Louise says.

Jon rubs a hand over his head, leaves his hair sticking up in tufts. 'That's the understatement of the year. Listen, you know I'll do anything I can to help here. Just ask.'

'We will,' Davie says. 'Don't you worry about that.'

* * *

Back in the car, Louise leans back into her seat and starts picking at her cuticles. 'What about this Lucas Crisp? What do we think about him going home early?'

Davie slaps her hand gently and she stops picking. 'I'd like to go and talk to him now, but if he's ill we're not going to get

123

much out of him. Let's go round and see if he's up to it, then we can go back to the station, try and work out where we are so far. We need updates from Steph Benedict and the uniforms back at the house anyway. And I need to talk to Malkie.'

Louise starts the engine. 'What about all the *first twenty-four hours is critical in a murder investigation* bit? Shouldn't we be talking to everyone who knew her?'

'Not tonight, Lou. Tonight we need to get back and regroup. See what the others have got. Work on a plan to decide who's doing what. It's been a long day. Nothing immediately obvious has jumped out at us yet, has it? Besides, I need to make a few phone calls.'

'Oh aye?'

'That lad in there – Pete ...'

'The janitor's assistant?'

'Aye, him. I don't want to jump the gun, but, well, there's been a few things about him in the past. He was questioned about approaching a wee girl in a park a few years ago. He had a bit of an obsession with my friend, Anne. And then he turned up with a piece of key evidence during all the business with the girls being scared up at the Track last summer.'

'But he didn't have anything to do with any of it, did he?'

'Nothing proven at the time, but I've always had my doubts. Problem is, his dad is Martin Brotherstone.'

'As in Councillor Martin Brotherstone, local Tory candidate?'

'For his sins. Makes it difficult to get anything concrete about Pete. But then again, now that Chief Inspector Hamilton has retired he's got no man on the inside, as it were. I might be able to push a bit harder. I know Malkie will agree. He always hated Hamilton and anyone associated with him.'

Louise's stomach flips. Pete Brotherstone. He'd been mentioned in the case notes from the investigations into what happened at Black Wood. Always a cloud hanging over the lad, but no one had ever been able to make anything stick. Interesting. It'd be nice if it could be this simple.

'Anyway,' Davie says, as Louise pulls out onto the main road, 'before all that I need to pop home. I need to eat, and so does the bloody cat. You coming with me?'

Louise feels a fluttering in her chest. 'Um, I was going to ask Malkie if I could borrow one of the pool cars to get myself back home—'

'You brought a bag, didn't you?'

'Yeah, but that was for an emergency – like if I had to kip at the station or something ...'

Davie laughs. 'I'm not going to twist your arm, Lou, but I've got a comfy bed in the spare room, and half a tray of leftover lasagne in the fridge. I might even be able to rustle up some garlic bread and a bit of salad. Plus, it would give us more time to talk about things ...'

Things? Jesus, did he know? Was she that bloody obvious?

'The case? We're still trying to solve a murder, in case it had slipped your mind.'

She realises she's been holding her breath. Lets it out in a whoosh. 'That sounds great, Davie.'

23

Polly

Polly flicks on the kettle and drops two pieces of bread into the toaster. She should be eating better. She knows this. She did a big shop on Sunday, filling the fridge with salads and yoghurts and chicken. The fruit bowl on the worktop is full to the brim with oranges and apples, a couple of bananas on top already starting to brown.

What she'd really like is a large glass of wine. A bottle, even.

Was it a mistake to come back here?

The house is warm, the darkness thick outside the windows. But the place feels empty and hollow. Memories of her childhood trapped in the walls.

Someone else's memories, too. The man who lived here before. The one who was killed at Black Wood cottage. He deserved it, and yet it still feels wrong. The man who caused so much pain, living here in this house – her house. Sleeping in her bed. She would have to buy a new bed. But money wasn't really free-flowing at the moment. She was still paying half the mortgage for the place in Edinburgh, even though Simon was there alone and could well afford it. Still, a small price to pay for being away from him.

So why does she miss him?

She checks her phone again. Nothing. No 'hope your first day went well'. No 'hope you're OK there on your own'. Why should he care? She left him. She's the one with another man's child in her belly – although he doesn't know this. Not yet.

She spreads a thick layer of Philadelphia on the toast and pours milk into the tea. Adds two heaped sugars. If she can't have wine, she'll have to get buzzed some other way. She takes a bite of the toast and leans back into the cushions on the sofa. Her mum made these cushions, years ago. She'd helped, holding the pins while her mother tacked the edges.

A small tear runs down her cheek and she wipes it away, angrily.

Fuck you, Simon.

If he'd just cared a little bit more. Thought about her instead of his bloody job all the time. Not to mention the golf. Jesus. Could there be a sport more boring than golf? Walking round a field chasing after a little ball? Discussing it over too many gins in the clubhouse where women were still forbidden to enter?

She rubs her belly. At least *he* isn't like that. *He* is nothing like that at all. For one, he doesn't drink. Isn't particularly interested in sports, either. He loves music, like she does. Books too. American boxsets. Walks in the woods.

She stares out of the window, towards the bridge that leads down to the woods where Claire and Jo had gone that day. Feels another tear slide down her face. This time she leaves it there.

She sends a text: **Did you hear what happened today?**

Stupid bloody question. Of course he'll know. She sips her tea; the sickly thickness of the sugar coats her throat. Waits.

Yes. Do you want me to come round?

Wind whistles through the air vent on the kitchen window. A high-pitched squeal: long, drawn out. A flurry of snow patters against the window.

The weather is awful. Don't come out in this.

He lives at the other end of the town. He doesn't have a car. She doesn't want him freezing to death out there.

Don't be stupid. I'm on my way.

She wants to reply, tell him to stay at home. Stay warm. She needs to think. Is it too soon? Does she want people to find out the real reason she came back to the town? Who she came back for? It's too complicated now – with what's happened. Mandy Taylor is back in her life. She's going to have to talk to her children. The two that she has left … And while she knows that they are not *his* children, he was there when they were little. She imagines that Mandy might need him more than she does right now. But she needs to feel his arms around her. She needs to tell him about the baby. Before it becomes too difficult to hide.

She swivels around, lies down on the sofa. Feels herself sinking in deep. The dream comes to her before she is even asleep. The woods. Darkness.

She doesn't hear the door opening. Doesn't feel the icy blast of air that he brings in with him. When he lies down beside her, holding her tight, she lets his coldness mix with her warmth and, finally, she feels safe.

TUESDAY

24

Louise

Louise bites into the bacon roll and feels the ooze of butter running down her chin. The diet is fucked for now, obviously. Lasagne and wine at Davie's, and now a breakfast of carbohydrate, saturated fat and too much salt. Bloody good, though. It's eat when you can and eat what's available, and thankfully Rav, one of the uniforms assigned to their team, had gone down to one of the local cafés – Landucci's? An Italian name, anyway. Something like that – and brought them all back their breakfast. If anyone was veggie, they were screwed, but judging by the happy faces munching away no one was disappointed with the choice.

'Right,' Malkie says. 'I'm assuming that you've all had some sleep, and you're now being well fed, thanks to PC Singh, so let's get on with it. Yesterday's developments ...' He pauses, flips the cover of the giant pad on the easel. He's clearly been busy with his theories, as the whole thing is covered in names, connecting lines. Some of the names are underlined, a couple have big red circles drawn around them. The team look on eagerly, desperate to get on with the day's work – desperate to find the bastard responsible. 'So,' he continues, 'here's the skinny. Door to door – that's Rav Singh and Al Patterson – spoke to all but one of the neighbours on Katie's street. So far, nada. A lot of them are elderly, and they were in bed early on Sunday night. Some of them were up early on Monday morning, but no one noticed anything suspicious. Problem is, the time of year – no one opens their curtains at 6 a.m. when it's still dark. According to the coroner, Katie was killed sometime between 5 and 7 a.m. – based on the bruising and the fact that she was only just going into rigor when the GP arrived on the scene.'

'What about the neighbour that no one spoke to?' Louise asks.

Malkie nods at her. 'Coming to that. Rav and Al are heading back there this morning, hoping we get an answer. The neighbour is a Mr Cooper Pembrey – he works at the carpet factory in Portobello. He often works double shifts, but it seems that he's something of a man of mystery. Sometimes he's not back for a couple of days at a time, according to the neighbour on the other side – Mrs Kendal – someone who was seemingly gutted not to have overheard anything. The street's gossip, apparently. Shame she'd gone to bed with earplugs and a sleeping pill after a dodgy stomach brought on by her Sunday evening meals-on-wheels. Anyway, we don't know if Mr Pembrey was around on Sunday night or Monday morning yet, but fingers crossed.

'Next: who's in the frame? Family first. The current stepfather, Brooke and Brett's dad, is locked up and he definitely hasn't escaped. We checked. We can't rule out the mother ...'

He is cut off by a series of groans and murmurs from the team.

'Come on, lads. You know how this works. I agree, she seems genuinely distraught, and we know she was working a shift at Barrett's on Sunday night, but we only have her word

132

about what time she got back – her shift finished at seven, she says she got home at eight-thirty, finding the house empty except for Katie – who was still in bed. Already deceased. Plus, there's the kids. Brooke and Brett. Where were they all of yesterday morning? We're still trying to establish this. We're going easy because of their age, but don't be fooled. There are plenty of damaged kids out there – they wouldn't be the first to do something horrific and run away.'

Another groan. Louise has a question to ask, but she's saving it. Something that kept her awake half the night. She and Davie had talked for hours, sitting together on the small sofa. She'd taken her shoes off, curled her legs up. Felt the heat of his thighs on the soles of her feet. He'd moved a bit closer then, or maybe she'd imagined it. She went to bed, stared up at the ceiling. Thought about Davie. Thought about Lucas Crisp. The teacher who'd gone home early. What about him? They'd gone round, but there'd been no answer at his door. He must've been asleep. They'd decided to leave him to it. Something had been niggling at her, but she'd shaken it away. She tries to focus.

'Just stating the facts. Next: boyfriend. We've still to properly question the boyfriend, Neil Price. Another likely candidate – lovers' tiff? Then there's the school – friends, teachers, anyone who's had any contact with Katie recently, or at all, even. In fact, it's the ones who haven't been in contact you might want to focus on. Who has she fallen out with recently? Talk to the kids. Get the school counsellor involved – you can use her as the appropriate adult, or you can let her take the lead. Karen and Sarah can deal with this. Louise – step in, if needed. See how it works best. Don't push them too hard, but find out what they know.' He pauses, takes a bite of his roll and washes it down with a glug of tea. 'Someone knows something, right? This is a small community. Use Davie as your point of contact – he knows better than anyone what this place is like.

Banktoun's turning into bloody Midsomer these days. Let's get this sorted out, soon as. Your sub-teams and tasks are on the whiteboard.'

Louise turns round to get a better look at the whiteboard. Sees Davie. He has a grim expression on his face. The others are moving into their smaller teams, sitting on the edges of desks, chatting quietly, working out what they need to do. The buzz is building up. Louise has been teamed with Davie. They're to go to the school and start talking to the children. But their first job is on there, circled in red. Twice.

Talk to Lucas Crisp. If he doesn't answer the door this time, they'll have to escalate things.

'Hang on,' Davie says. The room falls silent. 'You've missed a couple of people off this list, Malkie.' He walks over to the whiteboard. Draws a box in one corner. *Katie's dad???*, he writes. In another box he writes: *Jamie Quinn*.

'Care to expand?' Malkie says.

'Katie's dad has always been one of the town's biggest mysteries. Mandy was under-age. There were plenty of rumours, but nothing ever stuck. People got bored with it eventually. Plenty of other gossip to be getting on with. Might be worth revisiting this now, though. Someone must know who he is and if there's any possibility that he might be involved in this.'

'Have you any idea?' Malkie asks him.

Davie frowns. 'I wouldn't like to speculate, but I've always had my theories. I'll talk to you about this after the meeting, if that's OK?'

Malkie makes a 'hmmph' noise that Louise reads as his assent. 'And the other one – Jamie Quinn? Who's he, then?'

'Jamie Quinn, generally known as Quinn, is a chef at the Rowan Tree. He's lived here all his life, bar a couple of years at Her Majesty's pleasure.'

'And? He got form?'

'Not for this. Drugs. Petty offences when he was younger. He went into rehab. Sorted himself out.'

'Right. So what's he got to do with this?' Malkie's voice makes it clear that he is running out of patience. People are shuffling again, anxious to get on with their work.

'Well, possibly nothing,' Davie says. 'But he was with Mandy Taylor for a good few years. Lived with her when the kids were little. He was pretty much their stepdad, as far as I'm aware.'

A ripple of interested noises again.

'Right then,' Malkie says. 'You and Jennings need to talk to him too.'

LucasCrispIsAPaedo

🔒 Secret Group

289 Members (130 new)

Luke Crust

6h

As far as I know, Lucas Crisp still husnae been arrested. Does he have to kill another innocent girl before they do anything? Mind what happened last summer with those things up at the Track – nothing was done until it was far too late and that poor Laura got attacked. The polis are no doing anything here, are they? Has anyone got any updates?

Likes(189) Comments(77)

Big Jim Nailor I heard they went round last night and he wouldnae let them in.
Al Samson Bollocks, they'd huv kicked the door in.
Big Jim Nailor Not if he's no really a suspect.
Al Samson Whole thing's a joke – who else do they think might've done it?
Joe Crow Has anyone seen him?
Big Jim Nailor Nah – he'll be lying low.
Al Samson I say we get round there …
Luke Crust And do what? What're you suggesting, *Al Samson*?
Lou Peters Stop fannying aboot, lads.
Gary Niven I heard the polis wanted to talk to Quinn aboot it.
Pete Reed Fucksake. Quinn's sound. Nothing to dae wi him.
Big Jim Nailor Mind, he was inside for a bit …

Pete Reed For trying to rob the post office wi a fake gun in a Tesco's bag.

Big Jim Nailor Oh aye. Haha. Where's the lassies gone? Have they all left the page? They've no reported it, though, cuz it's still here.

Lou Peters That's cuz they dinnae think we're serious aboot this.

Joe Crow And ye's are serious, aye?

Big Jim Nailor Aye.

...

see 60 other comments

25

Neil

Neil turns over and yanks the duvet up angrily, covering his face. For a split second, he doesn't remember. It's just a normal Tuesday morning. Then it comes back. Thoughts of yesterday's events swimming into focus. He's sure he hasn't slept. It's been one of those sleeps where you're convinced you've been wide awake all night, staring at the wall, dreaming yet not dreaming. He screws his eyes tight. Wills himself to sleep. And he drifts off, just for a moment.

The buzzing of his phone wakes him out of whatever kind of trance he's been in. He wishes it was a dream. Wishes that the last thirty-six hours could be erased, that he could live them again. But he can't. Katie is still dead. He rolls over and picks up his phone. Bloody Facebook message notifications. He needs to turn the vibrate off. He opens the first chat thread, not wanting to but knowing he has to read it. Fuck. FUCK.

You can't keep ignoring me forever, loverboy

Fuck off. I'm not in the mood. And don't call me that.

Aww come on, just a wee joke.

How can you joke at a time like this?

What do you expect me to do? She's not coming back, is she?

Have some respect, Jesus Christ.

Like she respected me? She fucking hated me.

I'm not surprised. You're a bitch.

Now, now ...

Go away.

I need to tell you something.

FFS. What?

Go on Facebook. There's a group ...

There's loads of groups on there, fuckwit. What am I looking for?

😄 😄 😄

???

Patience!!!! Mr Crisp ...

Mr Crisp? What the fuck about him?

Well, we all know he's a dirty paedo.

Says who?

Says everyone. Wake up, you twat.

Look, I'm not in the mood for one of your stupid games.

My heid's like mince.

Go to: lucascrispisapaedo – I've already approved you so you can join the group ...

139

Wow.

??

Just fucking wow. Don't tell me you came up with that?

Just get on there, Neily-boy. It's already got 500 members ... there's loads of comments. People are getting right fucking ratty about it!

You're sick.

Not me that's sick! Anyhoo, I only did it for a joke, didn't expect so many people to get in a right huff about it.

A joke? Another one of your brilliant jokes? What the fuck is wrong with you??

You didn't think there was much wrong with me the other night ...

...

...

Oi. You there? You need to go and look at that group. It's gonna happen, whether you like it or not.

What is?

The battering, stupid. That dirty wee stoat's gonnae get it good.

He throws his phone across the room. It bounces on the carpet, slides under his desk. That girl ... that fucking girl. She's not even a girl. She's a monster. She's spent most of her existence making life hell for Katie, and for anyone else who doesn't agree with everything she says. What was he thinking? A moment of madness. Extreme madness. And now

140

this? What is he supposed to do? He's too scared to look at the Facebook group. He should tell someone. Mr Poole. His mum. The police. But if he does that, he'll have to tell them about how he found out, won't he? He doesn't want to search for the group on Facebook. Doesn't want to go anywhere near social media. He can already imagine the outpourings of fake grief … the little shits who couldn't stand Katie coming out of the woodwork to say how upset they are now that she's gone.

No, he's not getting involved in any of that. Fuck the lot of them. It's not like the bunch of dicks are actually going to do anything to Mr Crisp, is it? They can't be that stupid. Besides, Facebook will close the group down as soon as someone reports it, or maybe it'll get picked up in one of their scans, even if it is supposed to be secret. Surely the word 'paedo' is on their hit list. You can't go around accusing people of things like that when you've no idea what you're talking about. It'll all blow over before it starts. No one's going to actually hurt anyone. Nothing bad is actually going to happen. *Keep telling yourself that, Neil … And if you're lucky, you might be able to keep your head buried in the sand for as long as you want.*

26

Polly

Despite everything, Polly had slept well. She'd woken on the sofa, a blanket lain neatly over her and tucked in. A glass of water on the small table beside her; underneath was a note:

Didn't want to wake you. You looked so peaceful. I'm here if you need to talk to me xxx

She did want to talk to him. She knew he must be hurting too. But Mandy. How was she going to deal with Mandy?

She sits at her desk and waits for the first student to be brought to see her. The first one's going to be tough, she knows it. Sergeant Zucarro is with her, and she will be recording the interviews and taking notes. If there is anything that needs to be discussed further, the pupil will be taken to the police station and formally questioned. It seems quicker this way, and Polly is happy to do it. Apart from anything else, it is giving her time to get to know each one a bit better. To get to know them, full stop, since she has barely spoken to any of them yet. The other policewoman, Constable Evans, is spending time in the break-out areas and in the playground.

Keeping an eye on things – again, hoping to hear something that might be investigated further. Polly is not convinced that any of the children are going to be able to help. Despite their fights and falling outs, she can't imagine that anything more sinister could have happened. She trusts Lucas, too. Even though there's no sign of him again today. This is a worry, but she's going to leave Jon to handle that for now. Besides, maybe he's better off at home. She's already heard the stirring of rumours in the playground. The tiniest specks of dust have been kicked up into a whirl of dirt and rubbish. She's still giving him the benefit of the doubt. Why would he come to them so quickly and tell them about his friendship with Katie if he wasn't telling them the whole truth?

So if it wasn't one of the kids, and it wasn't Lucas, then it was someone else. In many ways, she would prefer it to be a stranger, someone who would just get caught and punished. Not someone that Katie knew and trusted. The thought of that makes her feel unbearably sad. Even though that is likely to be how it turns out in the end.

The school nurse, Mrs Blackhurst, has agreed to go and collect each child from their classroom and bring them to Polly for a chat. Polly is about to try and start a conversation with Karen Zucarro, who has been scrolling through things on her phone since she arrived in the office, but she doesn't get a chance. A knock on the door puts paid to that.

'Come on in,' she says.

The door opens slowly and a small face appears in the gap. 'Ms McAllister? Mrs Blackhurst said you wanted to see me.'

Polly hears a quiet click as Karen switches on her voice recorder.

The boy is small and pale. He is wearing a huge parka with a brown furry lining on the hood. He looks like he wants to disappear inside it and never come out again.

She hadn't expected this child to be in school today, but Jon had left her a note explaining it all. He'd wanted to come to school, and Mandy had let him. It made some sort of sense, she'd supposed. If the kid wanted to do what he could to take his mind off things, and his mum was happy to let him, then who was she to stop him? Besides, she knew exactly what his mum was like. She would be struggling to focus on anything right now. Reading between the lines, it was clear that Mandy's children did exactly what they liked.

So here he was.

'Brett, isn't it? Come in, please. Sit down. I've got some squash, if you like. And some biscuits.' She nods towards the jug of water and the bottle of Robinson's orange barley on the top of the filing cabinet. She shakes a box of biscuits at him. She'd stopped at Tesco's on the way in to pick them up, hoping it might make the atmosphere more informal. Hoping it might help the kids speak up. She needed them to see her as a friend, an ally. Not a teacher. Not for this.

He eyes her suspiciously before taking a plastic tumbler and filling it with juice. Then he sits in the chair opposite her and helps himself to a handful of biscuits, chocolate ones mostly. He doesn't remove his coat, and when he sits down his head disappears halfway inside, like a tortoise.

'You like chocolate?'

He nods, stuffs a chocolate finger into his mouth. 'Katie liked these ones,' he says. Tears form in the corners of his eyes. She hands him a tissue.

'I'm so sorry about your sister, Brett. It must be very difficult for you.'

He sniffs. 'Yeah. Well, I was really sad at first, and I *will* miss her, but Boggy says it's OK because she's an angel now.' He takes out another chocolate finger and crunches it in two bites.

Polly shifts in her seat. She has to remember that he is only a young boy. It probably hasn't quite sunk in yet. She doesn't want to push him too hard, but she hopes that he understands death, and that angels aren't real, but that's a conversation for someone else to have. 'Who's Boggy? Is he a friend of yours?'

Brett looks over Polly's shoulder and smiles. 'Sort of. I talk to him sometimes. We go in the woods together, hunting and stuff. Not really hunting, just playing. You know. He's good fun. I don't see him all the time, you know. But he likes to play with me sometimes.' He pushes a jammy dodger into his mouth and starts chewing.

Polly feels a tickle of something across the back of her neck. She shivers. The way he looked over her shoulder ... she wants to turn round, but that would be ridiculous. Karen is sitting to her right. Brett is in front of her. There is no one else in the room. Something tells her that Boggy might not be real. It's not uncommon in boys of this age, and it's not a name she's seen on the student transcripts or heard anyone else mention. Plus, with his mention of angels ... Polly knows this boy has had a difficult childhood. Imaginary friends are a way of dealing with that.

'Is he here now, Brett? Boggy, I mean.' She turns and glances quickly behind her chair, can't stop herself. She sees Karen do the same. The weather has turned gloomy, the air grey with a threat of a storm. She sees herself reflected back in the window, Karen too; the small shape of Brett behind her. She turns back to face him.

Brett coughs and pieces of biscuit fly out of his mouth. 'No,' he laughs. 'Not now. He was, though, a minute ago.'

Polly feels the hairs stand up on the back of her neck. 'OK,' she says. She'll investigate this more later on. No point in spooking herself, or Karen, for that matter. The woman has gone a strange colour of pale that could almost be blue. 'So, do you want to talk about Katie? Is there anything you want to tell me? Anything that might help us to find out what happened to her?'

He shakes his head and looks down at his lap. 'A bad man hurt her. That's what my mum says.' He sniffs again, wipes his nose on his sleeve.

'Did your mum say anything else?'

'No. Can I go now?'

Polly frowns. Wonders if it might be better to leave this to the police after all.

'Sure. Look – you know you can come and talk to me anytime you like, Brett? If you think of anything. Will you do that? If you want to talk about Katie, or Brooke ... or your mum. Anything at all. We need to help the police catch the bad man. Make sure he can't hurt anyone else. What do you think?'

'I can talk to Boggy. He understands. I don't think I need to talk to you. I don't even know you.' He stands up, sniffs again. 'Can I have another biscuit, please? To take with me? We never have this many kinds of biscuits at home.'

She pushes the box closer to him. He takes a handful and drops them into his coat pocket. A small smile plays on his lips. He glances over her shoulder again, and she spins round on her chair to see what it is he is looking at.

There's nothing there. No one.

When she turns back, the boy has gone.

27

Louise

The street is quiet, but Louise senses that there were people around not long before. Their essence hangs in the cold air. The appearance of the patrol car has caused them to skitter back under their rocks, like the cockroaches that they are. The officers who did the door-to-door on Katie's street said that there had already been murmurings. Suggestions that 'That Mr Crisp' had something to hide.

Does he?

Lucas Crisp should have stayed at the school yesterday with the others. Disappearing was a bad move, makes him look more guilty. Poole and McAllister should've done a better job of keeping him there until they arrived, but what could they do? Tie him to a chair? Lock him in an office? She hopes that they made the right call last night, leaving it alone when he hadn't answered the door. It *was* late, the man had gone home sick. Jon Poole had confirmed that it wasn't unusual – Lucas suffered from migraines.

Louise could relate to that.

It'd been years since she'd had one, but she'd gone through a bad spate where she had started to think she was going to have to give up her job. She was spending days on end in her darkened bedroom. Her GP was sick of seeing her. Started to question her on it. Was job stress to blame? Was she depressed? Codeine was the only thing that would touch the pain. Initially, the stuff you can buy over the counter in the chemist. Later, stronger stuff. Straight up. Prescribed by her GP. Then the rebound headaches had started and she had been forced to go cold turkey. Seek alternative treatments. Incredibly, it had been an osteopath who'd fixed her in the end. She still remembered the sheer terror when he had twisted up a towel, grinned at her and given her a knowing look – 'Yes, I know I look like I'm about to murder you ...' – before he'd placed it under her neck and given her a short, sharp twist. She could still hear the crack. Like he'd broken her neck. He hadn't, though. He'd re-aligned something at the top of her back, a facet joint, where her spine met her neck. Something she must've thrown out years ago, not realising the damage it would cause her in later life. 'Many people's migraines aren't migraines at all,' he'd explained. She's never had a problem since. Touch wood.

As they approach the front door, Louise sees that something has been smeared down the paintwork. She follows the slimy trail, sees the broken egg shells scattered on the doormat.

'Little bastards,' Davie says.

'You think this was kids?' Louise asks.

Davie sighs. 'Probably. It's a kids' sort of thing to do, isn't it? Throwing eggs, running away. They probably don't even know why they were doing it. Egged on by their mates ...'

'Is that supposed to be a joke?'

'Best I could do. Sorry. Sometimes you have to lighten the mood or else you'd drive yourself mad.'

Don't I know it, Louise thinks.

'Well, it was a poor attempt, DS Gray. I can only imagine that your brain is feeling a bit fried ... or scrambled ...'

He shakes his head. 'I thought my yolks were bad.'

They're still laughing when the door opens and they have to try hard to straighten their faces. The moment has passed. Back to reality.

'Lucas Crisp?' Louise states.

'Yes,' he says. Louise looks at his eyes, dark, red-rimmed. A man who is suffering. 'You'd better come in.'

He doesn't need to ask who they are. He's been expecting them. Perhaps Jon called him to let him know they'd be coming round. Or maybe he knows that whatever it is that is causing suspicion will bring them to his door, one way or another. Louise tries to shake the thoughts away. She doesn't want to jump to conclusions, but unfortunately, after seeing him, she already has. Good-looking young teacher. It didn't take much to work out why people had started throwing eggs at his front door.

'We came round last night,' Davie says. 'You didn't answer ...'

He ushers them into a small lounge. It's sparsely furnished. A decent sofa, TV in the corner. The rest of the space is taken up by bookshelves. He doesn't look at them. Ignores Davie's statement. 'They started last night. I was in my bedroom, I had the blinds down. Eye mask, earplugs ... I don't know if either of you have ever had a migraine, but, I can tell you, it's painful. There's not much you can do but wait for it to pass. I must've drifted off, I mean, obviously I did, because I didn't hear you knock ... but I woke up to hear the thump thump against the front door. The door's a piece of shit, I need to get it replaced anyway. A gust of wind could blow the thing in. It was eggs, I take it? Can I get either of you a drink?'

'Eggs, yes,' Louise says. She sits down on the couch. Davie stands. He's perusing the bookshelves. 'Tea for me, please. Milk, no sugar.'

'Same,' Davie says. 'You read a lot of crime. Like a mystery, do you?'

Lucas disappears into the kitchen. 'Complete escapism,' he calls through from the other room. 'I'm sure none of it's anything like what really happens, though, is it?'

Davie pulls out a hardback from the top shelf. 'Mo Hayder?' he says. 'I've read some of hers. Jack Caffery is a bit of a maverick, isn't he? All that supernatural stuff too, bit weird. All a bit dark for me.'

'I'm sure you get enough that's weird and dark in your job, no?' Lucas appears carrying a tray. 'Kettle was already boiled,' he says, by way of explanation. 'I think I must've sensed you ...'

'You probably want to steer clear of the true-crime stuff,' Louise says, taking her mug. 'Much worse than anything a crime writer can come up with.' She helps herself to a biscuit. 'Custards creams. Retro,' she says.

Lucas smiles and sits down on a footstool that seems to have appeared from nowhere. 'Modular furniture,' he says, nodding at the gap under the sofa where the extra seat has come from.

'Clever,' Davie says. He takes a sip of his tea.

All very jovial. Civilised. Louise doesn't want to ruin things by asking him the questions they needed answers to. Best just get it over with.

'So,' she says, 'you were Katie Taylor's teacher? Is there anything we should know?'

Lucas closes his eyes. Louise watches as he grips his mug tighter, trying to stop his hands from shaking. He's done well, up to this point, but she can feel it now. He's been going along with the charade. Keeping things light. It can't continue.

'She was my friend,' he says, so quietly Louise isn't sure she's heard him correctly.

Louise glances at Davie. Davie replaces the book he has

been looking at on the bookshelf, sits down on the sofa next to Louise.

'It's not what you think,' Lucas says, sensing the change in the atmosphere. 'She was a good student. A good person. We got on well, that's all.'

'Did you see her outside school?' Davie says.

Lucas looks up at the ceiling, then back down at his lap. 'A few times. I was helping her with her science prep work for university. She didn't need help with the curricula items. That stuff was too simple for her. I was trying to give her a head start with the uni work. It's a big jump from school to uni, bigger than some realise. Especially if she was to go to London, like she wanted. She'd be up against A-Level students there. The Scottish Highers and Sixth Year Studies are supposed to make things equivalent, but I'm not sure. I found it a big transition. But maybe that was just me.'

'Was there any indication of this being anything other than a teacher–pupil relationship, Lucas? I'm sorry, you know we have to ask this. What with you disappearing from the school yesterday too … Doesn't look good.' Louise knows she needs to push the point home. People are talking. That is clear.

He shakes his head. His expression is annoyed. Angry, almost. 'No. It wasn't like that. I'd tell you now, honestly. I don't want to piss anyone off. I don't want that lot outside my door shouting on the street, shoving things through my letterbox. Bunch of animals. Anything for a bit of drama. They need to be having a look at themselves. Trying to work out who might've hurt Katie. Why would I want to hurt her? I told you, right or wrong as it is, she was my friend.'

Davie nods. 'I think we've got enough for now, Lucas. Don't go anywhere too far though, eh. We'll probably have to come back and have a bit more of a chat, if that's OK. You might be able to help us. You'll know the type of people she hung about with.'

Lucas looks away.

'Just one last thing,' Louise says, standing up, wiping biscuit crumbs off her trousers. 'When was it you last saw Katie? Friday, was it?'

'That's right,' Lucas says quickly. Doesn't hesitate. Doesn't meet her eye.

You're lying, Louise thinks. *Question is: why?*

28

Polly

She knows that lunchtime is the worst possible time for him, but she can't wait any longer. She needs to talk to him, needs to find out if he's OK. She'd hoped to have had a conversation the night before, but she'd fallen asleep, and she was glad he'd let her.

She goes around the side of the pub, to the kitchen door at the back. She feels nervous all of a sudden. They haven't told anyone about their relationship yet. Not that she has anything to be ashamed of: she's single now, and he's been single a long time.

Their chance meeting that night at her brother's gig in town had been weird and brilliant and not something that she'd ever expected. She remembers the moment she recognised him, after he'd already been talking to her for twenty minutes, in the break between the warm-up act and the main event. He'd sat down opposite her. Didn't bother to ask if she was waiting for anyone else, or if the seat was taken.

'So you know this lot then, do you?' he'd said, gesturing at the band.

She'd glanced across at them, smiling. All five members of

Zohra Gee and the Quickies were sitting on stools at the bar, having a few preparatory pints. Ed, her brother, had come up with the name. Something to do with a sexy Afghan girl he'd met on a lost weekend in London when he was younger. She'd never got the full story out of him, but she knew it involved a party at a random celebrity's house and too much marijuana.

She'd turned back to the handsome stranger at her table. Despite his presumption that she was alone, she'd liked the look of him straightaway. Good looking, but with a neat scar running down the side of his face. A face that told a story. He was slim, but his arms were muscular. His eyes were bright. He was drinking Coke, and there was something she liked about that too.

Simon liked to roll back from the golf club in the early hours, stinking and gropey. It'd been a long time since she'd fancied him and could barely remember what it was she'd seen in him in the first place. This guy though, he looked like he had a story, and she'd decided to throw her usual caution into the gutter and talk to him. Going to the gig alone had been a big deal in itself, but Ed had assured her he wouldn't leave her on her own for long. That'd turned out to be a lie, straightaway. Or maybe not a lie, but she could see he was caught up with the rest of his band mates, the five of them standing in a row, laughing, getting ready to down a row of lurid green shots. She was nursing a bottle of Peroni, trying not to feel self-conscious in her newly purchased for the occasion skinny jeans and artfully faded (over-washed) Nirvana T-shirt.

'My brother Ed plays the bass,' she'd said. Swigging her beer, trying to look calm and cool. She'd slopped it down her T-shirt.

'Oops.' His eyes had flicked down to her chest, and back, and she'd felt herself flush.

'Bloody hell, can't take me anywhere,' she'd said. She'd given him a self-conscious smile and he'd grinned back.

'That an original, is it? From back in the day? Wasn't really a fan myself. I was into all that happy house rave back then. For my sins.'

For my sins.

Polly had looked into his eyes then and imagined there were many sins hidden somewhere deep in there. Something else too. A tiny spark of recognition.

'Jamie Quinn,' he'd said, holding out a hand. 'You're Polly McAllister.'

Polly had felt like she'd been slapped.

'You're not ... you're not *Quinn*, are you? You went to Banktoun High?' She'd felt like an idiot as she'd said it. She'd recognised him at last. He was about three stone lighter than when she'd last seen him, about twenty years before. He'd appeared at the swings at Garlie Park just after Mandy Taylor had ... She didn't want to think about that again. 'Jesus, you are! Bloody hell ... it's been, what—'

'Twenty years? I never saw you again after that day in the park. I, er, I was away for a bit.' He'd looked sheepish.

She'd heard some rumours that he'd gone to prison, others that he'd gone to rehab. Either way, she hadn't cared. Something about him was very different now.

'You, um, are you still with Mandy?' she'd said.

'No. I'm very much single,' he'd replied, winking.

That'd been the start of it. He'd filled her in with the rest over the next few times they'd met. Dates, she supposed they were. It was more than that now, though. She was carrying his baby now. She'd moved back to Banktoun to be with him. But now everything had changed, hadn't it?

She knocks on the window. It's steamed up, but she can still make out his form, moving back and forth inside. He appears at the back door, drying his hands with a dishcloth. He looks grumpy, distracted, but as soon as he sees that it is her, his face breaks into a grin.

'Hello you,' he says. He pulls her into an embrace, kisses her. He is hot, sweaty. He smells of chips. She steps back, scared suddenly that she's about to burst into tears.

'Are you OK?' she says. 'Have you seen Mandy?'

He frowns. 'I phoned last night. She didn't want to talk to me. She's in bits. I think the doc gave her some vallies. I spoke to the kids. It's difficult, you know. I still can't believe it's happened. I keep thinking someone's going to turn round and tell me it's all a stupid joke. Some idiotic prank. Katie's set it up to piss off her mum and Brooke. It'd be her style, actually. She was funny. Clever. I'm sure everyone's told you this ...'

'Of course they have. But it's different coming from you. You knew her—'

'She wasn't like a stepdaughter, you know. Not really. She was always just a good kid, someone I got on with. It was her who helped me get clean, you know. Did I tell you that? She told me she didn't want me to die.' He swallows, and she can see something pulsing in his cheek. He's trying hard not to let this get to him. He still likes to play the hard man, but she knows him. Katie knew him too. It's all just too horrible. She wants to tell him about the baby, but she can't. Not now.

'I was wondering if you thought it might be a good idea for me to go round and see Mandy, you know, sort of officially. See if she needs any help with the kids.'

'You can try, doll, but I can't imagine she'll want to talk to you. She's quite happy to wallow in it for now. She's got a couple of neighbours. All she's doing is saying the same things over and over. You won't get much out of her. Not at the moment. Maybe wait a few days. The police are still all over the place anyway. Best thing you can do is speak to the kids, try and find out what's going on with them. See if anyone knows anything, you know? Try and talk to that Hayley. Her and Katie were close, but I think they fell out. I don't know the details. To be honest, I hadn't seen Katie for a while. She used to pop round here sometimes, beg me for a bowl of chips. I think she's been pretty wrapped up with that boyfriend of hers ...' He turns away, steps back inside the kitchen. 'Put that back down, Jules. I'll be in the now. Fucksake.' He mutters the last word under his breath. Turns back to her. 'Sorry, got to go. Another two checks have just come in and if I don't get on with it, bloody Julie will start trying to cook fish again ...' He leans back inside the kitchen. 'And we know what happened last time you tried that, don't we, you muppet?' He ducks back out, blows her a kiss, closes the door.

Polly stands outside, feeling lost. Alone. Suddenly remembering how cold it is.

THREEWISEMONKEYSBLOG

Telling It Like It Is

Posted: 1st Dec 2016 by SpeakNoEvil
Status: Draft
Comments: 0

> *Say say old enemy*
> *Come out and fight with me*
> *And bring your BB gun*
> *And we'll have lots of fun*
> *I'll scratch your eyes out*
> *And make you bleed to death*
> *And we'll be jolly enemies*
> *Forever evermore.*

If I was one of those stupid girls that were prone to violence, I'd be doing everything it says in this rhyme ... You can fire anything you like, but I'd have much MUCH more fun scratching your eyes out and watching you bleed to death. But, hey, you know me. Far too bloody nice for any of that. So what do I do instead?

Cry.

Pathetic, eh? I wish I hadn't told you. I thought you would understand. I still don't really understand why you don't understand.

I'm not sure I'm even making any sense any more. I was supposed to be keeping it all anonymous. Talking about theoretical things happening to theoretical people. The point was it was supposed to be MADE UP – but no one would know that, would they? They'd all be reading the posts, wondering who knew their dirty little secrets …

They're going to kill me when they find out what I've been writing here.

29

Louise

Louise sits in Polly's office. She and Davie agreed that the questioning would be led by Polly, and this morning they'd let one of the uniforms sit in. Karen Zucarro: a decent PC, if a bit easily distracted. She's out monitoring the playground now with her colleague Sarah Evans. The younger of the two, she is constantly bouncing or tapping or fidgeting, full of nervous energy. Louise had planned to pull one of them in again for this interview, but she's seen Polly McAllister's list and knows that Brooke Taylor is next. This isn't one she can afford to miss.

In fact, she has a few questions of her own.

It had been a frustrating morning. Davie had dropped her off at the school after they'd finished at Lucas's house. They'd batted a few things back and forth in the car. Louise was sure he was lying about something, Davie wasn't so sure. He'd gone back to the station to catch up with Malkie and the rest of the team.

Louise makes tea for herself and Polly as Brooke sits in the chair opposite the counsellor, picking at her nails. Small pieces of bright orange varnish are piled on the desk in front of her.

She's paid no attention to the box of biscuits that Polly has slid over to her. She's slowly tapping one high-heeled foot against the back plate of the desk. Louise is irritated by the girl already. Call it instinct.

'Watch you don't pull off the surface of your nails, there,' Polly says to her. 'I had those gels once. They look good, but it's a nightmare to get the stuff off.'

Brooke ignores her.

'How are you feeling, Brooke?' Polly asks.

Louise admires the other woman's ability to talk calmly to the girl. Surely Polly's getting the same vibes as she is? Trouble. She looks bored, like this is all just a big inconvenience. Not like someone whose sister was found dead the day before. Louise had seen her at home. She'd been upset then. Could she really switch her emotions on and off so easily? Louise clicks the record button on her phone and lays it on the filing cabinet. 'Just for my own notes. Nothing official.' Not *yet* anyway, she wants to add, but doesn't.

Brooke stops picking for a moment, looks up. Her eyes flit from Polly to Louise and back again. Her mouth is curled into an expression of pissed-off disgust mixed with apathy, peppered with a smattering of disdain. It's a standard teenage-girl look. Louise was quite good at it herself, once.

'How the …' – she pauses, as if adding a 'blank' for the swear word she has decided not to use – 'do you think I feel? My sister's just been murdered. My mother is distraught. My wee brother doesn't know whether he's coming or going. So how would *you* feel, do you think?' She sniffs. Blinks. As if trying to squeeze some tears from her dry eyes. She's fooling no one with this act. Does she really not care? Louise is unconvinced.

'Were you close to your sister?' Louise asks. She knows that she wasn't. Polly has already filled her in on this, although it's second-, third-hand information. It would be good to hear it from the horse's mouth, as it were.

Brooke lets out a long, slow sigh. 'Katie was a pain in the arse. Sorry, 'scuse my French.' She gives them a half-smile. 'That's just a fact. No, we didn't get on. I'm not going to lie. Someone else will *obviously* tell you, anyway. If they haven't already. Wasn't her fault, I suppose. Or mine. We're just very different people. *Were*. Fuck.' Her face flashes suddenly, with what looks like genuine anguish, finally realising the implications of what's going on. Her sister might've been a pain in the arse, but she's a dead pain in the arse now. It had to sink in eventually.

She looks away, but Louise can see she is trying to fight back the tears. Genuine sadness? Or a brilliant actress? She's stopped from having any further thoughts on the girl by her phone buzzing.

'Jennings,' she says, snatching it up, 'just give me a minute.' Then to Polly, 'I'm sorry, I'm going to have to take this. It's important. Listen, I'd really like to hear the rest of this chat, or at least get one of the others in to take over, but I'm not sure where they are right now and I'd rather I had all of this conversation on the tape, you know – to make sure I've got the full picture—'

'Am I under arrest now or something?' The anger is back in Brooke's voice. Her moment of sadness – if it was genuine at all – has passed.

'Of course not, Brooke. Look, if it's OK with Ms McAllister, why don't you come back in tomorrow, have a proper chat then? Gives you a bit more time to think about things too.'

'What things?'

Louise has to try hard not to snap at her. 'Anything about Katie. Anything you think we need to know.'

Brooke shoves her chair back, hard. 'If you're trying to pin something on me, you better make sure you know what you're on about, yeah? I've got connections, you know.'

With that, she turns and flounces out of the room.

'What the …?' Polly says.

'Sorry. Get her back in tomorrow. I don't think it'll do any harm, giving her a bit more time. I think she knows something about all this, but she's confused. Never mind her brother, I don't think *she* knows if she's coming or going. She might've hated her sister, but she was still her sister. She's going to have to process that.'

Polly sits up straight. Her face is pinched tight. 'That's supposed to be what *I'm* here for.'

Louise hasn't got time to get into a psych-off with this woman, so she doesn't bite. She's still holding the phone. She can see the timer on the front, recording the call duration. Davie will have heard everything she said. 'Make sure you ask her about these so-called "connections", will you? I'll try to sit in again tomorrow, but if not, one of the others will be here. I'm sorry, I really have to go.'

She closes the door behind her and walks quickly down the corridor and out into the playground. An icy blast of air hits her in the face. She hurries towards the car, nodding at Zucarro and Evans as she passes. They are chatting casually to a couple of the kids. Evans has her baton in her hand and a serious expression on her face. No doubt they have been inundated with requests to see their various pieces of equipment, which isn't strictly allowed but if it's helping the kids to open up, Louise doesn't care too much about it. She nods at Evans, gesturing for her to go inside. She looks at the phone again. Nearly five minutes. Shit.

'Sorry, Davie. I wanted to get out of the school. Get some privacy. I've a feeling you're calling me with something important.'

She hears him sniff down the line. 'Five minutes, Lou? You could've called me back. Anyway. We've got the forensics results back. Confirmed as asphyxiation, most likely by a pillow being pressed down on her face. Signs of a struggle, the usual. Bruising, a broken nail. A few loose hairs that were lifted off her bed have gone for DNA testing. Results should be in tomorrow. Oh, and that insect you picked up. You were right, it's a damselfly. Or more specifically a Southern Damselfly, otherwise known as *Coenagrion mercuriale*. It got sent over to entomology at Edinburgh Uni. They couldn't tell us too much, other than that it had been preserved the traditional way, by drying, and that it had been done fairly recently, as it was still in good shape. They also confirmed that the insect has full legal protection under the Wildlife and Countryside Act of 1981, and it's illegal to catch and kill one like this without some sort of research permit. They're interested in finding out where it came from. They're keeping it. I reckon that's a dead end anyway ...'

Louise tucks the phone in under her chin while she buttons up her coat. She doesn't agree. That insect is significant, but she doesn't know why. Not yet. 'Right, so you're saying the DNA from the hairs might be the most important thing we've got, assuming it's not her own hair ...'

'Aye. We're going to have to take samples from her nearest and dearest. I've a funny feeling that Mandy's not going to be too keen on that. Having her DNA added to the National Database.'

'Unless it's already on there, of course?'

'Hmm ...' She listens to the sound of liquid being slurped, waits for him to say more. He doesn't.

'Anyway, I'd like to know where the board is. The one with the rest of the insects.' She pauses. She's about to take a leap. He'll dismiss it, but she's not giving in that easily. 'I reckon if we find that, we find our killer—'

'Hardly. We don't know if the two things are linked. Maybe her little brother nicked it and smashed it up or something.'

'Why would he do that?'

'I don't know. Isn't that the sort of thing that little brothers do?'

She thinks about her own brother. Remembers the time she caught him raking through her knicker drawer. Wee perv. 'Yeah, maybe. Although no one's said that Katie and Brett didn't get on—'

'Just because they haven't said it, doesn't mean it's not true. Maybe it's not just the sister that Katie didn't get on with. Has anyone spoken to the lad yet?' Another slurp.

She's dying for a hot drink. Even just for something to warm her cold hands. 'I've just left the school, but no, I don't think so. Just been in with the sister. She's a complicated wee creature. Can't quite work her out yet. Anyway, regarding the boy … I'll make sure it's done soon.'

'Right you are. Meet me back at the station. We've got another house call to make.'

'Oh? Who's that, then?'

'Jamie Quinn.'

Ah. The *ex*-stepfather. Was that a thing? Are you always a stepfather, even if you've split up with the mother? If the kids aren't yours? Louise wonders if they'll get anything interesting out of him. From what she's been told, he hasn't been a part of the Taylors' lives for a long time. She picks up the pace, trying to ward off the cold. 'I'm on my way.'

30

Polly

Polly takes a deep breath and knocks on the door.

'Come in.'

'Have you got a minute, Jon?'

He looks up from his desk, smiles when he sees her. 'Ah, Polly. Of course. Take a seat.' He takes off his glasses and lays them on the desk in front of him. Pinches the bridge of his nose. Blinks. 'How are you getting on with the interviews?'

Polly sits down opposite him. She finds herself pulling the sleeves of her cardigan down over her hands. Crossing her arms. Uncrossing them. She feels fidgety and unsettled. 'I don't think I'm getting very far. They don't seem to want to talk. Or else they've nothing to say. I'm not sure yet. I haven't managed to get hold of Hayley Marsh yet. I've heard that she was good friends with Katie until a few months ago ...'

Jon sighs. 'I expect she's off sick again. It's been a semi-regular occurrence, since her ex-boyfriend died last summer.'

'Oh ... right. I remember now. He was one of the ones who died at Willow Walk, wasn't he? Sean ...'

'Talbot. Yes. To be honest, she'd been going off the rails for a bit before that happened. She was picked up by the police at the shows. She'd been hanging round with some of the lads there. She's going out with one of the rugby lads in the year above now. Ross Hardy. I've heard some rumours about that too …'

'You hear about everything, don't you?' She smiles when she says this. It was always something she was aware of back when she was here as a pupil. Even with eight hundred pupils with eight hundred different personalities – good, bad and everything in between – Jon Poole always seemed to know absolutely everything. 'It would be good to talk to her, Jon. The police will want to see if she knows anything. I'm sure it's easier on the kids if we do the interviews here. So far they haven't had to follow up with any of them formally. At the station, I mean. Which is good – if none of them are involved – but not so good when it's not really helping them find who did this.'

'I'll ring her mother, ask her to bring Hayley in tomorrow. You're right, we do need to talk to her. Soon. I've no doubt she's feeling very low right now. She's been saying some bad things about Katie of late, but I don't think you can throw away a friendship that easily, can you?'

Polly's not so sure about that. She'd never been able to patch things up with Claire after her 'accident', as everyone liked to call it. And Jo had never really liked her in the first place. Can't say she blamed either of them. She wasn't particularly nice back then.

Polly blinks, snapping back to the present. 'I'm sure you're right,' she says. 'Oh, something else I meant to ask you … probably just nonsense, but Brooke said something a bit worrying earlier. She got a bit upset when Detective Jennings and me were talking to her. Said something about having "connections". Any idea what she might've meant by that?'

'I'd like to say I have an insight into that girl's mind, but I'm afraid I don't. I'm sure it was an idle threat. Nothing in

167

it. Hmm …' He pauses, frowns. 'I suppose she might've been referring to some of her father's dodgy friends. Not that I'm one to judge, but the man is in prison and it's not the first time. He doesn't mix with a particularly worthy crowd of humans, from what I've heard. Did you get anything useful out of her in the end?'

'Not really. We got cut short, as Louise had to leave. We're picking it up again tomorrow. Louise asked Brooke to have a good think about what she was planning to say. I think that's what got Brooke riled. Like we were accusing her of something – which we weren't, by the way – but the reaction … Well, now I'm a little concerned. She seems like a very troubled young woman.'

'Well, keep me posted.'

Polly takes that as her cue to leave. With no other children scheduled in for the day, she decides to go home early. Only half an hour, but she could do with a break. The whole experience has been draining and she knows that she needs to be looking after herself now.

Out in the playground, Evans and Zucarro are chatting to a couple of the sixth years. The teenagers scuttle off as Polly approaches.

'Was it something I said?'

'I think they were about to head off anyway,' Sarah Evans says. She's shifting from one foot to the other, rubbing her hands together. Polly's not sure if it's because she's freezing or just the result of her usual frenetic energy.

'Anything new come up?' Polly says.

'Nah,' says Karen Zucarro. 'None of them have much to say about anything, really. They're interested in knowing what we get up to on a daily basis, but they're not keen on reciprocating that info, no matter how casual we try to be.'

'Do you think they're scared?'

'I don't get that impression, to be honest. It's weird, but I thought they'd be more intrigued by it all. That's what kids are usually like when something awful happens. It's their natural instinct.'

Polly frowns. 'I think they all know more than they want to admit. They're just not too keen on voicing it, in case they get someone into trouble ... or get themselves into trouble, for telling tales.'

'Maybe,' Karen says. 'Anyway, that's us off for the day. We'll be back in the morning.'

The two of them disappear down the path just as the bell rings. Polly fumbles in her bag for her gloves. She senses a movement out of the corner of her eye and turns just in time to see a figure disappearing into the maintenance room at the edge of the building. Is it Pete? She's been meaning to have a chat with him. The police have already questioned him and Brian, his boss, but she wasn't there and she's interested to find out if he might know anything – considering he spends all day milling around different parts of the school. He must hear things. See things.

'Hi,' she calls, but her voice is lost in the crowd as the front door is slammed open, crashing against the wall, and hundreds of chattering children burst out onto the concrete, as if someone has pushed them all into a can and shaken it until it popped.

31

Louise

Jamie Quinn lives at the end of a row of neat, terraced houses. They all look the same, except for their various front doors. His is a polished dark wood, matching the window ledges, which look as if they've been recently painted. A knock on the door leads to barking and the sound of four excited feet pattering on the carpet behind the door.

'Calm down, Drummer, that's enough.' A tall man stands in the doorway. He has short cropped dark hair; a tight white T-shirt shows the lines of a muscular torso. He's bent slightly to one side, one large hand on the dog that is scrabbling to push its way outside the door. Louise recognises it as a springer spaniel – white body, brown velvety ears. Its long pink tongue hangs out of its mouth as it pants at them.

'Looks like the dog is excited to have visitors, even if you're not,' Gray says.

Quinn attempts a smile. He has the kind of craggy face that looks perpetually grumpy. 'Sergeant Gray – I was wondering when I might see you.'

'It's Detective Sergeant now, son. This is Detective Constable Jennings. Mind if we come in?'

Quinn steps back, hand still on the dog, trying to prevent its escape. They both step inside. 'You can call me Louise,' she says. 'Nice dog, by the way. We used to have a springer when I was a kid. It always makes me laugh when they start bouncing on all four feet.'

'Aye,' Quinn says. 'They bounce higher when they've eaten a plateful of sausage rolls. I don't recommend feeding them that though, unless you're particularly partial to dog sick. Party. Some clown decided he'd like to feed him the lot. Funny the memories that stick in your head, eh?'

Quinn lets go of the dog and it disappears down the hall towards what Louise assumes is the kitchen.

'Tea?' Quinn calls.

They put in the orders and take a seat at the kitchen table. Louise glances around. The units are freshly painted in pale tangerine. Wooden venetians on the small window look brand new.

'Been doing the place up? I noticed the door, and the window ledges too. Looks nice.'

Quinn sighs. He flicks on the kettle and lifts mugs from a shelf above it. 'My mum died last year. Sold her house and used the money to sort this out. She was always telling me to do the place up. She'd have liked it. Just wish I hadn't waited until she was gone.'

'Usual story,' Louise says. 'We never do things when we should.'

Quinn turns back towards them and Louise can see the strain on his face. In the dim orange light of the kitchen, the dark circles under his eyes are more obvious. 'I suppose you're here about Katie,' he says. 'I still can't believe it.'

Davie stands and walks across to the kettle. He takes teabags from the canister nearby. Quinn doesn't protest. 'I tried calling Mandy last night, but she's not answering the phone. Spoke to one of your lot. A Constable Benedict? Said Mandy's been on pills from the doc ...'

'That's right,' Louise says. 'Steph Benedict is the FLO. She's looking after her. The GP reckoned it was best to keep her on Valium for a few days at least. Try to take the edge off things.'

Quinn makes a sound somewhere between a grunt and a single note of laughter. 'Fine. I ken about that sort of thing.'

Davie places mugs on the table. 'How long's it been now, Quinn? Ten years?'

'That's right, near enough. Good thing too, or I doubt I'd have had ten years left in me. Things are going well now, in case you wondered. New girlfriend and all that. Well, things *were* going well. Until this. Poor Katie. I don't understand it at all. She was a model kid, that one. Not like the others. Maybe it's just because she was that wee bit older, I got to know her pretty well. She always had a mature head on her shoulders. She was always encouraging, when I was at my lowest. I had a rough time a couple of years back. Felt myself sliding under again. It was Katie that made me go to the doc's. Got me sorted before I found myself back on the smack. Christ ...' He pauses, runs a hand across his shorn head. 'I only saw her the other day. She was buzzing. Had some exciting news, she said. Only she wouldn't say what it was. I gave her a portion of chips in a polystyrene box and told her to bugger off. That was the last time I saw her.' He looks down at the table.

'So this was at work, I take it? At the Rowan Tree?'

He looks up, and Louise can see the unshed tears making his eyes shine. 'Aye. She often popped round to the back door of the kitchen to see me. It's where I am, most of the time. To be honest, when I'm home I'm usually asleep. You caught me just in time.'

Louise takes a mouthful of tea. 'Will you try Mandy again please, Jamie?'

'Call me Quinn. It's just Quinn.'

'Sorry, yes ... can you try to talk to her? She might talk to you. There might be things she's too scared to tell us, or things she doesn't think are important. She's in a bad way. But she needs someone. I understand you haven't been together for a long time, but, from what Davie's told me, you were close for many years. It's times like this she'll need all the friends she can get.'

'Mandy only likes friends who she can rely on to give her things that she wants. That's her way. She relied on me for the sex, mainly. Oh, and her Friday night eighth to see her through the weekend.'

'As in an eighth of an ounce of cannabis, is that what you mean?'

'Aye. Other stuff too. It was all fine with her as long as it was on her terms. She wasn't keen on me taking smack. Can't say I blame her. Anyway, it worked out better for everyone when Mandy was on the blow. It was the only thing that kept her consistently calm. That and the mind-blowing sex, obviously.' He gives Louise a wry smile and lifts a tin of tobacco from a fruit bowl in the centre of the table.

'When you say it kept her calm ... you mean she had a temper?'

Quinn takes out the packet of cigarette papers, slides one out, sprinkles in tobacco. She watches, entranced as he rolls it back and forth between his fingers. Runs his tongue along the edge. Her grandfather used to do this. The sweet smell of the tobacco takes her back to her childhood. He lights the cigarette, sucks it in. Blows out a neat stream of smoke. He turns to Davie. 'What do you reckon to that, Davie? Our Mandy? A temper?'

Davie sighs. 'You could say that. She was a feisty one, Lou. Still is. You're not really seeing her in full-on Mandy mode right now, but she was well known for her temper, that's for sure.'

Quinn turns back towards her. He holds the cigarette between

173

his teeth, closes one eye as smoke snakes up towards his face. 'See this?' he says. He pulls up the sleeve of his T-shirt to reveal a patch of shiny scar tissue. It looks old, healed. But wide and ragged, as if it wasn't stitched properly, if at all. 'She did this to me, with a Stanley knife I'd been using to rewire the plugs on her toaster and kettle. I took too long, apparently. She wanted a cup of tea. Wanted it right away. Fucking thing wouldn't stop bleeding. Katie came in just after it happened, when Mandy was pale-faced and rocking in a kitchen chair, muttering *sorry sorry sorry* ... Katie patched it up as best she could, but it needed stiches. I couldn't go into the hospital though, could I? Tell them how it happened. She tried her best, Mandy did. I couldn't have the social getting involved, know what I mean?'

Louise glances across at Davie, as Quinn rolls his sleeve back down and taps the ash off the end of his cigarette.

'Would you call her back tonight, Quinn? See if she'll talk to you. We've very little to go on at the moment, so anything you can do to help.'

'Sure,' he says. 'But I wouldn't hold out much hope. Mandy might fly off the handle now and again, but she's fierce loyal. If she knows who did this – I mean, if it's someone close to her – she'll protect them. She'll never grass. You know that, right?'

Louise lays a business card on the table. 'Give me a call if you hear *anything*. Day or night.'

Quinn nods. His eyes are shining again. He stubs out the cigarette, looks away. 'I meant to ask, did you talk to that teacher of hers? Katie always said they were just friends, but I'm not so sure. Katie's very different from Mandy, we all know that, but you know ... For every teenage girl who thinks she's "mature", there's a man who'll take advantage of that. Ken what I mean?'

Louise puts a hand on the back of the chair opposite. 'Are you saying you think something was going on with Katie and Lucas Crisp?'

174

'I never said that. I'm just saying ... Mandy used to try it on often enough, when she was Katie's age. Some folk reckon Katie's dad is one of Mandy's old teachers. Anyway, it's not Katie you need to worry about here. It's Brooke. She's the one who planted that seed. About Crisp, I mean. I'm assuming you've seen the stuff on Facebook? I'm surprised it's not been taken down yet—'

'Thanks,' Davie says, cutting him off. Louise can see the panic flashing in his eyes. They need to get out of here. They need to go back to see Lucas Crisp.

The dog pads behind them as they walk out of the kitchen. Louise bends down to rub its ears before they walk out of the door and leave Quinn to his sleep.

LucasCrispIsAPaedo

🔒 Secret Group

375 Members (100 new)

Lou Peters

3h

Right, seeing as you bunch of pussies are too shy to sort this out, how about I take control, eh? Ootside the Rowan Tree, 8.30 p.m. (but whoever needs a wee livener can meet inside before – I'll be there fae six, when the work's van drops us off.)

Likes(310) Comments(95)

Big Jim Nailor See yous there.
Al Samson Maybe we shouldnae say we're going, case the polis see this?
Big Jim Nailor Fuck it.
Joe Crow 😄
Luke Crust OMG I cannae believe it's really happening! Cheers for sorting this, *Lou Peters.*
Gary Niven *thumbs up*
Pete Reed 😄😄
Kev Mason F'kin A!
Dave Simon Ace.
Mike Sullivan YA BASS.

. . .

see 85 other comments

32

Neil

Neil is standing outside the Rowan Tree, waiting. A small crowd has already gathered outside the pub, huddled together in the recess between the wide pedestrian boulevard and the entrance to the pub car park. People are wrapped up warm in thick coats, gloved hands grappling with cigarettes and lighters. It's hard to tell who is smoking and who isn't, with the chilled air making everyone's breath into an icy mist.

Where is she?

He is already feeling jittery. Starting to wonder if this is such a good idea. But she was insistent. *You have to be part of it. You can't miss out on something like this*, she'd said. *This is going down in history.*

He rubs his hands together, trying to keep warm. Through the steamed-up windows of the pub he can see the silhouettes of bodies, crushed together in the warmth. Occasionally, the door opens and he hears the sounds of laughter. Raised voices. The incessant whine and rattle of the fruit machine.

He pulls out his phone to check the time. 20:20. Still time to change his mind. Still time to disappear into the darkness.

Pretend he has nothing to do with it. He's almost made up his mind to leave when he spots her. She appears through the alley off the little side road that leads to the High Street. She's in a thick black coat, hood up. Scarf pulled tight. Only her eyes are visible, the rest of her face obscured by the scarf and the furry edging of her hood.

Even from here he can see that she's smiling. The impish grin that she can change to a frightening scowl in an instant.

Fuck. Too late to back out now.

He shoves his hands into his pockets, trying to give off the impression that he's totally fine with all this. With what they're about to do.

He checks his phone again. 20:28.

He's only just dropped it back into his pocket when the door of the pub swings open and a long, steady stream of bodies makes its way outside. The laughter has gone now. No one's smiling. Their faces are fixed in steely determination. No one's smiling now. He envies them. At least they've had a bit of alcohol to ready them for this. Not like him. He'd tried to buy two cans in the Spar garage, but they weren't having it. Old biddy behind the counter gave him a look of disgust when he'd laid the cans on the counter. *You're not old enough, son. I know your mother.*

Fucksake.

The men and women from the pub merge into the crowd that's already outside. There are a few murmurs now. A nervous tension hangs in the air, as thick as their freezing breath.

Brooke appears by his side. Trailing along behind her, faces down as they frantically stab angry words into their phones, are several other kids. Some he knows, some he doesn't. Hayley is there, of course. She might be skiving off school, but she's not going to miss this. She refuses to catch his eye. She's turned into Brooke's sidekick lately. He wonders how

178

she feels about Katie? She was Katie's best friend until a few months ago, when she let Brooke poison her mind. He knows how that feels. He always thinks he knows everyone until it comes to something like this. People seem to appear out of the woodwork. Out of the grimy little hovels they spend their time in.

These are the kind of people who were made for something like this.

Fuck it. He wants to talk to her. 'Hayley—'

Brooke steps in front of the other girl, cuts him off. Clearly she doesn't want them talking. Worried about what he might tell? She shoves him in the arm. 'What's wrong wi' your pus? Thought you'd be excited.'

He shrugs. 'Dunno. Second thoughts, I s'pose. Starting to wonder if I can be arsed. There's plenty of other folk here …' He lets the sentence trail off when he sees the expression on her face.

'That bastard killed my sister. Your *girlfriend*, in case you'd forgotten her already. She was a pain in the arse, but fucksake. She didnae deserve to be killed. No by that freak.' She rolls the 'r' on the word freak and the small group behind her sniggers.

'Dinnae worry, hen. We'll sort oot the dirty nonce. Won't we, no?'

There are a few mumbled 'aye's. People glance around at each other. Neil can tell there's a few others who are as scared as he is, but now they're here, and they're all together. And no one's got the balls to leave.

Funny. No one would have the nerve to do something like this alone, but get a few together and all the bravado comes out. He'd been shocked when Brooke had first told him what they were going to do. That phone call, early afternoon. He hadn't wanted to pick up. Had almost turned off his phone after all the messages from earlier.

You're off your heid, Brooke. Just leave it
to the polis

**They've no' got a clue. They've got that
erse of a counsellor helping them oot,
but she's clueless an aw. It's taking too
long. My ma's bloody devastated. She's
no' sleeping. They've got her on vallies,
but even wi' them and the drink she's
up tae high doe!**

I know that. Do you think I don't? I'm
fucking devastated too. I loved her …
don't fucking smirk, you know I did … I
want this bastard caught as much as you
do. But …

But what?

What if you're wrong? What if it's no'
him?

**Somebody seen him. They seen him
outside our house. What else was he
doing there?**

I'm sure the polis are trying to find that
oot …

**Then what? He'll go to prison. Maybe.
He'll get a few do-ings in there, right
enough – but that's no' really enough,
is it? He needs to know what he's done.
He needs to know you cannae dae
things like that in this toon and expect
to get away wi' it.**

He won't get away wi' anything. He'll be
lucky to survive in prison.

Well, this way at least he'll understand.

They'd gone back and forth for half an hour before Neil had given up, defeated. He just wanted her to shut up. He hated that girl. Regretted getting involved. What had he been thinking? He had to go and see what was happening though, didn't he? What else was he going to do?

OK, I'll come.

And now here he was, standing outside the pub. Part of the mob that was heading to visit his biology teacher. The man who'd become a suspect after someone said they'd seen him outside Katie's house the night before she was found dead. The man who'd been accused of having an inappropriate relationship with the girl. But Neil wasn't convinced about any of it. He knew how much Katie liked the man. He'd been the one to encourage her to go to university. To escape her toxic roots.

He wasn't a paedophile, was he? Besides, Katie wasn't a kid. Not really. Crisp hadn't done what they were all saying he'd done? No way. Katie could never have kept that from him.

Well, he was in on it now. Nothing he could do. He'd follow them up there, but he wasn't taking part. No way. And if things went wrong, he had the number for that lady copper, Louise. She'd given him a business card round at Mandy's house. She'd seemed all right. Wanted to help. He should tell her about Brooke. About Hayley. But he was scared. Scared of looking like a complete shit. Not that it mattered much now. Not now that Katie was gone.

Fuck it.

It was OK, he tried to convince himself. No one was going to get hurt.

Just scare him a bit, that's all.

33

Louise

Davie waits until they are back in the car before he erupts. 'Shit. SHIT. Lou, get on Facebook. Why haven't we been alerted to this already? We've had IT scouring social media from the word go. How the fuck have they missed it? Get searching for anything to do with Lucas Crisp. We need to see what we're dealing with here.'

Louise starts tapping on her phone. She can almost guess what she's going to find. She's seen the sort of thing before. People setting up pages right after something like this. She types his name into the search bar. Waits while the connection speed catches up with her typing. Nothing. Nothing public, that is.

This is bad.

She realises it now, more than ever. Lucas Crisp is not safe.

The man is scared, she gets that. Louise knows what it is like to be a seventeen-year-old girl, although it seems like a century ago now. From what the others said, he's a popular teacher – just on the right level of geek not to seem like a real threat to anyone. But Louise had seen him for herself. He was smart. Cute. Looked young. Mix that in with some pubescent hormones and you have a potent cocktail.

Teenage girls always like older boys. Men. It's a fact. Girls mature quicker than boys, and it's not long before the boys in your year seem like children and you're ready for something more. Louise knows all this. Her first boyfriend was six years older than her. It caused a fair bit of jealousy from the other girls. She can understand why Katie might've been getting trouble from her friends, and her sister, if it seemed like she was hanging out with this older guy.

Nothing to do with him being a teacher. That's not how girls think. They see an older man. A good-looking one. Giving attention to someone. Attention that *they* want. It's jealousy, pure and simple. There aren't many girls who would turn down attention like that.

As for Crisp – he was naive, at best.

Louise hopes that is it. Hopes that he, perhaps, had a bit of growing up to do. He is only twenty-five: a young man being a young man. Had he overstepped the mark? Louise wasn't sure. It's funny how opinions differ on this. It's not black and white. It's fine for people to say he's the adult and he should know better, and a seventeen-year-old girl doesn't know her mind. But really? These girls are smart. Especially someone like Katie. Jesus, her own mother had her when she was barely sixteen. She knows what she's doing. *Knew.* Shit.

Louise glances at Davie. He's been silent since his small tirade when he got into the car. They've been driving in the dark for five minutes, and with some of these streets without streetlights (typical council cost-cutting measures) Louise has no idea where she is. Or where they're going. Davie does, though. He could navigate these streets in his sleep. She stares at the bright screen on her phone. Almost can't believe what's staring her in the face.

'Found anything?' he says.

No, and that's the scary part. That means it's hidden. A secret group, non-searchable. You need to be invited. She needs to call IT. Maybe they've already requested full access to the secret groups on the system, but there's always a delay. *Always* a bloody delay. And someone has been fast. And clever enough to hide it. *Fuck.*

'How far is it?' she says.

He turns to her and gives her a strange look. 'We were here earlier. Don't you recognise where you are?' When she doesn't reply, he continues: 'Not far now. A couple more streets.'

'Do you think we're too late?'

Davie smacks his hand on the steering wheel. 'What have you found? What makes you say that? You don't think he's going to do anything stupid, do you?'

Not him, maybe. Someone else might though. She doesn't even want to imagine what people have been saying. She taps out a quick text to her contact in IT, asking for an update.

What is *wrong* with people? What makes them so quick to judge? So nasty. She thinks about Polly – supposed to be a counsellor – a psychologist. What was she thinking, letting Lucas go home? Maybe if they'd spoken to him sooner they might've arranged for him to be elsewhere. As it is, he's at home, alone. A sitting duck. She doesn't want to think about it. Can't do anything until they get there.

'Polly's an interesting one,' she says. 'So you know her?'

'Not really. She went to school here. She used to be friends with Jo ... Well, not really. Friends with Claire. You know all about that, right?'

'Some of it. I know that Jo did something to the guy she reckoned pushed Claire in the burn when they were kids. That's right, isn't it? I don't know the full story.'

'I'll tell you all about Black Wood another time, Lou. It's a bit of a tale. I seemed to get myself entwined in the whole thing, somehow. Polly looked a bit scared when I arrived, didn't she? Not sure what she thinks I'm going to do. It was twenty-odd years ago, and really it's Jo and Claire she needs to be talking to. Anyway ... back to Crisp, just round this next corner ...'

He's about to say more as they round the bend into Elm Road, but he stops mid-flow. They both gasp.

The street is filled with people. All the houses on the street are in darkness, except there's a yellow glow coming from a house halfway up. Crisp's house. The one that was decorated with eggs this afternoon, and now something much worse. The door is standing open and there are people littering the front gardens all the way up. Others are hanging back on the other side of the road.

'What the ...'

Davie stops the car. Flicks on the siren. Just a single 'whoop'. Enough to make them all take notice. They start running before Davie can get out of the car. 'Lou ...' he says. There is a slight waver in his voice. He jumps out of the car.

'Already on it.' Louise tries to sound more confident than she feels. A heavy feeling of dread settles in her stomach. She wants to call after him, tell him to be careful, but he's already out of ear shot. Straight in there. No thought for himself. She swallows. Presses the radio on the console: 'All units, this is Twenty-Three Echo-Two-Delta. DC Jennings and DS Gray. We are at Elm Road in Banktoun, signs of a ...' She pauses. What is it? 'There's a rowdy mob. Fifty-plus. Possible vigilante attack.'

'How many victims, DC Jennings?'

'Just one. I think. I don't know yet. It's a local teacher – Lucas Crisp. We were en route to re-question him as a witness in the Katie Taylor case. Possible new information. DS Gray is approaching the premises. I'm going in now.'

She gets out of the car and follows Davie. Most of the bodies that'd been loitering near the teacher's house have run off already. A few are still hovering around on the opposite side of the street. Davie has disappeared inside the house.

'What's going on?' Louise addresses a cluster of young

women standing outside the house opposite, smoking. She has her baton in her hand.

'Dirty bastard killed that Katie, didn't he? Surprised you didn't lock him up earlier ...'

'Too late now, eh?' another one says.

Louise scans the small crowd. At the far end, she thinks she spots Neil Price. He's standing back from the others, not involved but watching. So many of them are watching. Jesus Christ.

By the time she gets to the house, the area is clear. There was no point in trying to catch any of them, stop them from running. There's only her and Davie. Besides, no one's going to tell them anything. Mob rule. Mob decisions. *Fuck.*

She walks up the path, noticing that the grass on either side has been churned up into mud. Even half-frozen, the amount of people who've been on it has made an impact. What have they done? she thinks. She's scared as she walks inside the house. Scared of what she's going to see. Scared of the realisation of what people are capable of. She's quite sure that not all of the people in this mob are bad ... but there are some who will push things further than others. Some who will make amoral decisions. And many who will follow behind, like sheep. Sheep might look a bit stupid, but a herd of them moving together can cause a lot of damage.

'Davie?' she calls. She feels stupid to be scared, but the house is silent, and the people left on the street have fallen silent too. She strains her ears, hoping that she might hear the sound of a siren in the distance. Not yet.

'In here,' he says.

She follows the sound of his voice. Smells smoke. He's in the kitchen. He drops a saucepan on the floor, black plumes of smoke curl up towards the ceiling from where he has put out a fire. Drawers have been yanked out. The place has been wrecked.

At first, it looks like they've interrupted someone doing DIY. There are pieces of broken wood on the floor, spatters of what looks like paint across the walls. But it's not paint. And the crumpled heap on the floor isn't a pile of dirty overalls. It's a man. Lucas Crisp, presumably. Although she'd be hard pushed to identify him by looking at the mess of his face.

Louise hears a whooshing in her ears, feels her heart pumping hard in her chest. She hears Davie's breathing, coming out fast. She watches, entranced, as he kneels down next to the broken man and whispers softly into his ear. 'We're here now, son. You're safe.'

Please be alive, Louise begs inside her head. *Please don't die.* A horrible feeling of foreboding floods her veins. An eerie silence falls upon them, until all she can hear is the desperate sounds of their breathing. Hers. Davie's … In the distance, the merciful sound of sirens.

WEDNESDAY

34

Polly

Sergeant Zucarro is waiting for Polly outside her office. Jon is there too, and the expressions on their faces aren't good.

'Morning,' Polly says, tentatively. She misses out the 'good' because it clearly isn't. 'Am I guessing that there have been some developments? Have you caught Katie's killer?' She wants the answer to be yes, but if it *is* yes, she is terrified of what the policewoman might tell her. She had tried calling Lucas Crisp before she left the school yesterday, but he hadn't answered. She hopes she wasn't wrong to trust him.

The policewoman and the headmaster follow her into the office.

'I'm guessing you haven't heard, then?' Karen Zucarro says. 'It's all over social media ...'

'I'm not really on social media,' Polly says. 'I email, of course, and I use Skype sometimes, but not a lot else. Not Facebook or anything like that. Not that many people I want to keep in touch with on there. I prefer my friends to exist in real life, you know?'

Karen's eyebrows disappear into her fringe. Probably thinks she's one of those freaks that doesn't know how to

191

use a computer. One of those 'old' people who don't like the internet in case it steals all their information or something. It's far from the truth. One, she's not exactly old. And two, she just doesn't see the point. Don't people use it to find their old school friends? That's the last thing Polly wants to do.

'Lucas Crisp has been attacked,' the officer says.

Polly sits down hard in her chair. 'What? What do you mean *attacked*? Is he OK?'

'He's in ICU. In a coma. He was taken there last night. We're still waiting for an update from the hospital, although I've already called them three times this morning. His parents are flying in. They've been travelling around Australia in a campervan for the last three months …' She lets the sentence trail off.

'There was a secret Facebook group set up on Monday called "Lucas Crisp is a paedo". We weren't aware of it until it was too late. Seems that a mob attacked him at home, last night. Officers went to question him earlier in the day, and there had been a bit of a disturbance then, but he insisted he was OK. And we didn't know about the group at that point—'

'Who set it up? The Facebook group, I mean. You must be able to tell that?'

'Someone used a made-up ID. Set up a fake account. Called themselves "Luke Crust". Our IT team are on it. They think they know who it is.'

Polly's stomach lurches, her boiled egg threatening to make an unwelcome reappearance. 'Who? Who would do something like this?'

'We can't disclose anything right now, Ms McAllister,' Karen says, 'but we just wanted to make sure you were aware. For when you talk to the children today. As before, one of us will be with you at all times. I think DS Jennings will be along later, but for now it'll be me and Constable Evans again, like yesterday. Are you OK? I know this must be a shock.'

Another shock, when she hadn't had time to process the last one. All part of the same sorry mess. 'I'll be fine,' Polly says. But when she looks down at her hands, she sees that they're shaking. Poor Lucas, she thinks. If only we'd kept him here. Discussed it with the police earlier. Maybe he shouldn't have been at home on his own. Not if there were people baying for his blood. What triggered it, though, she thinks? She remembers what Lucas said about Brooke, Katie's sister. About how he thought she was jealous of the attention that Katie was getting from him. But this? Is she really that bad? It seems so. She leans back in her seat and a thought hits her. Outside the office on Monday, when Lucas had been telling her things. Someone had been outside. Someone had overheard. Could it have been Brooke? No one had seen her for the rest of the day. Polly knew that she and Brett had turned up at home at lunchtime. Could she have come into the school afterwards? But why? Why wasn't she at home, comforting her mother? Grieving for her sister.

'I'll leave you to it,' Jon says. 'Just let me know if you need anything.'

'I'll get us a tea,' Karen says. 'Or would you prefer coffee?'

'I shouldn't really drink coffee,' Polly says. Her hand goes automatically to her belly, and she pulls it away again quickly, as if burned. She can't let Jon know about this. Not now. 'Goes for my stomach,' she continues, although it doesn't appear that the police officer is taking much notice, and Jon has already left the room. She's paranoid, she knows that. But it's not something she was expecting to have to deal with.

Polly is about to ask Karen if she can tell her any more about the case when there's a knock on the door. It opens, slowly, before Polly can tell whoever it is to come in.

'Hello, Ms McAllister.' She is pale-faced and the red of her hair seems brighter against the leached colour. Her voice is small and thin, and she seems to have shrunk in on herself since Polly last saw her.

'Diane. Come in.' Polly gestures to the empty chair in front of her desk. She hears the policewoman shuffle behind her. 'I've got Sergeant Zucarro with me. Karen. I hope that's OK with you, Diane.'

Diane shrugs. 'I don't mind. I don't really have anything to tell you.' She looks down at her lap, starts picking at the skin on her thumb.

Polly glances over her shoulder at Karen and widens her eyes in a gesture that she hopes conveys disbelief.

'You and Katie were close, were you not?' Karen pulls her chair closer to the side of Polly's desk. 'Can you tell us when you last saw her?' Karen lays her notepad on the desk and clicks her pen. Polly can see her from the corner of her eye. She's smiling at the girl, trying to engage.

Diane looks up. 'Yeah. Well ...' She lets the sentence trail off.

'Well ...?' Polly leans forwards, trying to shrink the space between them.

Diane looks up at the ceiling, then back to her lap. She's blinking, but she can't stop the tears from escaping. 'Yes,' she says quietly. 'We were good friends. I just ... I don't know what to say. I can't believe she's gone. It's ... it doesn't make sense. I saw her on Saturday. She'd just bought a new board for her insects, you know? They're in the biology lab in a box. Mr Crisp helped her to preserve them. Oh God. Mr Crisp! Is he OK? I heard—'

'Mr Crisp is in hospital, but we're all keeping our fingers crossed for a good outcome,' Polly says. 'So she was keeping the insects in the biology lab?'

'Yes. She was keeping her new insects there until she got a new board and frame. Like a box frame thing. The last one she had was cheap and the glass fell out, so she was making this one with a new sort of frame, and—' She stops talking, as if a sudden realisation has hit her. 'She won't be able to finish it now, will she?'

Polly leans across the table and places a hand on top of the girl's. 'Diane, did she say anything to you recently about anyone? Someone she had an argument with, anything like that?'

Diane shakes her head. 'No. Nothing. Really.' She blinks again. Looks up at the ceiling. 'Do you mind if we talk about this later? I just … I feel a bit sick.'

'That's fine,' Karen says. 'You get back to class for now, Diane. Thanks for coming in.'

Diane nods. She doesn't say any more. Just shuffles out of the room as quietly as she came in.

Polly says to Karen, 'Give me a minute.' There's something not right about this. Diane is upset, obviously. But she seems scared too. Looking away. Cutting their conversation short. Could she know something? Polly waits a moment for the corridor to be clear, then she steps out of the office and walks quickly in the direction of the classrooms. Diane is nowhere in sight. Polly continues along the corridor, glancing through the glass panes on the doors as she passes each room. There is little noise coming from anywhere. The classes are subdued. She wants to check that Diane has gone back to her class, wants to make sure she's OK. She rounds the corner at the far end of the building and sees the familiar red hair disappearing into one of the rooms. Not a classroom, though. It's one of the IT labs. Polly walks faster, keeping light on her feet, trying not to draw any attention to herself. She holds back when she gets to the door, tilts her head just enough to peer through the glass at an angle where she can see in but whoever is inside won't be able to see out, unless they were to come right up to the door. There are only two people in there. Diane and Lois Reibach. They're standing at one of the benches, an open laptop in front of them. Diane is frantically tapping at the keyboard, and Lois is saying something – leaning in close – not quite a whisper but clearly something that she doesn't want to be overheard. They're handling it in different ways: Diane trying to hold back tears, angrily bashing at the computer; Lois is calmer, but her eyes are giving her away.

What are they doing on that computer? She thinks back to what Karen told her about the secret Facebook group. No. Not these girls. Surely not?

There's something going on here, and Polly has no idea what it is. But both of the girls in that room look utterly terrified. She pulls back from the glass, hoping that they haven't seen her. What now? Should she go in? Find out what they're up to? She takes a deep breath. No. Leave them to it. For now, anyway. She makes a mental note to mention this to the police. The stuff on social media is probably nothing to do with the girls, but she should report it. Just in case … She'll have to talk to Diane again soon. And Lois.

But she has someone else to speak to first.

35

Neil

Neil shifts in the chair. He doesn't want to be here. Doesn't want this woman probing him, making him tell her things he doesn't want to tell. What's the point now? Katie is dead. She's dead, she's gone and she's never coming back. Lucas Crisp is in hospital. Whether he killed Katie or not is irrelevant right now, at least until the police have another suspect. And seriously, who else could it have been? He hadn't been sure at the time, but now it made some sort of sense. It had to be him. The policewoman has tried to engage him in conversation, but he doesn't feel like replying. He slumps down in his chair.

'Sorry I'm late. I got held up,' Polly McAllister says, hurrying into the room and shutting the door behind her just a bit too hard. 'I'm not going to ask you how you're feeling, Neil, because I imagine your answer is going to be "shit", am I right?' Polly sits down, blows a bit of hair away from her face. She's a bit pink-cheeked, as if she's just run along the corridor. She smiles at him and he thinks she's probably not a bad sort, he just can't really be arsed. Half of him wants to tell her everything he knows. The other half wants to say nothing.

'Yeah.'

'Is that it? Pretty short session, then. Do you want to send the next person in after you, please?' She turns away and bends down to take something from a low drawer in her filing cabinet.

Neil is confused. 'Um … don't you want to ask me anything else?'

She sits up again. Her face has gone bright red now, from the blood rushing to her head as she was bent half upside-down. 'Well, I'm not going to drag it out of you. I expect the police will want to talk to you formally, ask if you knew about the plans to attack Mr Crisp last night. Ask if you had any reason to want to kill your girlfriend …'

'Hang on, what do you mean? Of course I didn't kill her. I loved her! She was fucking amazing, and I wanted to move to London with her – away from this dump.' He feels tears prick at the corner of his eyes and he blinks them away.

'You seem angry, Neil. That's normal, of course. Forgive me – I didn't know Katie at all. Why don't you tell me a bit about her?'

'What's the point? It's not going to bring her back.'

'Well, of course not, but it might help you to process what's going on right now. In your head, I mean.'

Process it? How the hell is he supposed to do that? He needs to tell them about the thing that's really bothering him right now. He's disgusted with himself, but maybe telling someone about it will help him to push it out of his mind. He takes a deep breath, lets it out slowly.

'You know why I'm so fucking angry, Miss? I'm sorry for swearing, but … Jesus. I'm such a dick. I really am. I was horrible to her the night before she died, and I never got time to tell her I was sorry. And … and not only that—' He has to stop talking, feels like his breath is drying up in his throat. 'Not only that, but I cheated on her. I fucking cheated on her.' He stands up and the chair tips back, clattering onto the floor behind him.

'Neil, please. Calm down ... this is not helping.'

He's crying now, unable to keep the tears at bay any longer. 'If I hadn't been such a dick on Sunday, she wouldn't have kicked me out. I'd have stayed the night there. I'd have been there until just before her mum came back. I could've protected her. Whoever it was who came round and ... and ... fucking *snuffed her out*. I could've stopped it. I could've saved her—'

Polly has come round from the other side of the desk. She puts a hand on his shoulder. He wants to shrug it off, but really he wants her to touch him. He wants her to hold him. He wants Katie to hold him, but that's never going to happen again, and it's all his own stupid fault. He lets Polly put an arm around his shoulders, lets her guide him back into the chair. He pulls away from her, drops his head into his hands on the desk.

'I slept with Brooke,' he says. He whispers it. He whispers it because he needs to say it out loud, but he is so ashamed. He is so fucking annoyed with himself. He'd bumped into her as he was leaving Katie's house on Sunday. She was halfway along the road. She was like a younger version of Katie, a certain smile they both shared. She wasn't as sexy though, her tits weren't as good and she wore too much make-up, and basically, she was a fucking bitch. But he was horny, and she was there ... and she was smiling at him, in that way that she did. That way that she did to all the boys. But the thing was, it worked. It worked, and she loved it. She was jangling a bunch of keys, swaying them in front of him like she was trying to hypnotise him – and she *was* hypnotising him. He was angry and he was *so fucking horny*, and he followed her to the lock-ups around the corner ...

'Do you want to tell me about it?' Polly says. She is back in her seat now, back round her side of the desk. There is disappointment in her voice, and Neil doesn't blame her. Brooke is underage, for a start. Only just, but let's not even go there. Anyway, it's not as if he was her first. Fuck no. The dirty wee slag's seen more cocks than a rugby boys' stag party in Prague.

'I don't know what to say,' he says. 'It was a mistake. A stupid mistake.'

It'd been freezing in the lock-up. There was electricity, for the lights, but no heating. 'Is this yours?' he'd said. There was a couch in there, blankets. A shit stereo in the corner. 'Comes with the house,' she said. 'Mum gave me the key. She doesn't need it. Said I could do what I wanted with it.' She'd unzipped her jacket, smiled. Peeled off her top. He was mesmerised, watching the goosebumps skittering over her pale skin. She'd put on a lamp. Walked towards him, untucked his T-shirt from his jeans. Run a hand across his belly. That was all it had taken.

He felt so ashamed. Disgusted with himself. 'I don't know what to say,' he says. 'It was a mistake. A stupid mistake.' The tears are running down his cheeks. 'I don't want to tell you about any of it because I am a fucking dick, and it should never have happened. I should never have let it happen. And this is the thing I'm going to remember for the rest of my fucking life. So no, I don't want to tell you about it. I want to lock it away, forget all about it.

'But there is something else. Something I need to tell the police because I am fucking terrified this is all about that, and if it's all about that, then it's my fault too. It is my fault that she's fucking dead!'

'Neil, please,' Polly says, 'you need to calm down. Do you want me to get Jon in here?'

'Poole? No, Jesus fuck! Listen … there was some money. Katie won money on a scratch card. We were going to use it to help with a flat in London, start us off. I wanted to blow a bit of it but she said no – that's what the stupid argument was about, that and …' He pauses, remembering himself trying to force her to suck his cock. 'Nothing. It was about that. It was five grand. I said we could spend a couple of hundred, have a bit of fun. But she said no …'

'Does anyone else know about this?' Polly says.

Neil swallows. 'I don't think so. I don't know. Problem is, I don't know where it is. The scratch card, I mean. Do you think the police have got it?' He pauses, glances at the police officer in the corner of the room. Her face is expressionless, giving nothing away. 'Maybe someone else found it,' he continues. 'I'm just, I don't know. I think Brett might snoop about her room sometimes. She said stuff had gone missing before. Brooke too. I can't believe I touched that girl, honestly I can't. Fuck.' He leans back in his seat.

'So Katie had five thousand pounds? Did she have the cash, or did she still have the scratch card?'

He sighs. 'She told me she still had the card. We were supposed to cash it together, but now … now that this has happened. I don't know. If Brooke … or Brett—'

'Don't worry, Neil,' the policewoman says. 'You might need to pop down to the station about this, though. It changes things, I think. Gives us a motive to investigate. As far as I'm aware, there's been nothing concrete on this, as yet …'

Polly turns round to say something to the policewoman, but their voices are low and he tunes them out.

Neil closes his eyes. Wishes he never had to open them ever again. 'Is it OK if I go now? I need to clear my head a bit.'

The policewoman nods. 'Sure. I'll let DC Jennings and DS Gray know that you'll be on your way in to see them, shall I?'

'Now?'

Polly glances at the policewoman, who shrugs slightly. 'Not right now, Neil. Go for a walk first. Clear your head, like you said. But go in before you go home, will you? They're going to want to hear more about this.'

'Right,' he says. 'Fine.'

He leaves them to it. Walks out into the corridor. He lets out a long, slow sigh. Balls his fists. It's best that he told them about Brooke, isn't it? The scratch card, too. He's no idea what either of those things might have to do with what happened, but who is he to judge? He's not a detective. Plus, he has no idea what happened. Someone does, though. He didn't say anything to them about his suspicions. Why should he? Just more rumour and that didn't help Mr Crisp, did it?

He's just about to open the front door and walk out when he spots her coming through the gate. Fuck that. He's not speaking to her. Not now. He turns and heads down the corridor towards the side-entrance, hoping she hasn't seen him.

36

Polly

Polly suggests to Karen Zucarro that they take a break. Pop along to the staff room for a coffee and a snack maybe. It's been an intense morning. Polly hasn't even had time to process what's happened to Lucas.

'Any word from the hospital?'

Karen looks up from her phone. 'Not yet. Louise said she'd let me know as soon as he was awake. She's been there all morning. She says she's not leaving until he wakes up.'

'But ... she can't do that, can she? It could be hours. Days. He might never—' She stops. She doesn't want to say it.

Karen puts her phone on the table and brings her chair closer to Polly. 'Try not to worry. He's in good hands. They induced the coma to protect his brain, which means there's a good chance he'll be OK. Louise will text me as soon as there's any news. Come on, you're right. Let's get out of here for a bit. A coffee in the staff room sounds perfect.'

Polly puts her bag into her desk drawer and locks it. She wishes she hadn't said coffee. She'd love a coffee. Surely one wouldn't do any harm. As far as her mum had told her, pregnant ladies in the Eighties didn't particularly adhere to the rules and she'd turned out OK. She opens the door, just as it gets pushed from the other side. She jumps back slightly, startled.

'Oops, sorry, Miss. Didn't know you were hiding behind there. Mind if I come in for that chat now?'

Something about Brooke unnerves her. Polly wasn't prepared for this. She'd expected to have to coerce her into coming back into the office after yesterday's showdown with Detective Jennings. Polly had been furious at the time, but thinking about it overnight she'd realised the other woman was right. Brooke needed time to get her story straight in her head. Whether she was directly involved or not, she knew *something*. Turning up unannounced like this. Volunteering to talk … it didn't sit right. She either knew something or she was enjoying playing this little game, whatever it was. Polly was pretty sure it was the latter.

'Come in, Brooke,' Polly says.

Behind her in the corridor is PC Evans. She pops her head around the door, talks to Zucarro. 'Want to swap over?'

Karen is already standing, ready to leave. 'I guess that coffee will have to wait, Polly,' she says. 'Unless you want me to bring you something?'

Polly thinks about the cupboard in the staff room that is filled with various goodies, mainly things that people have brought in – biscuits, crisps. Sometimes boxes of Mr Kipling's. But there are often some confiscated goods in there, too. When Polly was a pupil, she'd always suspected that the teachers ate the contraband that they lifted during classes, but she hadn't really believed it was true until she'd seen it for herself. She'd asked Jon about it when they'd sat in there after her interview, and he'd told her where it came from. 'If you take half a Kit Kat away from them because they've been eating in class, they rarely ask for it back later.' She'd laughed at the very idea, but then she'd seen the packets of Nik Naks in a basket and her mouth had watered at the thought.

'Maybe just some chocolate, if that's OK?' she says. 'We can make some tea here.' Again, she thinks. More bloody tea.

'I'll have some chocolate, if there's any going,' Brooke says. 'Mrs Cohen still owes me a Bounty from last week.' She grins.

Polly holds in a sigh. Bloody girl seems to have read her mind. She pushes the box of biscuits across the table. 'I think there are a few chocolate ones left. Your brother's eaten most of them.'

Brooke reaches into the box, but at the mention of her brother she pauses, just for a moment, before taking a handful of bourbons.

Polly glances around at Sarah Evans, nods. Sarah switches on her voice recorder and lays it on the desk so that Brooke can see it. Brooke glances at it, then looks away. There is a hint of a smirk on her lips and Polly feels a brief surge of anger.

'Brooke ... have you heard what happened to Mr Crisp?'

Brooke shoves a biscuit in her mouth. Rolls her eyes. 'I heard he had an accident,' she says. 'Walked into a door.' Smirk.

'OK, so clearly you know what happened. We both know he didn't walk into a door ...'

'He was always a bit clumsy, old Packety.'

'He was attacked by a mob after an arrangement on Facebook. You wouldn't happen to know anything about that, would you?'

Brooke is wide-eyed. 'Me? As if. What kind of mentalist do you think I am?'

Jesus, this girl is good. She looks Polly straight in the eye as she says this – a blatant lie. She might not have been behind it, but there's no doubt she knew about it. Polly wonders if she's the kind of person who would study tells – make sure to do the opposite of what was expected. People who are bad liars tend to look away, fidget when they speak. Hesitate. Brooke looked her in the eye and didn't hesitate for a second. It was too well rehearsed. She turns, raising her eyebrows at Evans, who gives her a tiny nod in return that says, *Don't worry, I'm watching this too.*

'Do you like Mr Crisp, Brooke?'

Brooke snorts. 'What's that supposed to mean? He's all right, I s'pose. For a teacher—'

'What about *not* as a teacher – as a friend, maybe?'

Brooke folds her arms. 'Boring. Move on.' She looks away.

Polly suppresses a sigh. This girl is challenging, that's for sure. She decides to change tack, hoping she might reveal something while attempting to blame someone else. Polly has a feeling that this is how Brooke operates.

'Where's Hayley, Brooke?'

'How the f … hell should I know? She was Katie's friend, not mine.'

'That's not what I've heard. What I've heard is that you've been spending a lot of time with Hayley, ganging up on Katie. Spreading rumours about her.'

Brooke's eyes flash with anger. Her carefully controlled mask slips, just for a moment. 'Bullshit.'

'So you don't know where Hayley is?'

'No, I don't. But if you want me to guess, she's probably away being shagged or battered by that lunatic she's going out with. She thinks it's cool, you know. She shows off the bruises. She thinks it makes her look hard, but it makes her look stupid. She needs to get one of the other lads to batter the shit out of the creep. Teach him a lesson.'

'Like they taught Mr Crisp a lesson?'

'I told you. I had nothing to do with that.' She looks away.

'Brooke, did you send letters to Mr Crisp? Did you pretend they were from Katie?'

Brooke laughs, but it's a hollow sound. She squirms in her seat, and Polly wonders if she might have broken her at last. The girl lets out a long, slow sigh. 'This is so boring, Miss.

You should ask Hayley about these letters, though. Sounds like her sort of thing. Why would I bother?'

'Were you jealous of your sister?'

'Jealous? You're having a laugh.' She moves in her seat again. Won't meet Polly's eye.

'I think you were jealous of your sister's relationship—'

'So it *is* true, then? I heard him say it the other day, but to be honest I'd thought they actually *were* just friends ...'

'Hang on – you heard him say it where? Say what?'

'In here, talking to you. I was outside. He said they had a *relationship*.' She makes air quotes around the word with her fingers.

'You didn't stick around to hear the rest, then? The part where he explained that he was helping her with stuff for uni, and that they were friends ... and that someone had been sending letters, trying to cause trouble.'

'No ...'

'No, you just took what you wanted and went off to set up that Facebook group. You wanted to cause trouble, am I right? You couldn't have cared less about your sister, could you? Trying to say this was all for her – that getting revenge on Lucas was for her – that's rubbish, isn't it, Brooke? You did this because you're a nasty little girl who was jealous of her prettier, cleverer sister. You did this because—'

Sarah lays a hand on her arm and she stops talking. She'd been so carried away she hadn't even noticed the change in Brooke.

She was crying. Hard. Rocking back and forth in the chair.

'Brooke ...'

'I'm sorry, Miss,' she manages through sobs. 'I didn't mean it. I didn't mean any of it. It was just meant to be a laugh. I ... I miss her. I really do. I can't even believe it's happened. I can't ... I think I'm going to be sick—'

Polly makes it around to the other side of the desk with the waste paper bin just in time. She pulls the girl's hair back from her face as she vomits into the bucket. Rubs a hand gently on her back. She lifts her head, gestures at the voice recorder. Sarah turns it off.

Polly feels sick herself now. Not just because of the acrid stench of the vomit splashing into the bucket, but sick at herself for getting so angry, for pushing the girl so far. But, in some ways, she's glad. Brooke has finally grasped the enormity of the situation. She's accepted that her sister is dead. It's not a game.

It's Hayley that Polly is concerned about now – she doesn't know if the comment that Brooke made about her boyfriend hitting her was true or not, but she is worried that no one seems to have seen Hayley for the last few days … And no one seems to care where she might be.

37

Louise

'Are you sure it's OK for us to talk to him now?' Louise asks the nurse.

She's been sitting outside ICU for several hours now, after the initial call to say that Lucas had woken up. She and Davie had rushed to the hospital only to find that he wasn't ready for visitors yet. So she'd sat there, patiently. Waited with the uniformed officer who was placed outside for protection. Lucas had been given a room at the far end of the corridor, one that couldn't be accessed without getting through the secure doors and past the nurses' station, but they weren't taking any chances. He'd taken one hell of a beating, and if Louise had been a betting woman she'd have given low odds on the man waking up at all. Davie had left her to it after an hour, gone off somewhere with Malkie.

She texts him now:

Want me to go in without you?

He replies straight away.

Yes.

Louise hates hospitals. Well, most people do. But for her they bring back memories of her time spent in and out of them when her little brother was sick. Years of doctor's appointments and blood tests, seeing him hooked up to machines and drips, losing his hair, looking so frail it was amazing that he could actually hold himself upright. Incredible to think of that now, if you were to see him. A picture of health, a keen sportsman. With two little children that Louise spoiled rotten whenever she could, being the doting auntie that she was.

The nurse left her to it. 'Don't be too long, he's very weak still.'

Louise pushed open the door. The smell inside caught the back of her throat, just for a moment. That chemical shitty smell that seems to seep into your pores. The nurse has tipped the bed up at the top, just enough so that he's no longer lying flat out, so he can see what's going on. Should he open his eyes? She can hear his breathing, a weak rasp. His skin is grey, his complexion waxy. He has small bruises on his hand where the cannula has been inserted. His face is still puffy, one eye swollen shut. But other than that he doesn't look too bad. The rest of the damage is hidden under the covers.

'Hello again, Lucas,' she says. She sits down on the chair next to him, turns it in to face him. 'It's DC Jennings. We spoke before—'

'I remember,' he says. 'You like custard creams and you don't take sugar in your tea.'

'Ha. Well, to be honest, I've been having a few sugars the last couple of days. It's been—'

'Stressful? Tell me about it.' There is a hint of a smile, despite everything.

'I'm not going to ask how you're feeling ...'

'The mess that is currently my face is only superficial. Or so they say. I haven't looked, but I can feel it. Three cracked ribs, a punctured lung. My left arm is broken in two places. The right one is OK. They did their homework, I suppose.'

'What do you mean?'

'I'm left-handed. I guess they reckon kiddie-fiddlers can only fiddle with their primary hand.'

Louise swallows. 'We should've taken you somewhere, Lucas. I'm sorry. It just happened so quickly.'

'I know it did. You aren't to blame. If anyone is, it's me. I should've told you everything when you came to see me, then maybe you might've suggested I get away for a bit. I tried to bury my head in the sand. Hoped it'd be OK. I didn't count on the baying mob ...'

'They arranged it on Facebook. We didn't see it until it was too late. I'm shocked at how quickly the rumours spread, how quickly people got fired up ...'

'I'm not. Remember Chris Jefferies? Didn't take much for him to become suspect number one. Trial by media. I suppose mine was trial by smoke signals. You hardly need social media in a town like this. People seem to know bloody everything the minute it happens.' He pauses, starts to cough.

'Do you need some water?'

He nods, and she lifts the cup from his cabinet and directs the straw between his parched lips.

'Sorry, Lucas, but what did you mean when you said you should've told us everything? I thought you did tell us everything, about your friendship with Katie ... Was there something you missed? Something that might help?'

'A couple of things, yes.' He sighs. 'Katie won some money. On a scratch card.'

He starts to cough, and she holds the plastic beaker up to his mouth again. He sips. She places the cup back on the stand and pulls a tissue from the box. Wipes his mouth.

'Thanks. Kind of humiliating, this. Being helpless.'

She can feel his embarrassment coming off him in waves. Don't worry about that, she thinks. Just be bloody grateful the fuckers didn't kill you.

'This scratch card?' Louise says.

He nods, takes a breath. 'Her and Neil. They won five grand. She wanted to use it to help them get a deposit for a flat for university. They were both planning to go down to London. She was scared to keep the card at home, wasn't ready to cash it in yet. Her and Neil had a bit of an argument about it. He wanted them to go and spend some of the money – have a day out in Edinburgh – a night, maybe. In a hotel.' She could see his cheeks reddening slightly.

'When was this?'

'She texted me on Sunday night. Told me about the argument. Asked me to come round. I did. One of the neighbours saw me. I don't know his name. He nodded a hello, but he seemed to be in a rush.' He sighs. 'So, yeah. I was there. She asked me to look after the scratch card. She didn't explicitly say so, but I got the impression she was a little worried about Neil.'

'In what way?'

'That maybe he was getting cold feet about going to London with her. That maybe he'd been seeing someone else.'

'And had he?'

'I don't know. I took the scratch card, anyway. It's in a drawer, at home. In the kitchen. Don't worry. It's safe.'

Louise thinks about the fire that Davie was putting out as she'd entered the property. The kitchen was a state. Drawers yanked out and stuff strewn across the floor. Had someone found it? Had it been damaged in the fire? She decides not to worry him with it for now.

'Did anyone else know about it?'

'I'm not sure. I don't think so. I know she wouldn't have told anyone in her family. She'd be too scared they'd try to convince her to split the cash. She wasn't being selfish, you know. But this university thing … it was her big chance.'

'I know, I can understand that. What about her sister? Do you think she knew anything about the money?'

212

'If she did, it didn't come from Katie. Like I said, they fought like cat and dog. No, if anyone else knew about the money, it could only have come from one person because I didn't tell anyone.'

'Neil.' Louise says. Fuck. Five grand might not be the biggest sum of money in the world. But for a couple of school kids, or a poor family, it was a motive, definitely. Was Neil up to no good? He'd seemed genuinely distraught, but people could be good actors when they wanted to be. She'd seen it often enough. Something was niggling at her. Just something about the way Neil was. Upset, yes. But cagey too. Did he know something? Had he told someone about the scratch card?

'Thanks, Lucas. This has been really helpful.' She watches him close his eyes before turning away, ready to leave. Pauses for a moment. Turns back to him. Finds herself channeling Columbo.

'Just one more thing ...' she says. His eyes open slowly. 'The people who attacked you. Any idea who they were? Even one of them. If we could get the ringleader ... we've questioned half the town – everyone is pleading ignorance. Even the arseholes who threatened violence via the Facebook group are trying to tell us it was all just a joke, that it was nothing to do with them—'

'I'm sorry, DC Jennings,' Lucas says quietly. 'I'm really very tired now.'

He closes his eyes again. Her cue to leave.

Louise pats him on the hand and walks away. No matter what they've done to him, there's no way he's going to make things worse by grassing them up. She opens the door.

'Wait,' Lucas says. He blinks. 'I should've mentioned this earlier ...'

She holds the door. Raises her eyebrows at him. 'Yes?'

'You might want to talk to her friend Diane ... and Lois, too ...'

'Lois, the teaching assistant?'

'Yes. She and Katie were close. The three of them were doing an experiment of some sort. A psychology thing. I don't know if it ever happened or not, but they were talking about setting up some sort of blog. A sort of gossip column. I warned her she should be careful about that sort of thing. It's not always as anonymous as you think it is. The internet, I mean.'

Louise wanted to kick herself. Of course. Katie's laptop. So far the tech team hadn't found anything of interest – but maybe that's because they didn't know what they were looking for. Maybe it wasn't public yet. If they'd started a blog, but it hadn't been published yet, it'd be more difficult to find it. They might have found the blog provider, but with no live content …Maybe Katie had been good at keeping it concealed. One of Katie's friends must know something, though. Maybe more than one of them. This blog … this was going to answer a lot of questions. Louise was sure of it.

THREEWISEMONKEYSBLOG

Telling It Like It Is

Posted: 1st Jan 2017 by SpeakNoEvil
Status: Published
Comments: 0

> *Oh little enemy,*
> *I cannot fight with you,*
> *My mommy said not to*
> *Boo hoo hoo hoo*
> *I can't scratch your eyes out*
> *And make you bleed to death*
> *But we'll be jolly enemies*
> *Forever evermore.*

This is the last verse. This is the last you're going to hear from me. I'm not going to carry on with this shit. What's the point? It's a funny verse, this one – as if my mum would tell me not to fight with anybody. Bloody loves a fight, my mum. Nice of her to pass down her shitty genes to my little sis, eh? Cow. You and her are well suited as mates, actually. You're both as bad as each other.

Fucking hell – I have *loved* writing these posts – so cathartic. Better than a diary, 'cause I can just scrub the lot and no one ever has to know. I feel better just writing it. I push all my

215

anger and disappointment onto the screen and I read it back, and I feel better. Until I see you ...you, HAYLEY. Hanging out with my sneering little bitch of a sister, BROOKE.

OOPS – not so anonymous now, is it?? See, that stuff I told you about LUCAS – you're just fucking jealous. Jealous that someone interesting wants to be my friend. Jealous that I get to spend time with someone who knows more about the world than any of you fuckwits from this crappy little town. Yeah. Well, fuck you. Fuck you for trying to ruin things. Guess what? YOU FAILED.

One day, you little bitch ... one day I might actually publish these blogs ... and I'm not going to make them anonymous again, Hayley Marsh. I'm going to let everyone know what a two-faced disappointment you really are. You and Brooke are welcome to each other. My only question is: whose life are you going to fuck up next, before someone calls you on it?

You know, it was Lois who had the idea for this experiment. Her and Diane and me, we all came up with it together. They're doing their own posts too – SeeNoEvil and HearNoEvil. Bet they won't be as honest as me, though, will they?

**Girls, if you're reading this in drafts, I'm sorry – don't worry – I was never going to publish them 😑

---Comments are open---

38

Polly

PC Sarah Evans tells Polly that she will be sending in Karen Zucarro to replace her again and asks if she can photocopy any notes she has been taking from the students' talks to pass on to the investigation team. Even with the recordings of each session, they want to make sure they aren't missing anything that might need to be followed up. Polly closes the door and breathes in a sigh of relief. Finally, a bit of time to herself. She's been non-stop all day and she really needs to gather her thoughts. She picks up her handbag, checks that she hasn't left anything important on her desk and she's about to head out and finally get that break – her stomach has been making loud gurgling sounds for the last ten minutes and she's starting to feel a little lightheaded – when the door bursts open.

'Miss, Miss – please … you've got to help us!'

'Diane, Lois … what's wrong? What's happened?' She steps back into the room and lets them follow her inside.

Diane's voice comes out in short gasps. 'Oh God! We didn't mean it to happen, but now it's too late and we don't know what to do – please – you've got to help us, Miss—'

'Lois?' She cuts Diane off and addresses the teaching

assistant, hoping for a calmer response, but the young woman's face is entirely devoid of colour. She looks like she's about to burst into tears.

Diane drops into a chair and holds her head in her hands. 'I knew we should've kept it as one username for all three of us. Then we'd have seen it before—'

'Seen what before?' Polly has no idea what the girl is talking about. 'Lois?' She tries again, hoping to shake the woman from the trance that she seems to have fallen into.

'The blog,' Diane says. 'It was ...' She looks at Lois, then back at Polly. Her face holds a guilty expression. 'It was Lois's idea. We all thought it would be fun ...'

Polly sighs. 'Right. Can you just slow down a bit and tell me what's happened? What blog? I'm not sure I follow—'

'It's called Three Wise Monkeys, you know ... See no evil, hear no evil, speak no evil?' Polly nods, and Lois carries on. 'It was supposed to be ironic. Just a bit of fun. It's the kind of thing I see a lot back home, but there's not so much of it here, so we thought ... I thought it might be a good psychology experiment for the girls. It was supposed to be ... it wasn't supposed to contain real names. It ... wasn't supposed to contain real things – it was meant to be anonymous. It was meant to be a trigger, to see how people would react to things. You know, like horoscopes – you read them and you apply them to yourself, even though the person who wrote them made them completely general – it's all down to the individual's interpretation.'

'I get it,' Polly says. 'So what was on this blog?'

'That's the thing,' Diane says. She steals a sideways glance at Lois. 'Nothing was meant to be on it. Not yet. We were all working on different pieces. They were drafts – as in, unpublished. We were going to talk them through before we started publishing them – before we made them open for comments. We wanted to start slowly, gauge people's reactions. If there was no interest, we'd stop. We, um … we had a username each. I was See No Evil, Lois was Hear No Evil—'

'Who was the third one? Who was Speak No Evil?'

'It was Katie,' Lois says. 'Only … we just found out that she wasn't making it anonymous—'

'What do you mean? Found out how?'

'Diane borrowed Katie's old laptop because hers was broken. She went over there and got it on Saturday. We decided to look at the blog today. We weren't sure what to do with it, what with … now that Katie's gone.'

'We hooked it up to the screen in the IT lab,' Diane says. 'Not on purpose. I didn't realise the Bluetooth was on. It popped up on the screen automatically. Anyway, then we realised that Katie had written a load of posts, and she was talking about Brooke, and Hayley … and it was angry stuff. We were scared. We didn't want anyone to see them, so we decided to delete the posts …'

'Only something went wrong,' Lois continues. 'Instead of deleting them, we published them. They're live. We've been scrabbling about for the last half-hour trying to take them down again, revert them to draft, delete them, whatever, but there's something messed up with the blog server – it won't let us update it. We can't get the things down.' Panic is back in Lois's voice.

'OK. OK,' Polly says. 'Let's not panic too much yet. No one else knows about the blog yet, is that right? So no one else has seen the posts. They've only just gone up. Unless anyone knows where to look for this blog, they're not going to find it, are they?'

Diane's voice is barely a whisper. 'It auto-posts to the school magazine page on Facebook as soon as they're made live … that's how we planned to spread the word. Anyone who asks can get admin access to that page. It's what we all use for announcements and stuff.' She drops her head into her hands again.

'That's not all of it, is it?' Polly says.

Lois takes a deep breath, blows it out slowly. 'We think someone saw it on the screen in the IT room. Someone was in the anteroom – you know, that connecting room between the two labs?'

'Who?'

'The only person who could've been in there was Mr Hennessy,' Diane says.

'Or Pete,' says Lois.

Pete. That name again. Damn it. What had he seen? If the girls were this upset, it was highly likely it was bad. Really bad. Maybe he hadn't seen it. If they'd slammed the laptop shut as soon as they'd realised …

'That last blog,' Diane says. 'I don't know what had got into Katie, but she was so angry. The things on there – she accused Hayley of all sorts. I just hope we can get it taken down before Hayley sees it. I know they'd fallen out, but Hayley was upset. She was scared of her boyfriend. Too scared to tell anyone. She just kept up this bravado all the time … But, oh God! If anyone has notifications switched on for the magazine page on Facebook, they might be reading it already.'

'Jesus,' Polly says, under her breath. She picks up her phone, starts scrolling through for Louise Jennings' phone number. Spots that she already has a missed call from her. Ten minutes ago. *Shit.* 'Have you seen Hayley today? Have you any idea where she might be?'

Diane shrugs. 'She hasn't been in school all week, but I doubt she's sick. She's a mess. She's got herself mixed up in all sorts. I feel really bad now. I should've gone round, maybe. Seen if she was OK—'

'She probably wouldn't have spoken to you, Diane. Don't beat yourself up about it—'

'But if she sees these posts … we need to calm down. I'm sure we can remove them before anyone else sees.' She pauses, as if a thought has struck her unexpectedly. 'You know, Miss … if you're wondering where to find her, she's probably not even at home at all. She'll be hanging out in the same place that everyone goes to when they're skiving off.'

Polly frowns. 'And where's that?'

Diane glances at Lois, a worried look on her face. 'The river.'

39

Neil

Neil feels sick. Everything inside his head is swirling round and round like draining bathwater. His stomach is churning. He feels like he hasn't slept for days. Last night he'd taken a bottle of vodka from the back of the kitchen cupboard, mixed it with Ribena. It had knocked him out for a bit, given him nightmares, and he was suffering for it now.

Going into school had been a stupid plan.

But it was better than being at home. His mum's been giving him a wide berth. She must've known he'd taken the vodka from her stash, but she didn't bother mentioning it. She doesn't know what to say to him. She's never been very good at all that stuff. His dad is better, but he's away and Neil isn't sure when he's coming back. Mum says he's working on the rigs again, but Neil is sure he's banged up. The two of them are useless, really. Neil's used to getting on with things himself.

He walks around the edge of the playing fields, heads towards the river – hoping that the fresh air will remove the cotton wool from his head. Take away the memories of the visions. He couldn't work out if they were real or not. Last night, Katie had come to him. She was perched on the end of his bed, wearing black knickers and a faded Soundgarden T-shirt. One of his. She'd smiled at him, and he'd reached for her, but just as his fingers were about to touch her shoulder she'd blown him a kiss then disappeared.

He'd barely slept at all after that, even with the drink to numb his brain. He'd tossed and turned, throwing the duvet off, sweating like a pig despite the chill in the air.

His eyes feel scratchy. Too small, suddenly, like dry stones pushed into his head. He takes a pouch of tobacco from his pocket, pulls out the pack of papers from inside. He'd taken it from his brother's bedside table, and even that grumpy bastard hadn't given him a hard time. No sympathy there either, just stunned silence.

What are people supposed to say, anyway? Katie's gone. She's not coming back. Except in his dreams. She'll never leave those.

He rolls a cigarette. Stops and turns into the thick bough of an oak tree to light it away from the wind. Takes a drag. It's quiet here, down by the river. The surface is frozen over in parts, and the sound of the water flowing underneath is barely noticeable. He walks along the path, crunching broken twigs and small clumps of ice underfoot. He's not even sure where he's going. He's just walking. Keeping away from all of it.

Thinking about what happened to Lucas Crisp makes his stomach flip again. That wasn't supposed to happen. They were meant to stand on his stupid little patch of lawn, bang on his windows. Post a fresh turd through his letterbox. Scare the crap out of the fucker.

No one was meant to go inside.

It hadn't taken long for the thing to get out of hand. People were hammering on the window. Battering the door. Neil hadn't been able to see what was going on inside. He'd stayed well back, across the other side of the road. He was there because he felt like he'd no choice. But he wasn't getting involved. They were wrong, anyway. It wasn't him who killed Katie. He'd never have done that. But once the rumours had started – once *Brooke* had started them – there was nothing that anyone could do.

Guilty. Paedo. No trial required. That fucking Facebook group. Bunch of sick animals, jumping all over it. Desperate for something. Who knows what.

Once the door got kicked in, that was it. They filed in. Those angry men from outside the pub. Riled by drink and anger. Bravado. Mob rule. Katie would've been fascinated and horrified. They were insane, driven that way by each other.

The poor bloke didn't stand a chance. Neil had hoped that the teacher might've been quick enough to leg it out the back, but he'd seen a trickle of blokes disappear round the back, just before the door went in. There was no way out.

They were armed with planks of wood, bricks wrapped in bags-for-life. Where the fuck had they got them all from? He hadn't seen them at the pub, but then he remembered that there was already a gang in wait when they arrived on the teacher's street. The news had spread. The proper hard men were in attendance.

'What if it was your daughter? Your girlfriend?' someone had shouted before they piled in. Any murmurs of dissent were ignored.

Because everyone was too fucking scared.

He wipes his hand across his cheek, getting rid of the angry tears that can't seem to stay inside his head. Where does it come from? All that liquid? It shouldn't be there any more. He feels like he's dried up inside. Desiccated, like coconut. Katie loves coconut.

Loved.

He's about to cut up the bank, to climb over the broken wire fence and head back into the playing fields, when something catches his eye.

Something is bobbing amidst the shattered ice of Digby's Deathhole. Someone's chucked something in there. Shards of thin, broken ice float slowly across the deep pool, catching the last of the sunlight through the bare trees. He roots around until he finds a decent stick. Rips it away from the frosty bank.

He walks to the edge. What the hell is that? He pokes the stick at a large jagged sheet, and it slides into the dark floating lump. He feels his breath quicken. Is it an animal? Has some poor dog trotted onto the ice and slipped through? Maybe someone's gone to get help. He doesn't sense anyone nearby. He moves closer to the edge, pokes at another piece of ice, tries to use the stick to guide the floating lump closer to the water's edge so he can see what it is. It's probably just a rubbish bag. People are arseholes.

The thing bobs closer to him, and with a bit of a stretch he reaches it with the stick. He hooks the stick onto the edge and pulls. Black bag full of clothes? Why would someone chuck it in here?

His mind is trying its hardest to come up with a rational explanation, but it's a waste of time. He can see quite clearly what it is. Because it isn't an 'it', it's a 'she'. He stumbles backwards. The thing in the water seems to swim towards him now. Hooked, still, on the stick that he's gripping tight, so tight that he feels like his knuckles might snap and break through the pale skin of his icy cold hands. He watches in horror as the thing in the water bobs and flips, long hair swirling like tangled reeds. He sees her face now, and a strangled sob escapes his frozen lips.

Oh Jesus, no—

It's Hayley. Katie's best friend.

Katie's *ex*-best friend.

'Oh fuck ... oh fucking hell.' He falls to the ground, lets go of the stick. He scrabbles back towards the trees. He doesn't want to look, but he can't stop staring. She's dead. She's already dead. There's nothing he can do now. He can't risk going in the water – he'd end up drowning himself. No. He has to phone the police. That's all. He takes a deep breath. Lets it out slowly. Fumbles in his pocket for his phone. 'It's OK, Neil,' he says to himself. 'You can do this. Keep calm.'

He's pressing the second '9' into his phone when he hears the rustling in the sparse bushes behind him. Twigs snapping and falling. He doesn't want to turn round. He closes his eyes. Waits for the blow. It doesn't happen.

'She was a bad girl,' the voice behind him says. 'A bad, bad girl.'

He opens his eyes. He recognises the voice. He turns around slowly, finger pressing the third '9' into his phone. He hears the tinny voice, far away: *Which service do you require?*

'Police,' he says into the phone. 'I'm at Digby's Deathhole. You better send an ambulance too, although I think it's too late.' He hangs up. Addresses the man standing next to the bushes. 'Hello, Pete,' he says. 'It's OK. Help will be here soon.'

Pete gestures towards Neil's coat pocket, where the pouch of tobacco is poking out. 'You shouldn't smoke, you know. It's really bad for you.'

40

Polly

After calling Louise to tell her about what Diane and Lois had said, Polly is relieved to hear that the police had already been aware of the blog. They'd set up a notification on the school magazine page and had seen the posts as they'd come in. They'd already been collaborating with Facebook about the Lucas Crisp group – which had now been taken down – and they were able to disable the school page straight away; and they'd accessed the blog server, explaining why the girls were struggling to make the updates. The police knew that someone outside the team had viewed the blog too, via the Facebook links, and they were close to finding out who that was.

Polly is glad to have this taken out of her hands, and although she's annoyed that the girls didn't come to her sooner, she understands why they tried to keep it all a secret. She manages a break, at last. A cheese and pickle sandwich and a hot chocolate from the machine in the staff room. She's missed lunch, and thankfully, no one else is in there. Afterwards, she heads back to her office, feeling slightly more refreshed but more anxious than ever about what is going on in the school. She'd like to take the rest of the afternoon off, but there is a note on her desk letting her know that she'll be getting another visitor very soon. She leans back in her chair and waits for him to arrive.

★ ★ ★

'How are you feeling today, Brett? Mrs Cohen said you'd been a bit quiet in your classes. She was wondering if you were OK, or if you wanted to talk to someone?'

'What about? Can I have a biscuit, please?'

Polly lifts the box of biscuits out from where they've been stored, on top the footstool under her desk. She pushes them across, takes off the lid. He goes for the chocolate fingers again.

'Brett?'

He sighs. Munches on the biscuits. 'Boggy says I've not to be sad any more about Katie because she's with the angels now and she's OK.'

'Does he now? What else has Boggy been saying?'

'Oh, just the usual things, really. He's not happy with some of his insects. He says it's too cold and he can't wait for the summer so he can get some better ones. Also, he thinks that it's a shame that Mr Crisp is in hospital because he didn't do anything wrong. He says he hopes that Mr Crisp is OK and that he'll be able to go home soon.'

'I'm sure he will. It was a nasty thing that happened to him, but he's awake now and recovering in bed. You can tell Boggy that, if he's worried.' She smiles. 'He's not here now, is he?'

Brett frowns, scratches his ear. 'Who?'

'Boggy, of course. Is he here?'

Brett barks out a strangled noise. 'Of course he's not here. You'd be able to see him if he was. He's not invisible.' He shakes his head, then reaches forward for another biscuit.

Polly decides to change tack. 'How's your mum, Brett? Has she got anyone round, taking care of her? I was glad that she said it was OK for you and Brooke to come back to school. Sometimes it's better to be around people when you're sad, so that you can talk. Have company.' Polly decides that she will go round and see Mandy later. She's been dithering over this for too long.

'Mum's OK. She's crying a lot. There's a police lady sort of living there, in our house. She's called Flo, or something.'

Polly smiles. He means *the* FLO. The Family Liaison Officer. She imagines that's not enough, though. Not for Mandy. Mandy was always over-emotional, especially when she was meting out slaps and punches. Long time ago, though. Will Mandy want to talk to her now? Perhaps she won't bother going round after all. What can she do, anyway? And maybe with the situation ... her own situation ... she doesn't want to make things any worse.

'Do you miss Katie?' Polly asks.

He stares at her then, silently. She watches as he tries hard to keep his mouth tightly shut, his nostrils flaring gently as he breathes. His lip wobbles. 'Of course I do,' he says. A tear runs down his cheek and he sniffs, wiping it away along with his snot on his sleeve. 'Boggy says I'll see her again one day. He says maybe she's with his mum, 'cause she's with the angels too. He says his mum was really nice, and that he wishes she was still here because sometimes his dad shouts at him too much.'

Polly is intrigued. He's invented a friend who has no mum, and a domineering father – which is the exact opposite of his own situation. She should ask about his dad, or his stepdad. But she's not sure she wants to go down that route just yet.

'Boggy sounds like he knows a lot. Do you speak to him often?'

'Hmm. Yeah. Most days. Mostly not during the day, though, in case he gets in trouble. I meet him in the woods after school and we do stuff like foraging. He knows loads of things about

229

the woods. He knows the animals and the plants and even the name of the stuff that makes up the floor, you know, that mulchy stuff? He can tell you all the things that are in it. He knows the flowers, too, and the insects. He doesn't shoot things now, because he got in trouble before, but we sometimes make catapults and we can catch some of the flying insects in nets. The stuff that crawls on the floor and on the trees, we get that with bits of sticky tape and sometimes beakers and things. We like it when we can catch them and watch them die, instead of squishing them too much. It's better that way, if you want to keep them and pin them to the board. But so far we've not had much luck with that, which is why I said Boggy could come round and talk to Katie about hers …'

A chill runs down Polly's spine. 'Brett … you need to tell me the truth now, and don't be scared … but where does Boggy live? Is he … is he a special friend that only you can see? That only you can talk to?'

Brett laughs. 'Are you mad, Ms McAllister? He's not an imaginary friend or something. That's for little kids! Did you think I made him up? You know him. Everyone knows him. But some people think he's weird, so that's why he hasn't got any friends his own age—'

'His own age? What do you mean, Brett? Who *is* Boggy? What's his real name?'

The boy sighs. Shakes his head. 'It's Pete, silly. I thought everyone knew that. Pete. P-E-A-T. Bog. Get it?'

'Pete? Not Pete, the man who helps Mr Hennessy with the school and the gardens?'

'Yes, of course. Pete, the jannie's helper. Who did you think I was talking about?'

41

Louise

The phone call from Polly McAllister had been enlightening. Neil sleeping with Brooke. Katie's scratch card. Brooke stirring up trouble for Lucas. Diane and Lois – all this stuff about the blog posts ... and Pete Brotherstone. Poor Neil. There were so many things to unpick, but the scene at the river had presented itself fairly intact. They'd been on their way to see Mandy, but that would have to wait now.

He hadn't put up a fight. He'd looked shell-shocked. Sad. But he'd let them lead him away, put him in the car. He said nothing in the car, but as soon as they arrived at the station, the floodgates had opened. Like he knew exactly what was expected of him now.

'Well, Pete. Do you want to tell us what's been going on?' Louise says. She and Davie are in the small interview room at the back of the station. There are only two in Banktoun, but the larger one has been their HQ during the investigation. This room is bleak, windowless. The walls are a dirty grey that looks like neglect rather than a chosen shade of paint. Davie switches on the recorder, says the things he has to say.

Pete sits straight in his chair, looks directly ahead. 'Hayley was a bad girl.'

The room is silent. Outside, Louise can hear raised voices. Someone has arrived at the station. Someone that doesn't sound happy. Pete has waived his right to a legal representative, but they have called one, nonetheless.

'Should I?'

Davie nods. Louise walks out into the corridor, just as the solicitor turns the corner.

'Rob Bates,' he says. 'I hope you haven't started without me.'

'What's going on round there?' Louise says.

'Martin Brotherstone is what. Don't worry, you can talk to him later. DI Reid has it in hand.'

Louise gives the solicitor a wry smile. They both know what this means. Malkie will shut him up and shut him down. Martin's councillor credentials don't wash with Detective Inspector Reid. Rob seems very matter of fact, and that's not a bad thing. His name sounds familiar, but she doesn't think she's come across him before. Best they deal with this as quickly as possible. Of course they're hoping that Pete is responsible not just for Hayley but for Katie too, but that seems too neat somehow. Louise isn't convinced. She walks back into the room, with Rob following her.

'Hello, Davie,' he says. Louise was right – he is familiar. She makes a mental note to ask about him later on. He seems intriguing, somehow, she's not sure why.

'Rob, do you need to speak to Pete on his own first?'

'I don't need to do that,' Pete says, before the solicitor can answer. 'I just want to tell you what happened. It's better that way. I thought it was good fun having all the secrets, but I don't like them any more.'

'Which secrets are those, Pete?' Davie asks. His voice is gentle. He has told Louise who this boy is, and Louise's feelings are mixed – but she knows he needs to be handled carefully.

'About *The Collection*. You want me to tell you about that, don't you?'

A shiver runs down Louise's neck. The Collection. Louise doesn't know what the boy is referring to, but there is something chilling about the way he said it.

Davie is calm. 'I do, Pete. I do. But first of all I want you to tell me what you were doing down at the river today. Can you tell me that bit first?'

Louise glances across at Rob. His face is stony. Should he intervene? Tell his client to keep quiet?

Pete sighs. 'I did a bad thing. I'm sorry. But I told you … Hayley is a bad girl. She hurt Katie.'

'Katie Taylor?'

'Yes. Katie. She likes butterflies and dragonflies and she's got a damselfly too. I've looked and looked but I've never been able to catch one. I wanted to talk to her, to ask her how I could catch one. But I was scared to. I always get it wrong when I try to talk to girls. So I asked Brett to help me …'

Rob coughs. 'Pete, can you answer Sergeant Gray's question first of all, please? Then we can talk about the other things. If we need to.' He gives Davie a look. Davie nods.

'Pete? Can you tell me what happened to Hayley?'

Pete starts to clench and unclench his fists. He stares down at the table. 'She was bad to Katie. I read the things—'

'What things?'

'I saw it on my phone! It pinged. I'm not meant to use my phone at work, but it's OK with the stuff that's about the school. Mr Hennessy helped me do it on my phone. So I could read the school magazine? It's not really a magazine. It's on the computer. My phone went ping ping ping. I think it was six times, or maybe it was more. It was on the big computer screen too, but only for a minute. I didn't have time to read it

233

on there. The girls were looking at it on the computer. I went in to sort out the cables in the little room between the rooms because Mr Hennessy said they were a tangled fucking mess. Sorry—' He pauses, his cheeks flush. 'He said the bad words, I didn't.'

Louise understands now, at least she thinks she does. She doesn't want to make assumptions, but it seems pretty clear that Pete has learning difficulties of some sort. This is why they are being careful with him. He is very literal in what he says, what he does. He is vulnerable. She feels sorry for him, despite what it is they think he has done.

'The girls were playing with a laptop. It wasn't a school one. It was black.'

'Which girls?'

'The American lady teacher and Diane. The ginger nut.'

'Lois Reibach and Diane McBride?'

'Yes. They were reading the things. Then Diane pressed a button and Lois started shouting and Diane started crying and they pressed more buttons, and then my phone started pinging so I clicked on the links, and I saw.'

'What did you see?'

'Things that someone had written about Hayley. Things saying she was bad. Lots of bad words. I don't want to say them.'

Davie leans back in his seat. Louise takes over.

'Who wrote the things, Pete? Do you know?'

He sniffs. 'It didn't say. But I heard Lois say "oh Katie" and then Diane was crying. I wanted to speak to them. I wanted to say "who wrote that?" But I was too scared. I stayed in the little room until they'd gone. They slammed the lid shut and when they were walking out they said, "Oh God, Hayley will go mad when she sees this" and the other one said, "Yeah, but it's true, she did make Katie's life hell. She's a bad apple, that one." And then they were gone.'

234

Davie says, 'So then what? Did you tell anyone what you'd seen or heard?'

'No,' Pete looks confused. 'I'm telling you now. I wanted to go home after that, but I didn't get to go home because I walked down by the river and I saw Hayley and I said to her, "What did you do to Katie? Katie was nice." And she said, 'Fuck off, retard." Sorry, but she did say that. And then I don't know, but I think I pushed her out of the way and then there was a splash.'

Louise says, 'You pushed her into the river? Did you try to help her get back out again?'

Pete laughs, a strange mechanical sound. 'Of course I didn't. I told you. Hayley was a bad girl. I went and sat in the bushes and I watched her for a bit. She was loud, really loud. Shouting all the things at me. So in the end I threw her a stick, but it was too heavy and she didn't catch it. It hit her on the head. She went under the water then, and I couldn't do anything because I can't swim.'

'Did you call for help? Did you phone someone?'

He looks sad for a moment. 'No,' he says, 'my phone ran out of battery. I'd left it on the internet for too long. It always runs out when I do that. I'm waiting for my dad to buy me a new one. I closed my eyes then, because I didn't want to see her any more. She looked scary, floating there in the water. And it was so cold. But she was bad, wasn't she? She was a bad girl.'

No one speaks for a moment, trying to take it all in.

Davie says, 'Interview terminated at 14:37.' He switches off the tape. 'I think we need a break, don't you?'

Rob nods.

Pete says, 'Could I have a cup of tea, please? And a cheese sandwich? I'm hungry.'

Louise nods. 'Sure, Pete. I'm going to get someone to come in and look after you for a bit. They'll take you to another

235

room, and then they'll bring you some food and a drink. Is that OK?' She looks at Rob, waiting for a reaction.

'Sounds good,' Rob says. 'Let's do that, and then we can sort everything out later on.'

'Then I can tell you about The Collection?' Pete says. 'About Katie's board with the butterflies and the dragonflies? I wish I had the damselfly ...'

Louise takes a deep breath and walks out of the room.

The damselfly.

42

Neil

'Is it OK if we go through here?'

Neil nods and follows Detective Jennings to an area behind the front desk. There is a small kitchenette and a couple of chairs. A partition separates it from the desk and the rumbling hubbub of the station's reception area.

'Sorry,' she says, 'we're a bit short on space at the moment. I'd take you into one of the interview rooms, but we've, er ... Pete is in one of them and the other is our HQ. This station isn't big enough for an investigation like this.'

Neil sits down and lets his shoulders drop. He'd been feeling tense and scared since his meeting with Polly and then the bloody awful thing down at the river, but Jennings is making him feel at ease. They all know he had nothing to do with it, but he still has to be questioned. He will have to sign a statement.

'Tea?' she says.

He nods again. What is it with these grown-ups and their constant cups of tea? He used to think it was ridiculous, the way everything seemed to be made better after a hot drink, but he realises now that it's not just about the drink. It's the ritual – the boiling of the kettle, waiting for it to brew, deciding on milk and sugar. Choosing a biscuit. Delay. Delay. Delay. Then you can talk, right? He's not complaining, although maybe a wee shot of whisky in the tea would help relax him further.

He zones out as Louise goes through the familiar ritual. The bubbling of the kettle sends him off. He thinks about Hayley, floating towards him in the water. Imagines her screaming, distorted face as she realised she was going to drown. Imagines Pete, crouched there in the bushes, watching. Did he watch? Or did he close his eyes and put his fingers in his ears and hum *la la la* and pretend that it wasn't happening?

He closes his eyes, clenches his fists. Wills the images to go away. Katie comes to him then. That smile, head cocked to the side. A wink. Beckoning him with a curled finger.

'No. No!'

'Neil, are you OK?'

He opens his eyes. Realises he has shouted out loud. Jennings looks alarmed. Her hand hovers over the cup, spoon inside, teabag halfway out.

'Sorry, I don't know what happened there. It's like I'm having nightmares when I'm awake now.' He runs a hand through his hair, mutters, 'Fuck.'

'Don't worry. This won't take long. You've already told us what happened, but I just want you to go through it one more time so I can write up a report, then you can sign it off and we're done.' She drops the teabag onto a stained saucer. 'Listen … do you have anyone you can talk to about all this? If you need us to sort something out for you – we've got victim support, who can help. They aren't counsellors; they'll just be there to listen. Or if you need more, it might be worth speaking to your GP. I'm sure that they can get you a speedy referral for trauma … and grief, of course. I'm so sorry, Neil. You've had a hell of a few days.'

Neil gives her a small smile, then looks away. He can't deal with the pity in her eyes. He knows that they know about Brooke. What a shit boyfriend he was. Polly will have told them. He's sure they know about him being there when Mr Crisp got attacked too, but they haven't asked him. Either they're waiting for a better time, or maybe they know that he's not going to tell them anything. There's no way he'll tell them that Brooke was responsible for that. Despite her failings as a sister, he's not going to add to the shit. He's got a feeling she's going to wake up soon. See what a stupid little bitch she's been.

'I'll be OK,' he says. 'Let's get this over with.'

★ ★ ★

Neil walks out into the biting wind and makes his way down the High Street. He'd normally be tempted to walk down by the river, but the place has lost its appeal. He's not sure if he will ever go back there. Not after what he saw. He wonders what will happen to Pete. There have been rumours about him in the past, but he's never been found guilty of anything. Could this be it, after all? Could the police have been wrong about him before? Maybe he *was* involved with those girls at the Track last summer ... maybe. No. He didn't want to think it. Could he have killed Katie too? No. No. Hayley was an accident. He didn't mean it. He panicked ...

Don't think about it. He can't think about this shit any more. It's going to drive him mad. He's walking, rolling a cigarette. His head is down. He's not paying attention until he walks smack into something and the something shouts at him and shoves him out of the way.

'Oi, watch it ... Oh, Neil. It's you ... fuck ...'

'Quinn? Sorry, pal. What's up? You look like shit.'

Quinn grabs him by the arm and pulls him into an alleyway,

off the street and out of the wind, which has picked up again, throwing icy blasts down the street. 'Neil, I'm so glad I bumped into you. I need to talk to someone, but I don't know who … I spoke to the police yesterday.'

Neil frowns. 'Oh yeah?'

'They wanted to know if there was anything I might know that might help them work out what had happened to Katie. I said I doubted it. She was the only one of that lot who spoke to me, but I didn't have anything to tell them that they didn't already know. Anyway … actually, can I have one of them?' He nods towards Neil's cigarette.

'I'll roll it. Carry on.'

'So, they asked me if I could try speaking to Mandy. Jesus. You know what she's like. I *did* phone on Monday night, but she wouldn't speak. I decided to go round last night. Wasn't really expecting her to let me in.' He pauses, takes the rollie from Neil and bends towards him while Neil lights it. He takes a long drag, then takes it out of his mouth, peers at it like David Attenborough discovering a new species. 'Knock off baccie?' he says. Neil rolls his eyes. 'There was a copper there. She let me in.' He takes another drag.

'And? Get on with it, will you? I'm fucking freezing. I was going down Landucci's for something to eat.'

'I'd come with you, but I have to get to work. Not that you were inviting me or anything. Right, sorry. Where was I?'

Quinn is fidgety, nervous. Neil wonders if he might be back on the smack, but, looking at his eyes, it doesn't seem likely. They are clear and alert. It's just the rest of him that's jittering like a road worker with a Kango hammer.

'I spoke to Mandy. She was … fuck. She was out of it. Off her face. Drink, I think. Not drugs. But too much, you know? I think she might be on vallies too. The two combined has quite an effect. Anyway, she was rambling. Talking shite. At least I think it was shite. I don't really want to believe there was any truth in it. She was confused. That's all it was—'

'Spit it out, Quinn. Fucksake!'

'She said ...' He takes another drag on the cigarette. Drops it on the ground and grinds it with his heel. 'She said that she saw someone leaving the house ... and that ... *fuck*. She said that Katie was still alive when she came back from work.' He gives Neil a look. A look that says, *I don't want to think about what the fuck this might mean.*

'Jesus Christ,' Neil says. 'Jesus fucking Christ.' He pokes his head out from the alleyway, out onto the street. No one is nearby. No one has heard. But this changes everything. If it's true, it means that Mandy was in the house when Katie was killed. It means ... that Mandy knows the killer. *Fuck.* No wonder she's been in such a state. 'We need to go to the police, Quinn. Right now.'

'But—'

'I'm not arguing. Come on. I'll walk back with you.'

43

Louise

They pull up outside Mandy's house. The street looks dull, desolate. A piece of broken crime-scene tape flaps in the breeze. The snow has gone now, leaving dirty grey pavements, leached of life and colour. The bare trees look bored. Indifferent. It's only been a few days since they first came to this house, saw Katie in her bedroom for the last time. Less than twenty-four hours since Lucas Crisp was set upon by a mob of ill-informed yobs. No time at all since the body of Hayley Marsh was found floating in an icy pool.

'Well?' Louise says, as they walk together up the path to the front door. 'What's all this about?'

'We'll soon find out,' Davie says. He holds his finger down on the doorbell.

No answer.

'Go round the back,' Davie says.

Louise is opening the side gate when the front door squeaks open. 'What do yous want?' Mandy's voice is tired, slurred. As Louise walks back towards the front door, she can detect the smell of stale alcohol in the stilled air.

'OK if we come in for a minute?' Louise says.

Mandy opens the door wider. Louise is shocked by what she sees. On Monday, when they'd first arrived here, the house had been tidy. Mandy had looked as normal as she could, under the circumstances. She was clean, in decent clothes. Today is a different story. She stinks of fags and booze. Her hair is hanging in greasy clumps. She looks like she's slept in her clothes.

They step inside and close the door behind them. Mandy has already retreated to the kitchen, where the air is tinged with smoke. Inside, the place is littered with empty cans, bottles. Several ashtrays heaped with fag butts. A few polystyrene chip wrappers are scattered around.

'Are you going to sit down? I'd offer you a tea, but I don't think we've got any milk. There's beer in the fridge ...'

'No, thanks,' Davie says. 'We won't be long. Just wanted to check a couple of things with you.'

'Like what?' Mandy lights another cigarette off the end of the last.

Louise sits down opposite the woman. Tries for a soothing tone. They don't know how much she's had to drink. They have to try and keep her calm. 'We've uncovered some new information ... we just wanted to double-check with you what time it was you got home on Monday morning. You know, in case you'd got confused with the times, what with everything happening. If you came back a wee bit earlier than you thought you did, you might've seen something. Maybe you didn't realise ...'

'That bastard.' She said it under her breath, and Louise wasn't sure she'd heard right at first.

'Sorry, what—'

'That bastard. Fucking Quinn. I thought I could trust him.'

Louise glances at Davie, and he pulls out the other chair and sits down. 'Trust him with what, Mandy?'

She starts sobbing. The hand holding the cigarette falls

243

towards the table and Louise reaches across and removes the cigarette, placing it in the ashtray. She squeezes Mandy's hand. 'What did you see, Mandy? Quinn told us he came round to see you... said you told him you'd come home earlier than you said ... said you'd seen someone leaving the house.'

Her sobs turn into a wail. She starts to cough. Davie pushes his chair back, goes across to the sink and finds a cup, rinses it. Returns with a cup full of water for her. She tries to take it, but her hand is shaking too much.

'Who did you see, Mandy?'

She stops crying. Gives Louise a hard stare. 'That fucking weird kid. Fuck knows what's wrong with him, but he clearly got it from his mother's side of the family.'

'Who, Mandy?'

'Pete! Pete Brotherstone!'

Davie puts a hand on Louise's arm, indicating that he's going to take this. 'Where did you see him, Mandy?'

'Walking down my path. Happy as fucking Larry – he had our Katie's beasties under his arm. I couldn't work out what was going on. Why did he have it? She'd never have given that to anyone. Not unless ...'

'Unless what?'

'Unless she was shagging them, or something. I couldn't believe it. Her and that bloody freak? He's no' right. Everyone knows that. Gets away with God knows what, all 'cause of that father of his.'

'Martin?'

'Aye. Martin.' She spits out his name like it's given her a bad taste in her mouth.

'So then what happened?'

'Well, I marched upstairs to see our Katie, didn't I? I had to find out what was happening. I mean, she wasn't to know, but still ... I couldn't understand what she was doing with *him*. I'd seen Brett hanging about with him, warned him off too. But Katie … and she had no idea who he was …'

Louise feels her heart start to beat faster.

'And who is he, Mandy? Apart from being Martin's son …'

Mandy snorts. She nods towards Davie. 'He knows. He must fucking know.'

'Know what, Mandy? You've lost me …'

'Mandy … was Katie alive when you went upstairs?'

Mandy looks away. 'I need a drink,' she says. 'OK if I get myself a drink in my own bloody house?' She stands up and wobbles towards the fridge. That's when Louise realises how drunk she really is, although she has been handling it fairly well up to now.

'Mandy,' Davie says. He stands up. Walks round to where Mandy is pouring lager into a glass; her hand is shaking and she is sloshing most of it on the worktop. 'Was Katie alive when you went into her bedroom?'

Mandy picks up the glass and downs it.

'No, of course she wasn't. I already told you. I came back home, and I … I held her wrist, but it was too late,' she says, eventually. Her voice is shaking almost as much as her hands. She won't look Louise in the eye.

'Are you sure, Mandy? Can you make sure you have a good long think about this before you answer, because this is really, really important, OK? Was Katie alive when you came back to the house?'

Mandy pours more vodka into her glass and starts to cry.

44

Polly

Polly feels sick. Pete Brotherstone. The janitor's assistant. The one that Brooke called a retard. Horrible word, but kids are cruel. She knows plenty about that. Polly has only met him briefly. He'd seemed quiet, maybe a bit strange. But was there something wrong with him? Was he dangerous? She wants to call the police, tell them about this. But first she wants to hear it from Brett.

'Tell me about Boggy then. About Pete. You said you played in the woods sometimes. Went hunting?'

'I told you. Not real hunting. He hasn't got a gun or anything. He used to hang round with a guy called Jake. They used to shoot stuff. Little things, like voles and rabbits. But one time Jake caught a badger. I've seen it. It's gross.'

'What do you mean, you've seen it?'

'They stuffed it. Well, sort of. I don't think they had the proper chemicals and things you need to do it properly. Most of the stuff they have in The Collection is just bones now. It stinks a bit, but it's cool. Maybe he can bring it in to school one day, to show you?'

Polly shudders, imagining this. And the mention of Jake scares her too. Jake was mixed up in what happened at Black Wood. He was mixed up with Jo and Claire too. Everything seems to be turning full circle.

'I'm not sure that would be a good idea,' she says. 'But tell me more about it. You said something before, about insects.'

His face lights up. 'Yes – the insects were really, really cool. Katie knew how to fix those up properly. Mr Crisp taught her, she said.' His face grows dark again. 'I miss Katie. I never thought any of this would happen. I just wanted him to be my friend. Wanted him to think I was worth hanging out with.'

'Why wouldn't he?'

'Because I'd never caught us anything good. But then I told him about Katie's damselfly, and he got really excited then. He wanted to see it. I knew Katie wouldn't let me bring the board into school, especially not when the glass was broken on the front of her display. She'd smashed it herself, by accident, trying to hang it up. Mr Crisp was going to help her fix the glass, but they never did it. So I knew there was no way she would let me bring it in to school to show Pete. Can I have a biscuit, please?'

Polly has a horrible feeling in her stomach now. A twisting, turning in her gut. 'Brett, did you ever take Pete back to your house. To show him Katie's board? To show him the damselfly?'

Brett takes a biscuit, stuffs the whole thing in his mouth. He won't look at her. Polly stares at him. Sees that his shoulders are shaking, that he's trying to make them stop.

'I'm sorry, Ms McAllister,' he says. His voice is a cracked whisper. Polly feels a shiver run right through her body. 'I told him he was only supposed to look at it. He wasn't to take it away. But she didn't see. She was fast asleep, I promise. That's all that happened.' He's crying now. There is more to this.

247

'Brett, did Pete hurt Katie? You have to tell me the truth now.'

'No, I swear he didn't. I swear on my life. I promise. He didn't. He just took the board. I let him in and we went upstairs to Katie's room. We tiptoed, but there's always that one creaky stair ... Mum was at work and Brooke wasn't in. I know she wasn't because her shoes weren't at the front door. We went in Katie's room, and I was going to ask if he could see it but she was asleep, proper asleep. So we sneaked in and Pete took the board off the wall, and I grabbed his arm and tried to say no, he couldn't take it away – I thought he only wanted to look at it ... and we sort of had a bit of a fight and he dropped it on the radiator and I think a bit of it came off and then he just grabbed it and ran out the door.'

'And what did you do?'

'I was scared that she would wake up and notice me and shout at me, but she didn't. It's like she was—'

'Why didn't she wake up, Brett?'

'I don't know! I think she had headphones in. She was lying on her front, facing the wall. She couldn't see or hear us. She was always like that when she slept. Sometimes I'd go into her room in the morning and I'd think that she was dead.'

Polly feels the hairs on the back of her neck stand up.

'And this time, Brett,' she says, quietly, '*was* she dead?'

'No!' he says. 'No.' He starts to cry. 'Not then ...'

She thinks she has misheard. The tickle on the back of her neck runs right down her spine. 'What do you mean, *not then*?'

He looks up at her, his eyes round and wet. He looks like a kicked puppy. 'I don't want to get anyone into trouble, Miss. Do I have to say?'

'Brett ... this is serious stuff. You can say it to me now, or I can phone the police and they'll come and take you down to the station. Which would you rather?'

'OK,' he says. He takes a deep breath. 'But please, don't tell them it was me who told you. Please?'

Polly nods. 'I'll do what I can to help, Brett. Just tell me, OK?'

He looks away, like he can't tell this right to her face. He doesn't want to tell her at all, but he's going to try. She watches him shaking and she wants to go round and give him a big cuddle, but she can't. She sits back. Waits for him to speak.

'I was standing on the top landing. Pete had run outside. I was half watching downstairs, to see if he might come back, and I was half watching Katie, to see if she was going to wake up and go mad at me. Nothing happened for a few minutes, so I crept into her room. I took her photo off her dressing table – it's one of those collage ones with lots of different photos stuck together. Anyway, I hung it on the hook where the insect board was meant to go. I thought then maybe she wouldn't notice the space on the wall where the bugs were meant to be. She would eventually. Obviously. But I thought I might be able to get it back from Pete before then. Something fell off and went down the back of the radiator, but I couldn't find it. I was just sneaking back out again when Katie moved a bit, one of her legs was hanging out of the bed, and her arm on the other side was tapping against the bedframe. She was awake, but she was listening to music. She hadn't heard me, or sensed me. I thought I'd got away with it ...' He pauses, looks at her as if to say, 'Am I doing OK?'

'Carry on,' Polly says.

'I managed to get out of her room without her noticing me. I was on the landing, then the front door banged open and my mum shouted "This bloody door!" – sorry for swearing – that's what she said. She was always shouting at us for leaving the door open. There's something wrong with the catch, I think.

I tried to fix it one day, but I couldn't. I didn't want to get in any trouble, so I went into the airing cupboard at the top of the stairs and pulled the door shut. Not all the way, just enough so no one would see me. I was going to wait until she'd gone in the bathroom, then I was going to go to school. I could hear her in the kitchen, banging cupboards and stuff. She was in a bad mood. It was best to stay out of her way when she was in a bad mood—'

'Was she often in a bad mood, Brett? Did she ever ... did she ever hurt you when she was angry like that?' Polly hates to ask, but knowing Mandy it's not such a big leap. She hoped she'd never taken her rage out on her children, but who really knew what went on behind closed doors?

'No. No. She just shouts. That's all she ever does. I don't think she likes her job very much. I think she wants a boyfriend too. She's always moaning about not having anyone round to help her. Anyway, she came thumping up the stairs. She was shouting on Katie, asking her where her washing was. She always washes the bed covers on a Monday morning and we all have to strip our beds. Katie was still in her bed. I couldn't see from the airing cupboard if she'd surfaced yet. Mum stormed past me and when she did she kicked the door of the airing cupboard so that it shut tight. It nearly hit me in the face, but I didn't cry out. It was dark in there. So dark. I wanted to come out, but I was more scared now.'

He stops talking and Polly can see tears running down his face.

'I don't want to remember any more, Miss,' he says. He wipes angrily at his cheek with his sleeve.

'You're doing well, Brett. Nearly done ... Just one last bit, OK? Did your mum go into Katie's room? Was she still shouting? I know you couldn't see anything now that the door was shut, but what did you hear?'

'Mum was yelling. She was shouting, "Where's your bloody

washing, you lazy cow?" and "What the fuck was that boy doing in this house?"'

'Boy? Did she mean Pete?'

Brett nods. 'Yes. Mum was really angry about Pete. I don't know why, because I didn't even think she knew who he was.'

45

Louise

Louise takes a deep breath. 'Davie, can we have a quick chat outside for a minute?' She looks across at Mandy, who is now sobbing gently. Trying to light yet another cigarette.

Davie gives her a tiny shake of his head. 'Mandy … Mandy, love? Can you tell us what happened? We're a bit confused. You told us before that when you got back Katie was already dead. That you held her wrist to feel for a pulse, but there was nothing there. Then you called the doctor. Is that not what happened?'

Mandy starts to cough, takes a sip of the water that Davie has left for her in the mug. 'No,' she croaks. 'No, am I in trouble?'

Louise's mind starts to whirr. They weren't expecting this. They'd eliminated Lucas, they'd ruled out any involvement from Neil – he might not have behaved like the best boyfriend, but he hadn't hurt her. Not like this. They already had Pete in custody. He'd all but confessed to pushing Hayley into the river, but he hadn't told them why yet. Did Mandy have the final piece of the puzzle? Had Pete left Katie for dead and she'd died while her mother was there? Maybe the pulse was very weak. It didn't make sense.

'Mandy … what do you mean, she was still alive?' Davie says. 'Did she have a pulse? Did you try to save her, but you couldn't? You don't need to feel bad about that. If you tried, and there was nothing you could do … sometimes it happens like that. Was it just that she was still warm, maybe? That she didn't seem dead to you. I don't know if you've seen a dead body before, Mandy, but it's not always like it looks on the TV.'

Mandy laughs. A single, hoarse bark. A horrible sound, somewhere from the back of her throat. 'No, Sergeant Gray. It wasn't like that at all.'

Davie turns to Louise and gives her a look. She can't tell what he's thinking, but she's scared. She's scared of what Mandy is going to say next.

'Mandy … Mandy!' He bangs his fist on the table. The woman seems to have gone into a trance. She's smiling, but it's a strange smile. Her eyes are unfocused.

'I saw that laddie leaving the house,' she says. She closes her eyes for a moment. When she opens them again, they seem clearer. Like she's woken up. 'I went upstairs. Katie was still in bed. She had her headphones stuck in her ears. One of her bare legs was hanging out the side. She was tapping her foot on the floor. She was wearing bright blue nail varnish. It's funny the things that stick out in your mind, isn't it?' She pauses to sip the drink. 'Maybe a coffee would be good. No milk, mind. Would you …?' She offers her mug to Louise, and Louise stands up, walks around the table and checks that there's water in the kettle before switching it on. 'I shouted at her because I knew she couldn't hear me with those things stuck in her ears. She always played her music too loud.'

Louise busies herself making coffee, looking for a clean spoon, rinsing mugs for her and Davie. She can almost sense what is coming, but she doesn't want to hear it. Doesn't want to be looking at Mandy's ruined face when she finally says it.

'I says to her: Katie, what the fuck was that lad doing in here? I saw him with your board. What the hell did you give it to him for?'

'You mean the board with the insects?' Davie says.

'Aye. That thing. I couldn't work it out. Anyway, I must've given her a fright, because she flips up in the bed like it's a broken sun lounger. The duvet falls off and I see that she's half naked. No jammies or nightie, just a wee bra top thing. One of the shoulder straps is hanging off ...'

'And this was unusual? How do you know that she didn't wear this in bed every night?'

Mandy sighs. 'Because she's always freezing, that one. Every Christmas and birthday, she asks for the same thing. Cotton jammies. And it was a cold night. What would she be half naked for, unless she'd been up to something?'

'You know that Neil was round on Sunday afternoon. Maybe ...'

'I know what you're saying, officer. Davie. But it just struck me as odd. Maybe I was reading too much into it. Anyway ...' She pauses, pulls a rumpled tissue from her sleeve and blows her nose. 'I'd had a bad night at work. Two of the machines were broken, so we ended up doing half the stuff manually.'

'You work in the laundry, over at the business park, is that right?'

'Barrett's. Aye. Anyway ... I said, what was that laddie doing in your room? And she looks at me like I'm mad. What laddie? What're you talking about? He took your board, I said. She jumps out of bed then. Get the fuck out of my room, Mum, she said. This is how she talks to me. Her own mother! I said, I don't want you hanging around with that boy, he's no right. He's dangerous. And Katie goes: what fucking boy? And I shout, Pete. Dopey Pete. I hate to think what he's been doing

254

to you in here, you make me sick! She looked confused for a minute. Then she looks at the wall where the board's meant to be and she starts shouting at me: what have you done with it? What fucking half-cocked story are you trying to spin at me now, you mad bitch ...' She stops talking. Looks down at the table. Louise can see her shoulders shaking.

'And then what happened?' Louise says, quietly.

'Well, I lost it,' Mandy says. 'I just lost it. I was exhausted. I was ... I was worried what might've happened if she'd ... I slapped her across the face. And the little bitch pushed me! I fell back, knocked my elbow on the door. It bloody hurt. Funny bone, you know? But it wasn't bloody funny. And then she laughed. And she turned away, and when she turned she went: Fuck off, Mum. And that was it. That was it.'

'What was it? Why were you so worried about her being with Pete, Mandy? What was it to you if they were friends?'

Mandy snorted. 'Friends? They weren't bloody friends ... I spent my life trying to make sure they never had any reason to be friends. I didn't want to be associated with that ... that bastard.'

Louise is confused. 'Pete? Are we still talking about Pete?'

Mandy shakes her head. 'No.' She nods at Davie again. 'He knows.' She turns to him. 'You KNOW, don't you?'

A shadow passes across Davie's face. He runs a hand over his chin, and she hears the faint scratch of stubble. 'Martin,' he says quietly. 'Martin Brotherstone is Katie's dad. No wonder you never told anyone—'

'No shit, Sherlock,' Mandy mutters.

Louise says, 'So I take it Katie didn't know any of this. That Pete was her half-brother?'

'Give the girl a coconut!' Mandy says.

'What did you do, Mandy?' Davie says. His voice is low, solemn. Louise thinks she knows now. She thinks Davie does too. They need Mandy to say it.

255

Mandy lights another cigarette. She sits there, that strange smile on her face again. 'You two work it out, if you're so fuckin' clever.' Her words are harsh, but the bravado is slipping.

'Quinn worked it out, didn't he?' Davie says. 'You told him something ...'

'I told him fuck all. I was drunk. I was upset about Katie—'

'Mandy, don't start to backtrack now. It'll be easier if you just tell us what happened. We don't want to make assumptions. Get the wrong end of the stick ... if it was an accident ...'

Mandy starts to cry. Huge, racking sobs. She rocks in her chair. 'It WAS an accident,' she says, her voice thick with phlegm. 'It was. I never meant to kill her, I swear. She just made me so angry. I was so tired ... I pushed her back on the bed and I was screaming at her – you filthy little cow – and she was pushing at me and kicking and trying to slap me off, so I sat on top of her, and I pinned her down ... and when she was wriggling around, I grabbed the pillow from the top of the bed and I put it on her face ... and I ... I just lay on her. And I could hear her screaming at me, to get off, get off, and it was all muffled through the pillow ... and I tried to stop. I tried. But I just froze. I froze. It's that thing, you know ... the red mist? I used to get it a lot when I was young, when I was Brooke's age. I was a proper nasty wee bully at school. I was angry, so angry.'

Davie leans across the table and lays a hand on Mandy's hand. He mouths silently to Louise: 'Call it in'. Says to Mandy: 'And then?'

Mandy sighs. She looks up at them both and her face seems to have collapsed in on itself. 'She stopped wriggling, eventually. I thought she'd given up. So I climbed off, and I lifted the pillow off her face ... I knew – I knew right then. I didn't need to pick up her wrist to check for a pulse. She was gone.'

Louise takes her phone out of her pocket and walks through to the hall to call Malkie. As she closes the door, she hears Davie's voice, strong, unwavering ... 'Mandy Taylor, I am arresting you on suspicion of the unlawful killing of your daughter, Katie Taylor. You do not have to say anything, but anything you do say may be used against you in a court of law ...'

Louise opens the front door and walks outside into the freezing air, trying to breathe. Trying to hold back the tears. That poor fucked-up family.

That poor, poor girl.

46

Polly

Polly can't face going home. She's heard too many awful things today. The thought of being in that house on her own is too much to bear. She's glad that the pub doesn't do food tonight, or else he wouldn't be at home. She's hardly seen him since she got back, still hasn't told him the news. But it's not the right time. Especially not now, after what she's just found out. Part of her hopes it's not true, but the main part of her knows that it is.

She knocks on the door, waits. Clouds of breath float in the air in front of her. The weather has been bleak all week, but at least the snow and the ice are mostly gone now. She's always terrified that she's going to slip and fall. She's never fallen on ice in her life, as far as she can remember, but her safety mechanisms have gone into overdrive now that it's not just her own body she has to worry about. She's about to knock again when the door is pulled open.

'Hello you,' Quinn says. 'Sorry, I was having a kip. I wasn't expecting you.' His eyes are bloodshot, the lines on his face more prominent than usual. She smells a hint of beer on his breath and feels a momentary rise of panic. He disappears inside and she follows him. From the other side of the closed kitchen door, she can hear scratching and a sorry sounding whine. Polly has only met Drummer, the springiest springer spaniel, a handful of times – but she's never known him to be shut in the kitchen. He's normally bouncing around the house, or straining to be let off his lead in the park, tongue hanging out with breathless excitement.

'Ignore him,' he says. 'He's been doing my head in today, so I've shut him in there for a bit.'

'Not like you. Everything OK?'

'Hardly—'

'Sorry, stupid thing to say. Of course it isn't. I've had a hell of a day myself …'

'Come here,' he says.

He pulls her close and hugs her hard. She lets herself be crushed in his embrace for a moment. She leaches his warmth. Then she pulls away.

'Beer?' she says, eyes questioning.

'Just one. Honest. Listen – I've been down at the police station …I, ugh. This is hard. I spoke to Mandy last night. She was a mess. A total mess. She said some stuff … I don't even want to think about it being true, but it kind of made sense, you know. I had to go to the police – well, actually, I told Neil first, and he made me go. I felt like shit, but it was the right thing to do. She—'

'I know what she did.' Polly sits down on the sofa. She unzips her boots and lets them fall off her feet. 'I've just been speaking to Brett. He … he heard it all.'

'Heard it?' Quinn sits down beside her, takes one of her hands and squeezes it.

'He was hiding in the airing cupboard. He heard Mandy and Katie fighting, then he heard Mandy run down the stairs and back outside. He waited for a bit before he came out – he looked in on Katie and he knew—'

'Fucksake. That poor kid!'

'He left after that. Went and found Brooke and said he wanted to skive off for the morning. He didn't tell her why and she didn't ask. The two of them went up town on the bus and mooched about in the Waverley Market until lunchtime. Both of them ignoring the calls from friends, and from Mandy – assuming they were going to get into trouble for bunking off ... they only came back because one of their friends texted them saying that something had happened to Katie.'

'And Brett knew what had happened, and he kept it all in? He must've been terrified ...'

'I think he just blocked it out, somehow. He was focusing on other things – he knew he needed to get the insect board back from Pete – he still hasn't, incidentally, but that doesn't really matter now; he had that at the forefront of his mind, and it helped him to *forget* about Katie – to push it away. But eventually it had to come out. It didn't take that long, really. I've seen things like this happen before. Sometimes it can take months, even years for a child to pull back that memory and deal with it.'

Quinn rubs a hand across his short hair. 'I'm sure he was terrified of Mandy, too. If he worked out what had happened – even if he didn't see it – he'd be scared of her finding out that he knew. Christ, no wonder Mandy was such a mess. I mean, I always knew she had this awful temper, but I never thought ... She did things to me, you know.'

'Me too,' Polly whispers. 'I can still remember that day at the swings.'

'I remember seeing you after it. You were bright red. Beetroot. And trying so hard not to cry. Mandy was sneering. She never did tell me what happened ...'

Polly takes a breath, blows it out hard. 'I was on my own, just swinging. I was miles away – off somewhere in a little daydream in my head. Probably something to do with a boy,

260

but I can't remember who. Funny how little things disappear from your memory like that, isn't it? Anyway, I felt an arm around my neck. The swing juddered to a stop. I tried to turn round, but I was trapped. Two arms. Then the swing twisted round and I was face to face with her. She laughed in my face. I thought she was going to spit on me, but she didn't. She was popping gum in her mouth. I can still smell it. Strawberry Hubba Bubba. Then I was facing away from her again. Then I was looking at her again. She kept twisting. She laughed more when I begged her to stop. I felt the chains crushing my chest first, then my throat. I begged and begged. *Please stop it, Mandy, I'll give you anything you want.* It just made her laugh more.' She feels Quinn squeezing her hand again. 'Then I couldn't beg. I started to cough. I felt like my whole head was on fire. And still she kept twisting ...' Polly feels a tear run down her cheek. 'I really thought I was going to die.'

Quinn is silent. His jaw is set and she can tell he is angry.

'I asked her what happened. She said you fell off the swing ...'

Polly makes a hmph sound and shakes her head. 'There was a flash of something in her eyes, just before she let go. It wasn't fear. It was ... it was excitement. She let go and stepped away. The swing spun round fast until it was untwisted and I fell off into a heap underneath. I was gasping, choking. Holding at my throat ... and you know what I said? I said "thank you" – like I was thanking her for not making it any worse, or something. I don't know. She laughed then, and kicked me in the stomach. Then she bent down and said, "If you tell anyone about this, I'll kick your head in, you stupid stuck-up bitch" – and then she walked away. I suppose that's when you turned up.'

'Aye. Fucksake. I'm so sorry, Polly. I had no idea ... If I'd known she was that bad – that *evil* – I don't think I'd have stayed with her. Christ, I'm as much of a mug as you – I was with her while she went and had three bairns to two different

261

dads. Well, seeing her on and off. Some stretches were longer than others. I don't think she actually cheated on me when we were properly together, but who knows.'

'I suppose she'll get the help she needs now, at least.'

'Help? I hope she gets battered to a pulp in prison. They don't tend to like people who kill their kids in there. I've seen it with my own eyes.'

Polly curls her feet up onto his lap and leans into the arm of the couch. 'I don't want to talk about any more violence, Quinn. There's been far too much of that lately. Can you do me a favour?'

'Anything ...'

'Go and get Drummer. I could do with some pet therapy right now.'

'You'll regret that when he starts licking your face and trying to sniff your fanny ...' He lifts her feet onto the couch and disappears through to the kitchen.

Polly closes her eyes, and smiles.

47

Louise

'You can't do this, you know. You can't question him on his own like that. He's not ... Pete's not like other boys. You lot know that. Isn't he supposed to have an appropriate adult or something? Why didn't anyone phone me? How come I had to hear about this from some sneering little bastard who decided to phone and tell me?'

'What sneering little bastard was this, Mr Brotherstone? I hope you're not implying that one of our officers—'

'No. That's what I just said, isn't it? Where's Gray? He knows Pete. He knows what I mean.' He scratches at his arm, distractedly. The raised voices of earlier have faded away. He's just a dad now, looking out for his son. Louise would feel sorry for Martin, if she hadn't heard all about him. Heard what he was like. He wasn't the best father, she knew that for a fact.

'Detective Sergeant Gray is busy right now.'

'Oh, Detective, is it? When did that happen? Going up in the world, is he? Bored of hanging about on the streets trying to pick up innocent people and accuse them of things they haven't done, is he? Off to the town, detecting things now, is he?'

Louise holds in a sigh. He really is an odious man.

'No, he's here. He's just finishing up in the other room. Look, why don't you sit down? I'll bring you a cup of tea. Pete is fine, I can assure you. He has Rob Bates looking after him. I've heard he's very good ...' She'd asked PC Singh just after she'd come out of the interview room. He'd filled her in, briefly. Rob was the partner of Craig McNeill. A friend of Jo Barker. Sort of. He'd managed to get her a very lenient sentence, despite the enormity of her crimes. Mitigating circumstances. She ended up with five years. She'd already served nine months. Louise gave it another two before she was out on parole. She wondered why Rob hadn't been involved with Marie Bloomfield's case, seeing that Davie knew him. But maybe Marie hadn't wanted that. Maybe Marie hadn't wanted a lenient sentence. She wanted to ask Davie about that, but it was still too raw. Her sentence had only been a couple of months ago. Complicated, what with her brother and all.

'Who was it that called you, Mr Brotherstone? Did you want to make a complaint?'

He waves her away. 'A tea would be nice. Thank you. I'm sorry. It's just that Pete ... well, he's been through a lot.'

Louise stares at him. 'You know why he's here? What he's confessed to?'

Brotherstone scratches at his arm again. The skin is red, inflamed. Eczema or psoriasis. Louise doesn't really understand the difference, but she knows both can flare up when someone is stressed. Brotherstone has good reason to be stressed.

'He didn't do it, you have to believe me ... Look, people don't really get Pete. Not like I do. He's always been different. We had so many tests done when he was a kid, but they were all inconclusive. He had all these odd little quirks: behavioural issues, they called them. I know some people call him slow, or they think he's autistic, but it's not that. If it was that, I'd know how to deal with things. Well, I could try at least. With Pete – it's always so difficult. I'm never really sure what he's thinking, what he's feeling. He takes some things so literally. And he can be quick to judge. He gets it wrong, though. A lot. His mind doesn't reason things out properly. He thinks before he acts, then his mind seems to shut down. He's done some stupid things, I know that, but he's not bad. Not really.' He pauses. Sighs. 'Maybe they'd know what was wrong with him now, if we took him back in. If I did, I mean. My wife's dead now. I don't know if you know that, Detective ...'

'Jennings. DC Jennings. Call me Louise, please.' She takes him by the elbow and guides him to the bank of chairs at the other end of the reception hall, away from the prying eyes and ears. She'd take him into another room, but there isn't one free right now, and she hardly thinks he'd like to chat to her in a cell. Besides, that'd be taken too, in a minute. Once Pete was processed and sent through there. She sighs. Nothing is ever cut and dried, is it? She'd been set to condemn Pete, and his father, but after hearing what he's said about his son, she's not so sure any more. She realises that she feels sorry for him. For both of them. What a mess. 'He's confessed to pushing Hayley Marsh into the river, Mr Brotherstone. The girl is dead. Whether it was an accident or not is yet to be determined. But I can assure you, we're looking after him. He's safe here.'

Brotherstone looks at her, confusion in his eyes. 'Hayley Marsh? But I thought ... the Taylor girl ... he wasn't—'

'No. No. We have someone else in custody for that, Mr Brotherstone. We're still trying to get to the bottom of it all.'

Brotherstone leans forwards, drops his head into his hands. She lays a hand on his back, not sure if she should or not, but the man is distressed. Whatever he's like as a father. Whatever his son has done.

'Please,' he says, 'I can't lose another child.'

Louise closes her eyes. It's true, then. About Katie.

'I'm so sorry for your loss,' she says. It sounds inadequate. It sounds like nothing. But right now, it's all she has.

THURSDAY

48

Neil

He buys a packet of chocolate digestives, a couple of newspapers and a bottle of Coke from the small shop inside the entrance of the hospital. He was going with the usual grapes and flowers but, apart from them being useless and a bit clichéd, the shop didn't sell either. He did ask about them, out of interest. Grapes were finished, apparently. And flowers not allowed on the wards. Besides, it might look a bit weird, him bringing a man flowers. He didn't really know how these things worked.

He checks the ward details at the reception desk and is told that Mr Crisp is now out of ICU and recovering in a side-room off the general admissions ward, on the second floor, right at the back. Follow the lines, she'd said. Painted lines on the floor. Red, yellow, green, blue. He followed blue.

He hesitates outside the door, butterflies in his stomach now, thinking about it all. Wondering if he's making a mistake. He's about to turn round, dump the biscuits on the vacant nurses' station that he passed on the way in. He reckoned they'd be pleased to come back from whatever it was they were doing – cleaning up sick, emptying bedpans, taking temperatures – to find a packet of biscuits waiting for them.

He can see the man through the slice of criss-crossed glass that's built into the door. Why is it criss-crossed? Another of life's mysteries. He's about to leave when the man looks up, suddenly. Catches his eye. He smiles.

Neil takes a deep breath, inhaling that sickly sweet stench of disinfectant, cabbage and shit, and pushes the door open. No going back now.

'Hello, Sir,' he says. 'I brought you these.' He offers his wares but doesn't see anywhere to put them. The pedestal next to the bed houses a water jug, a plastic tumbler. A glasses case. The swing-out table which is halfway across the bed still holds a tray with today's lunch offering. Red crusting around a soup bowl; yellow crusting and crumbs on another suggest apple crumble and custard. His stomach roils. He'd forgotten about breakfast today.

'Well, hello,' the teacher says. 'What a nice surprise. And please, it's Lucas today, OK? Would you mind taking that tray off? Just lay it down near the door. Then I can see what goodies you've brought me.' He sounds surprisingly chipper, despite half of his face being purple and yellow, his eye swollen half-shut. His voice is a bit croaky, though, and he's struggling to sit up straighter, although he is trying his best. 'Sorry,' he says again. Neil can't work out what it is he thinks he needs to apologise for. 'Would you mind?' He gestures towards a small plastic control box, which is attached to the bed by a white cable. 'Don't know how it ended up down there.'

Neil passes him the control, and Lucas clicks a couple of buttons until he has whirred himself into place, sitting upright. His sheet drops down his chest and Neil can see that he is heavily bandaged.

'Cracked ribs,' Lucas says. 'Bugger to heal. The rest is just bruising. It'll go away.'

Neil notices, seeing him in this state, just how young the man is. He's not that much older than himself. Neil is nearly eighteen. This man is, what, twenty-five? He was Katie's friend. Neil understands this now. She didn't see him as a teacher, although perhaps she should've done.

'Take a pew,' Lucas says. He starts trying to open the biscuits, but he is struggling. His hands shake.

Neil sits down, takes the biscuits and opens them.

The other man smiles gratefully. A tear pops into the corner of his eye. 'I was wondering if you were going to come in. I haven't had many visitors, to be honest. I think people are ... I don't know. Maybe a bit embarrassed?'

'Ashamed, more like,' Neil mutters. 'I'm so sorry, Mr Crisp. Lucas.'

Lucas shoots him a look. 'You didn't ... you weren't?'

Neil closes his eyes, lets out a long, slow sigh. 'I was there. I'm not going to deny it. I got caught up in the whole ...frenzy. Brooke—'

'Ah yes. Brooke.'

'I stood outside your house. I didn't do anything to stop it.'

Lucas laughs and it turns into a coughing fit. He holds a hand up to Neil to signal that he's OK. That it will pass.

Neil feels like the lowest of the low. Like a slug. Or something even worse than a slug, if there is such a thing on the earth that is more useless and disgusting than a slug. He is repulsed and revolted by himself. He wants to make things better. He's not sure if this will help, but it's a start.

'What could you have done, Neil? You'd have ended up getting a kicking yourself. What would be the point in that? Besides, it's my own stupid fault. I panicked, running off home from school on Monday. I should've gone straight to the police, told them I was scared. Told them I'd been stupid. I let Katie get too close, I know that now.'

Neil shakes his head. 'No. You were her friend. There's nothing wrong with that.'

Lucas sighs. 'I was her teacher. I should have kept the lines drawn more clearly. But she was such a great girl, you know? I wanted so much for her. I wanted her to do well. I was so excited when she got the place at King's.' He pauses, and Neil sees a shadow fall across his face. His smile fades. 'But I was scared too. Brooke was causing trouble. I should've gone to see Jon earlier ...'

'Brooke lives to cause trouble, Lucas. I know that better than most. I got sucked in by her too. I'm not proud of myself. Anyway, I'm not going to dwell on things. I just wanted to come and see you. See if there was anything you needed.'

'I'm fine. Really. I'll be home in a few days. Take a bit of time off work. I have a long queue of journalists who want to come and interview me – ask me how it felt to be targeted by vigilantes. Plus, the police aren't going to leave me alone. They want me to name names.'

'Are you going to?'

He chuckles. 'What am I? Mad?'

Neil smiles. He takes a couple of biscuits out of the packet, hands one to Lucas. Eats the other in two bites.

'It's good that you came in today, actually,' Lucas says. 'I wanted to give you something.'

'Me? What?'

'It's in my wallet, inside my jeans. On the top shelf of that little pedestal cupboard thing. Can you take it out for me, please?'

Neil opens the cupboard and takes out the jeans. He finds the wallet in the back pocket. Hands it to Lucas.

'No, open it. Inside. It's in the back part, there's a little popper button thing. Do you see?'

Neil fumbles with the wallet. Manages to open the popper. He pulls out a piece of folded cardboard. He hears her voice in his head: *Just think, baby! Me and you... we can get a nice place with this, can't we? Even in London ... Five grand, baby! I can't wait, I can't bloody wait! I love you so much, Neil. We're going*

272

to have a great fucking life, and we can forget this place, forget all of it …

A tear rolls down his cheek, splashes onto his hand. 'Katie's scratch card! But, how did …?'

'She called me on Sunday. Asked me if I would look after it for her. That's why I was at her house that day. I wasn't keen. That's a lot of money. I didn't want to be responsible for it. But I realised she needed it to be kept somewhere safe, until she worked out what she was going to do. I told the police it was in a kitchen drawer. They think it burned in that pathetic attempt at a fire—'

'And?' He doesn't even want to ask, but somehow he does. 'What are you going to do with it now? No one else knows about it, you know. I didn't tell anyone. I promised Katie. It was the one thing I promised and I swear I didn't let her down.'

'You had a ritual, right? She told me,' Lucas says. 'You took it in turns to buy them. You met in the park. You scratched them together, and you talked about your plans for when you became millionaires …'

We can travel for a year, then buy houses in London and New York and … Cambodia? Why the fuck would you want a house in Cambodia? It'd be hot, it'd be fun … they have great food there! Can I get a Ferrari? Ha ha, no way … too expensive. We need to live on this forever, you idiot. I think we should blow it, Kates, no one lives forever, do they? Me and you do. Always. In our hearts. You soppy cow … I love you, Neil. I love you too, Kates …forever.

'It's yours now, Neil. Take it. Go to London. Live the life you were supposed to. I can't imagine that Katie would want anything else, can you?'

He closes his eyes, lets the tears run down his face. Realises that's he's still gripping the scratch card, and that Lucas's hand is resting gently on his.

49

Louise

Louise lets Davie pour tea into her cup. It's been an eventful week. There is still a stack of paperwork to be done, but for now they are taking a break.

'It's quite nice, this place,' she says, glancing around at the white stucco walls, the red leather booth seats. 'Has it been here long?'

'Landucci's has been here since the dawn of time. Well, maybe since the Fifties. Always been my favourite café in the town,' Davie says. 'Cake?'

He's bought a huge slab of Victoria sponge. It looks far too big to be a single slice, but, judging by the grin on the face of the little old lady behind the counter, Davie might be in receipt of some special treatment.

'So,' she says, 'if you'd asked me a year ago, I'd have said that Banktoun was one of those quiet, sleepy towns where nothing ever happens. Where everyone is trapped by their own dull, boring lives. I got that a bit wrong, eh?'

He takes a huge bite of cake and seems to swallow it whole. 'Not sure boring is the right word. It's always been a good place to live, you know. A solid community. Peaceful. That's not to say that nothing ever happens.'

'Oh, come on. Before that murder at Black Wood last summer, and then that awful thing at Willow Walk, what actually happened here, Davie? Anything? Ever?'

He smiles. 'I've always liked it here.' He looks into his teacup. 'But things have changed. It's like a darkness has fallen on the town. I don't know why ... something triggered it, and then it's taken hold. People are more wary now. Wondering what other secrets are about to be unearthed.'

'That thing with Martin Brotherstone. Mandy. She was only a kid when she got pregnant with Katie, wasn't she? Do you think ...'

'Do I think he raped her? I hope not. I don't think so, if I'm honest. Mandy was a firecracker when she was young. I think she knew what she was doing. Although Martin should've known better. Twenty years isn't much if you're older, but a fifteen-year-old with a thirty-six-year-old man? There aren't many who'd be OK about that. It explains a few things, though, to be fair. Why Mandy was never completely desperate for cash over the years. She always worked, but she never seemed to struggle, if that makes sense.'

'And Quinn? Where does he fit in?'

'He and Mandy got together when she was eighteen or nineteen. He was with her a long time. Helped bring those kids up. Until the drugs took hold and she threw him out. I'd never have put him and Polly McAllister together though, not in a million years. Just shows you, eh? You can never tell who might end up with who ...'

He winks at her, and she feels a fluttering in her stomach. *Jesus, Lou – this is your chance. Say something, will you?*

'Er, Davie?'

He slurps tea. Picks up his Blackberry and scrolls through his messages. He's not looking at her.

275

'I was wondering if you might like to come out with me sometime? In Edinburgh, maybe? Away from here … just for a drink or something?'

His silence unnerves her, and she starts to regret asking.

'Davie?'

'Sorry … I was miles away. I just got an email from one of my old mates at the Police Training College. They've asked me if I want a job. To be honest, it's something I've been thinking about for a while. When the station was on the verge of shutting down, it was early retirement, transfer to CID or do something completely different – like this. I sent an email months ago, but there was nothing going … That's him just saying there's a training post available now. I might be able to do something on the physical side too, self-defence …' His voice trails off. He has finally noticed her expression. 'Sorry, Lou. What did you ask me?'

She hesitates. Thinks about whether she wants to say it again or not. *This is your chance to back out, Lou-Lou. Forget you said it, forget him. He's going to move away anyway, if he takes this job. You don't need this. Don't set yourself up for heartache, 'cause that's what you always seem to do, isn't it?*

He leans across the table and puts a hand under her chin. 'Lou? Ask me again. Please.'

She blows out a long sigh, feels a smirk pulling on the side of her mouth. He's playing with her.

'Do you want to go out for a drink with me, Davie?'

Her heart thumps. It's going to be OK. That heavy feeling she'd had before, that feeling of fear … dread. It's gone now. Her smirk turns into a wide grin. She can't stop it. Feels like a kid at Christmas.

He takes his hand away from her chin. He's still looking into her eyes. He picks up her hand, kisses it. His lips are soft, so soft. She holds her breath.

'That'd be lovely, Lou. I think I'd like that very much.'

50

Polly

'Well, well, well. You're probably the last person I imagined seeing on my doorstep today. Or any day, in fact. How did you find me?'

'It wasn't exactly hard, Claire. You've only moved next door.' Polly smiles at her old friend. 'So, can I come in?'

Claire wheels herself closer to the open door, looks up and down the street. 'Are you leaving him outside? I thought he was housetrained these days ...' She nods at Quinn, who is sitting on the low wall at the end of the garden.

'What're you doing?'

'Thought you two needed a wee while to yourselves.'

'You'll freeze to death.'

He has already taken a packet of tobacco from his coat pocket. He winks at her.

'You'd better come in then,' Claire says. She spins the chair around and disappears back inside. Polly follows.

'I like what you've done with the place,' she says, taking in the low units, the various handrails that are dotted around the place.

'Fuck off,' Claire says. 'I see you haven't changed much, eh?'

'I was kidding. It's great. I mean—'

'I know what you mean. Tea?' she calls through from the kitchen. Polly takes her time, taking in the collections of framed photographs on the walls.

'Did you take these?'

'Yep. How do you take it?'

'Milk and one,' she says. The photographs are stunning. Eerie. Most of them are in black and white, grouped into various collections: animals, birds, buildings, gravestones. Woodland. Polly shudders. The town is surrounded by woodland. So many opportunities for photographs. She is surprised, though. Not just about the logistics – it must be difficult for Claire to get in and out of the woods, unless someone takes her there – but more that she is happy to have photographs of the woods. Of the burn. Even the culvert, and the pipe crossing into the dark part of the woods, the part to which Polly vowed she'd never return, after what happened to Claire and Jo in there. And she hasn't returned, not once. She is reaching out, her hand on the edge of the frame of a beautiful shot of the water running over the weir, just past Digby's Deathhole. *Hayley. Poor Hayley.*

Claire appears at her side, hands her a mug. 'You like them?'

'Jesus, Claire. These are brilliant. Really brilliant. I hope you, I don't know, have you entered them in competitions or anything? I mean, they are so good ...' She lets her sentence trail off. Claire is holding a square hardback book. She offers it to Polly.

Beautiful Banktoun. Claire Millar.

'I sent a couple of photos into one of the big papers a few years back. Ended up commissioning me to do this book. Didn't pay much, but it was a nice experience. It's always cool when I go into a bookshop and see it there in the local section. They've asked me to do another. People this time. I'm not so sure, though.' She turns and disappears down the hallway.

Polly follows her into the living room. Out the back window, the garden is protected by a high fence. Exactly the same as her parents' fence in the house next door. The same as this whole street. A thousand memories rush into her head. Playing in the garden. Playing in the burn. Having fun, until she ruined it all for herself, for everyone. Being a nasty little bitch. What had she been thinking, acting like that? She's ashamed, thinking about it. She has been for a long time.

'I'm sorry, Claire,' she blurts. Her voice sounds thick. The tears are ready to break free, the dam about to burst.

Claire laughs. 'What for, Polly? It wasn't *you* who pushed me in that bloody burn.'

'No. I know. I wasn't even there, was I? But ... but if I hadn't been such a bitch to Jo, she wouldn't have made you leave like that. She practically dragged you out of the house. I can still picture it.'

Claire sighs. 'I felt bad too. We were so mean to her. But I shouldn't have let her take me down to the woods. That was a stupid thing to do. And what happened ... well, it happened. No point thinking about it now, is there?'

'I admire you, you know. How you've got past all that ... how you haven't let it affect you—'

'Oh, I wouldn't go that far, Polly. But, you know. It's life. You cope. Sometimes it's not even that shit! I mean, look at you, you look like you've found a penny and lost a pound. What's wrong?'

Polly gives her a small smile. 'You're right. I've no reason to be miserable, not really. I've been so scared to come back to this place, and then when I did, well ... It's been a bit of a challenging week, that's all. An awful week, actually. You must've heard everything that's gone on.'

'Of course I have. I'm not trying to be insensitive to that. Those poor girls. Their families. That poor teacher! None of it has really sunk in yet, to be honest. But I'm asking about

279

you ... and *him*, outside ... You could've brought him in, you know. '

Polly places a hand on her belly. 'He's my new beginning, Claire.'

Claire holds up her mug, chinks it against Polly's. 'I'll drink to that. So ... does he know?' She nods towards Polly's stomach.

Polly walks back to the front door and lifts the net that covers the small pane of glass. He's still sitting there, looking quite content. He's rolling a cigarette. He lifts his head and spots her peering at him through the window. He smirks. Blows her a kiss.

'Not yet,' she says. 'But I think he might be just about to find out.'

EPILOGUE

Friday, 20 January

Davie stops to take his gloves out of his pockets next to the Tron Kirk and Louise takes the opportunity to check her phone. They're more than halfway up the High Street; what the tourists call the Royal Mile. There are plenty of people about – the last of the shoppers heading into the pubs to reward themselves and soak up the atmosphere. The early evening revellers crawling out of their holes ready to start their next night out. There is a nice buzz about Edinburgh tonight, despite the cold weather and the inky skies. It's taken him a long time, but Davie is beginning to wonder if he might be outgrowing Banktoun at long last.

'I don't know the last time I had a night up town, just strolling about.'

Louise drops her phone back into her bag. 'Yeah, well, maybe it's about time you started thinking about yourself for a change. It's not like you're getting any younger.'

'Oi you. You're one to talk after your shock confession the other day ...'

'It was hardly a confession. I never pretended to be younger than I am. I'm not ashamed of my age. It's not my fault you

281

assumed my youthful good looks meant I was only thirty-one. I'm flattered. I can assure you, though, the paintwork might be in good nick, but there's still a forty-three-year-old engine purring away inside.'

'Purring, eh? I like that. Maybe you should purr more often.'

She spins him round to face her and looks up into his eyes. She kisses him, hard, and he doesn't hesitate. He holds her tight, and they stand there under the monument, snogging like teenagers. She tastes of spearmint, with an underlying hint of Earl Grey tea.

'Oi, yous old bastards, get a room, eh?'

Laughter.

They pull apart, catching sight of the small rabble of teens that are jostling their way up the street, shoving each other, laughing. Being young.

'Maybe you could—'

'Let's get chips,' Davie says, cutting her off. He grins. Touches her cheek. A squally blast of wind lifts her hair, whipping it around her face. She puts her hands to her face, pulls hair away from her mouth. Very carefully, he lifts a few remaining strands and tucks them behind her ear. He knows what she's going to say. She's going to invite him back to hers, and he's more than happy with that idea. But just for a wee while longer he wants to enjoy the courtship.

He wants to ask her if she knows the legend of the wee boy's ghost trapped under the old church, but decides it's maybe not a story for now. Too morbid. With everything that's happened recently.

They walk arm in arm up the street. They'll get a bag of chips, then maybe a quick pint in Deacon Brodie's, then he'll let her seduce him. Any way she likes.

He steers her by the arm into the Clamshell. Best chippy in town. It used to be anyway. Back in the day. Davie's pleased to see it's still open and busy and not been struck down by the curse of high rents or the influx of the health police. The Old Town seems to have more juice bars and salad places now than pubs and chippies.

'What you having?'

She's staring up at the menu board, which has everything on it from fish to sausages to chicken to pies, plus a few things he's never heard of. It's all fried. Even the pizzas. On the other side, there's a list of burgers and oven-baked pizzas. This is a new thing. Chippies never used to have things like that. When he was young, if it wasn't fried, it wasn't an option. He glances across at Louise, reads the frown as the battle between good and evil going on inside her head. He knows she's on a diet, but he knows she likes food too.

'Go on, treat yourself,' he says, nudging her. 'You only live once.'

'Not very long, eating this stuff,' she says, but her voice is light. 'I'll have a smoked sausage supper,' she tells the white-overalled woman behind the counter. 'Just salt, please.'

'Mince pie supper for me,' Davie says. 'A pickled onion. Salt and sauce. Loads of sauce.'

They grin at each other as they sit down at one of the Formica tables, waiting for Davie's pie to be cooked fresh. Louise picks up a paper and starts to flick through. Davie's happy to sit there people-watching for a bit. An old man in a long coat that's seen better days has been handed a wrapped parcel and he smiles in anticipation, giving Davie a small nod as he passes. Davie hadn't realised at first, but he looks homeless. He's about to get up, give him a few quid, but as the old man approaches the door, a gang of teens push their way in. Davie recognises one of them as the lad who shouted at him and Lou earlier.

'Mince pie supper, smoked sausage supper.' The woman behind the counter shouts in her usual foghorn way, despite the fact that Davie is sitting mere feet away from her. He stands up, picks the parcel from the counter. Behind him, he can hear the start of something down at the door. Louise has put the paper down now and she's standing up, a frown on her face.

'Get oot the way, ye stinkin' auld shite.'

'Oi, Lenny – grab his chips. This is the dirty old goat who tried to feel up my Pauline the other night, mind?'

'So it is! He's no sae pissed the night, though. Early yet. De ye no' ken eatin's cheatin'?'

One of them pushes the old man out of the door, onto the street. One of the others, the one they called Lenny, tries to grab hold of the chips, but the old man is refusing to let go.

'Gerroff me. Leave me alone, ye wee bastards.'

They're outside now, and the pushing and shoving continues on the street. People are walking in an arc to avoid the scuffling. No one wants to get involved.

Davie hands the parcels of chips to Louise and heads for the door.

'Davie,' she says, a warning. What is it, though? Leave them be? Don't get involved? You're meant to be off duty? All of those, but he can't stand about watching this man get pushed around, no matter if he did feel up Pauline, which is highly unlikely, unless she had a bottle of vodka going spare.

'All right, lads, that's enough, eh?'

At that, one of the lads grabs the old man and shoves him hard. The parcel of chips flies from his hands, landing with a soft thud on the pavement. One of them kicks at the chips, while another lad shoves the old man again. The old man, who probably weighs half of the youngest of the gang, falls hard against the post box on the edge of the pavement, his head colliding with the cast iron with a sickening crunch.

'Aww fuck, see what you've done now,' one of the lads shouts.

Several of them back away, but the one who pushed him is standing in the middle of the pavement, hands balled tight into fists. 'Old bastard deserved it.'

Louise sprints out of the shop and crouches down beside the old man. A long, slow moan seems to be escaping from his chest. Blood runs down the side of his head.

Davie walks up to the boy on the pavement. 'That was stupid, son,' he says. But there is anger in the young man's eyes. Davie tries to read him. Thinks there are two ways it can go. He's going to kick off, or he's going to start crying, realising what he's done.

'Lou?' Davie shouts, 'what's happening?'

'I'm calling it in,' she says. She takes her phone out of her pocket, but it looks like she's struggling a bit, trying to dial and keep her hand on the old man's head, which seems to be pumping out more blood than it should.

'Right,' Davie says. He takes a step closer to the boy on the pavement. 'What's your name, son?' He seems to be in shock. His friends are now huddled in a doorway, next to the chippie. They know there's not much point in running, but they're unsure what to do. Davie puts his hand in his pocket, feeling about in the depths for his phone.

The boy puts his hand in his pocket, takes a step back.

Davie puts a hand up in a 'wait just a minute' gesture. Takes a step back towards the boy.

'Oi, Kev, look!' One of the boys from the huddle speaks to his mate, the one who is facing up to Davie, a dark look in his eyes. The boy doesn't look away. 'Kev, look,' his mate tries again.

'What,' he says. 'What the fuck is it?'

Louise is on the phone. With one hand, she's taking things out of her bag, laying them on the floor. She's looking for gloves, Davie thinks. Or maybe her resuscitation shield mouthpiece. The man is lying on the floor now, in the recovery position. Is he breathing? She has left her badge on the pavement, and he knows now that the boy in the doorway has seen it. They should've identified themselves as police right at the start. Stupid mistake. But he knew that Louise was thinking the same as him. Try to keep it calm. Don't let them run off. Because that's what Davie had expected them to do, and he was slightly shocked when they didn't.

The boy takes a step towards Davie, and Davie can smell stale alcohol on his breath, or maybe seeping out of his skin. Up close, his eyes look bloodshot and dull.

'You a pig?' he says. Spittle lands on Davie's face. 'Pig killed my dad, you know.'

'Kev, fucksake. Leave it. Let's go.' The boy from the doorway sounds scared now. He's the only one to have found his voice, and no one is backing him up.

'Calm down,' Davie says. 'No need to get aggro. Just an accident, eh? We can sort all of this out. Just let me—'

He reaches into his pocket for his phone. But as he does, the boy reaches into his pocket too. Steps closer, until their faces are almost touching. Davie doesn't even realise what's happened at first. A warm feeling spreads across him, and he instinctively raises his arms, hugging the boy. But the boy steps back, a strange grin on his face.

Davie falls forwards, lands on his knees. 'What the—'

He is confused. He looks down at the pavement, sees the trickle of dark red as it drips through his shirt.

'Kev, ohnoohnoohno,' screams the boy from the doorway, who is shouting from somewhere far away now. Somewhere underwater maybe? But no, that doesn't make sense. There's a muffled sound of metal on stone. A knife spins across the pavement. Some of the boys are running, their figures blurred. Louise. Where's Louise? Somewhere in the distance, he hears an ambulance. Voices are coming to him, people all around him. No one around him.

He falls to the pavement, but it doesn't hurt. He feels numb. What was that song again? *Comfortably numb …Is there anybody in there?* Or was that *The X-Files?* Louise … he tries to call for her, but his voice doesn't work any more. The pavement is cold against his cheek. He can see feet – trainers. Cobbles on the road. Feels the wind. A cool breeze fluttering against him.

'Davie? What the fuck? Davie?'

She's grabbing at him. Pressing on him. Her voice is far away.

'Get me a coat, someone. Please. Here, you … come here. You need to press down on this … no, don't touch that. Please …' He sees her blurred form bending, picking up the knife, getting it out of the way. He hears whimpering, from somewhere nearby. In the doorway? Was there a boy in the doorway?

He feels cold. So cold. He should've buttoned his coat.

The sirens are loud now. The old man. They need to help the old man. He hit his head. *You need to help the old man*, he shouts, but it is only in his head. He closes his eyes. Feels tired. So tired.

'Davie? Can you hear me?'

He smells her. Spearmint and Earl Grey.

'Davie? Stay with me … come on. They're coming to help you. You're going to be fine.'

He tries to open his eyes, but they're heavy, so heavy. Someone is pressing down on his eyes. He giggles.

Bubbles of blood come out of his mouth.

'Oh Jesus,' she says. 'Hold on, Davie. Please hold on. Grab my fingers, Davie. Grab them …'

He grabs them, but there's nothing there. He grabs at air. He can't. Fingers not working. No. Try, Davie, try.

She's crying. He can hear crying. 'Please, Davie. Please.'

A door slams. Footsteps. How many? Count them.

One. Two. Three.

'Davie, squeeze my hand. Squeeze it. Davie … Davie!'

She's fading away. It's all fading away. He hears the sound of his scooter, somewhere deep inside his head. The cat!

287

Someone needs to look after that cat. Sees his mum, smiling at him. Sees nothing. Black. Red. White. Dark, just dark.

'Stay with me, Davie …'

A warm teardrop falls on his face.

He feels a hand. A small, soft hand. Long fingers, nails dig into his skin.

'I love you, Davie.'

Something flutters. Stutters. A cold engine. Turning. Turning.

'Davie?'

He squeezes.

Acknowledgements

A huge thank you, as always, to my publishers, Black & White for their excellent work in putting together such a beautiful looking book – kudos, especially, for the cover (got to love a creepy insect)! Massive thanks to Phil Patterson, who continues to keep me on the edge of sanity, and to all at Marjacq for being truly excellent.

Ginormous gratitude to AK Benedict. You know why.

Thank you to Lois Reibach, who bid for a character name and helped to raise money for the lovely Erin Mitchell in the process. I hope you like what I did with you!

Thank you to the people who have helped in any way, large or small, during the writing of this book: DS Darren Stewart from Police Scotland College; Amanda, Steph, Alexandra, Ava, Jenny, Louise, Rebecca, Tammy, Elizabeth, Jane, Angela, Graeme and Ed for the right kind of encouragement at the right times; The Cockblankets, for services to the crime writing community; Liz, Gordon, Vicki and Anne for your unflinching support; Daniel, Mark . . . I'm sure you two have done *something*? Jackie 'The Raven' for reminding me that Quinn had a story to be told; Craig, for letting me steal *fucksake*; everyone who has encouraged me, bought a book, come to see me waffle on a panel, left a review, bought me a drink or given me a hug; to the wonderful bloggers and the excellent online book clubs – THE Book Club, Crime Book Club, UK Crime Book Club & Book Connectors for helping to spread the word; The Shire Gang – who I miss every day, and who I have immortalised in print (if your name is not in here in some way, please send me a *Points of View* style complaint and I will rectify in the next one); and a big bouncy thank you to Ian for insisting that Drummer appear in this book – he fitted in perfectly!

If I have forgotten anyone, I'm sorry. It's not you, it's me.

Lots of love, as ever, to my gorgeous family and fabulous friends who continue to shout about me from the rooftops; and finally, because it's the way I always do it: To JLOH, for everything.